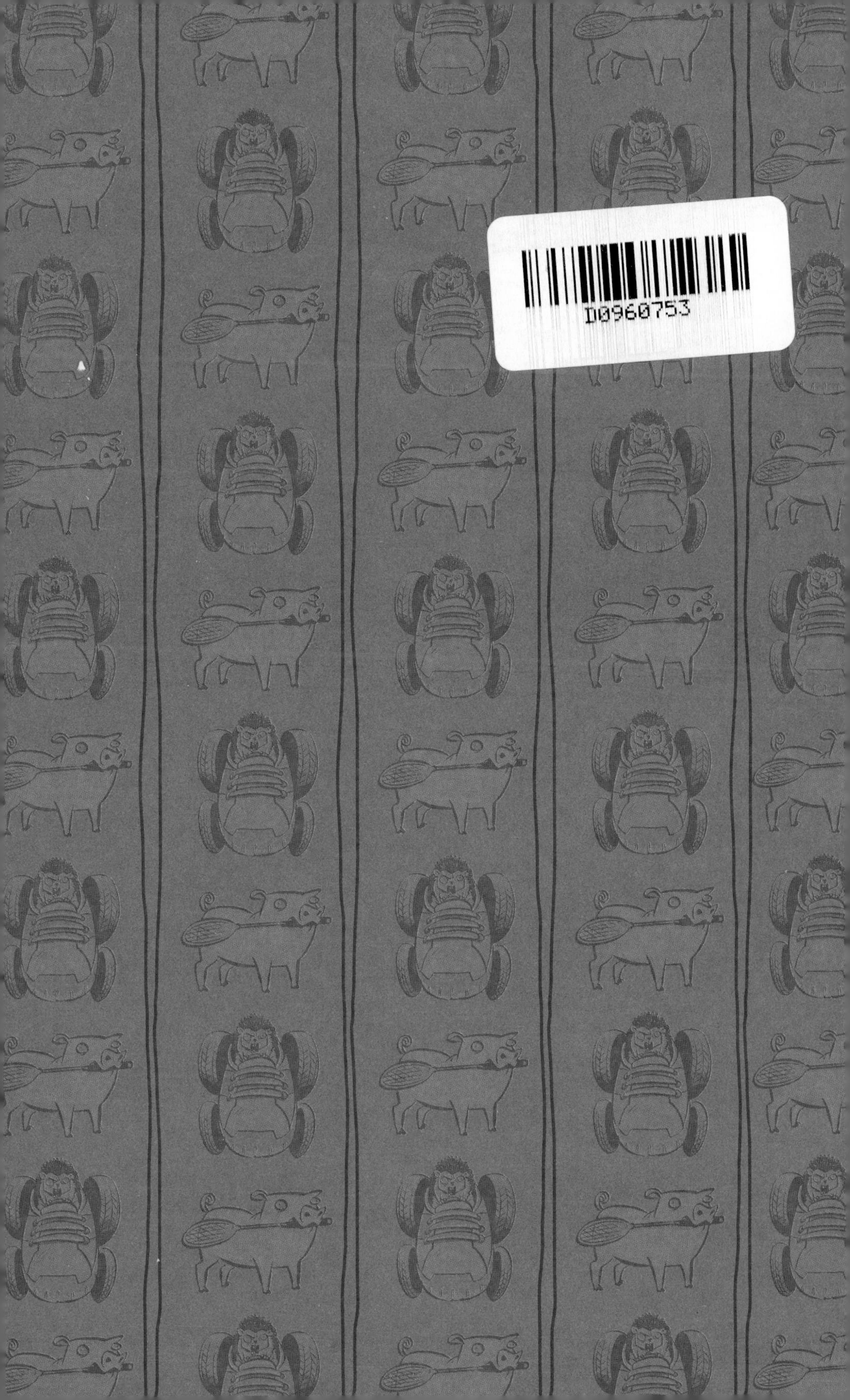

PLANTS VS. ZOMBIES™

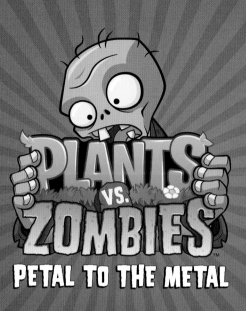

PETAL TO THE METAL

Written by **PAUL TOBIN**
Art by **RON CHAN**
Colors by **MATT J. RAINWATER**
Letters by **STEVE DUTRO**
Cover by **RON CHAN**

DARK HORSE BOOKS

PLANTS VS. ZOMBIES

PETAL TO THE METAL

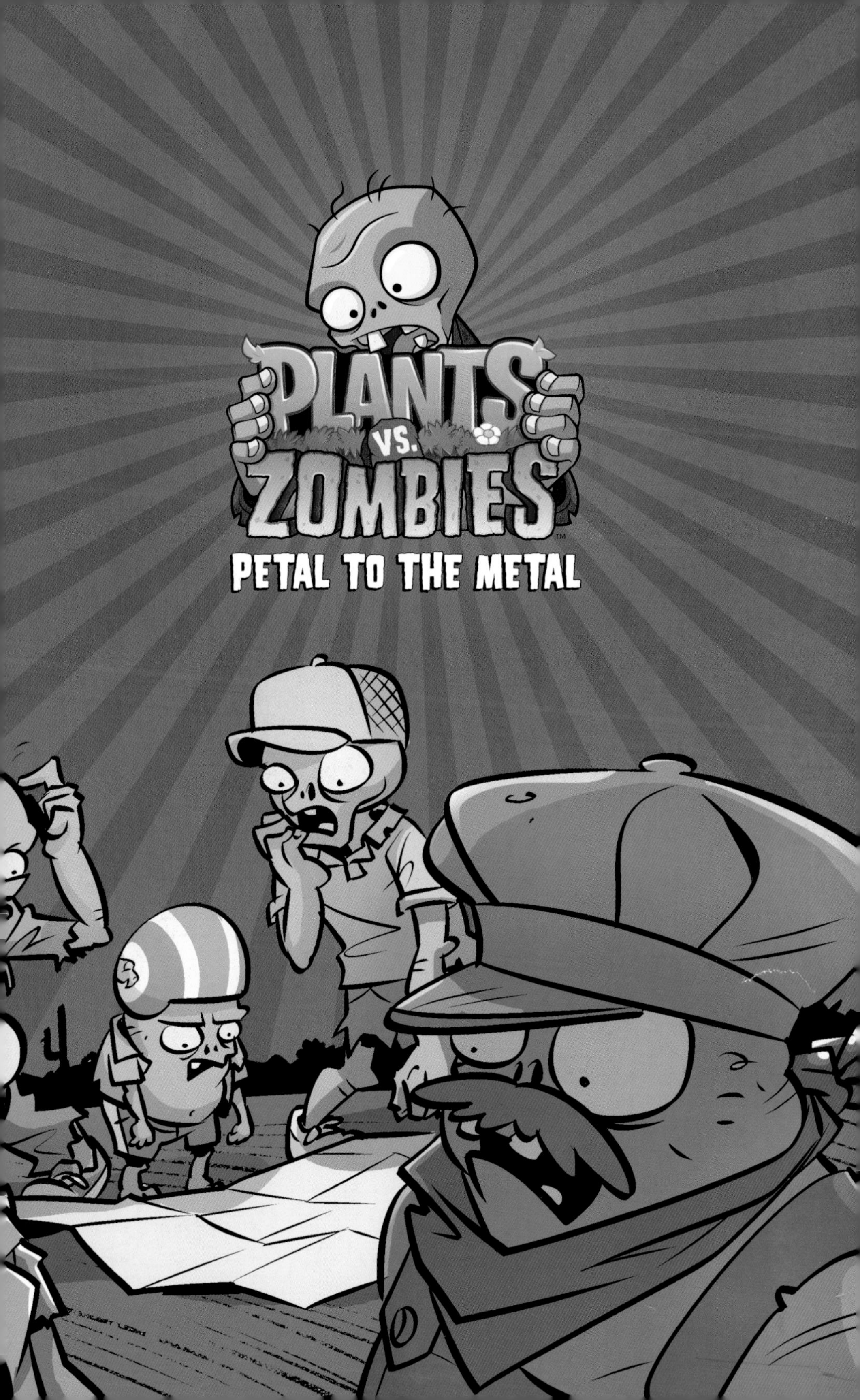

President and Publisher **MIKE RICHARDSON**
Editor **PHILIP R. SIMON**
Designer **BRENNAN THOME**
Digital Art Technician **CHRISTINA McKENZIE**

Special thanks to LEIGH BEACH, GARY CLAY, SHANA DOERR, ALEXANDRIA LAND, A.J. RATHBUN, KRISTEN STAR, JEREMY VANHOOZER, and everyone at PopCap Games.

First edition: September 2016
ISBN 978-1-61655-999-1

10 9 8 7 6 5 4 3 2 1
Printed in China

DarkHorse.com | PopCap.com

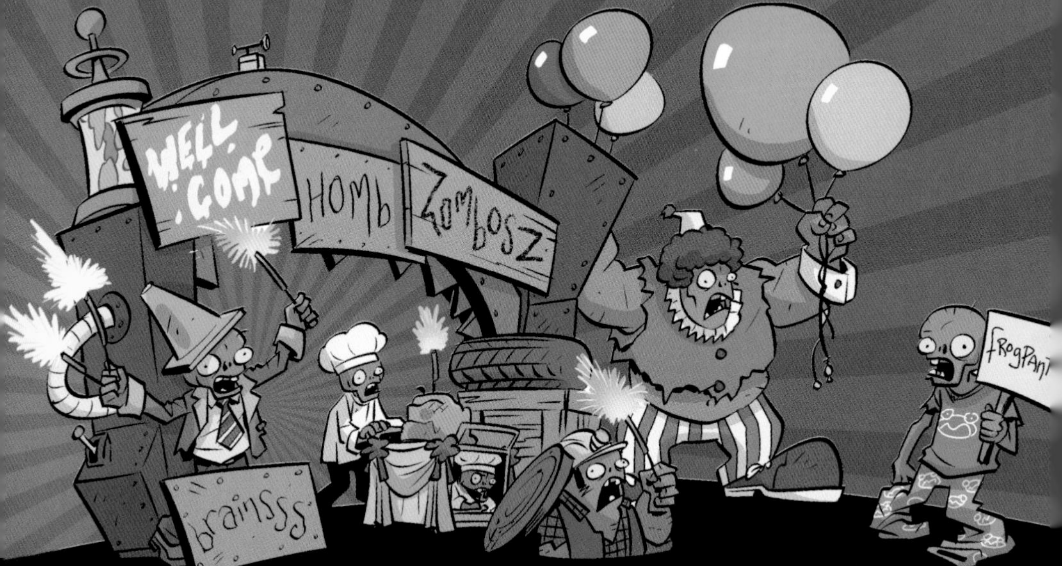
HOMb
Zombosz
brainsss

No plants were harmed in the making of this comic. Numerous zombies, including all the ones who can drive, pump gas, or unfold a map, however, definitely were.

This volume collects the stories found in *Plants vs. Zombies* #7–#9: *Petal to the Metal* Parts 1–3 and the "Plants vs. Zombies: The Lady in Red" short story that appeared in *Free Comic Book Day 2016: All Ages*, originally published by Dark Horse Comics in 2015 and 2016. | Published by Dark Horse Books, a division of Dark Horse Comics, Inc., 10956 SE Main Street, Milwaukie, OR 97222 | International Licensing: (503) 905-2377 | To find a comics shop in your area, call the Comic Shop Locator Service toll-free at 1-888-266-4226. |

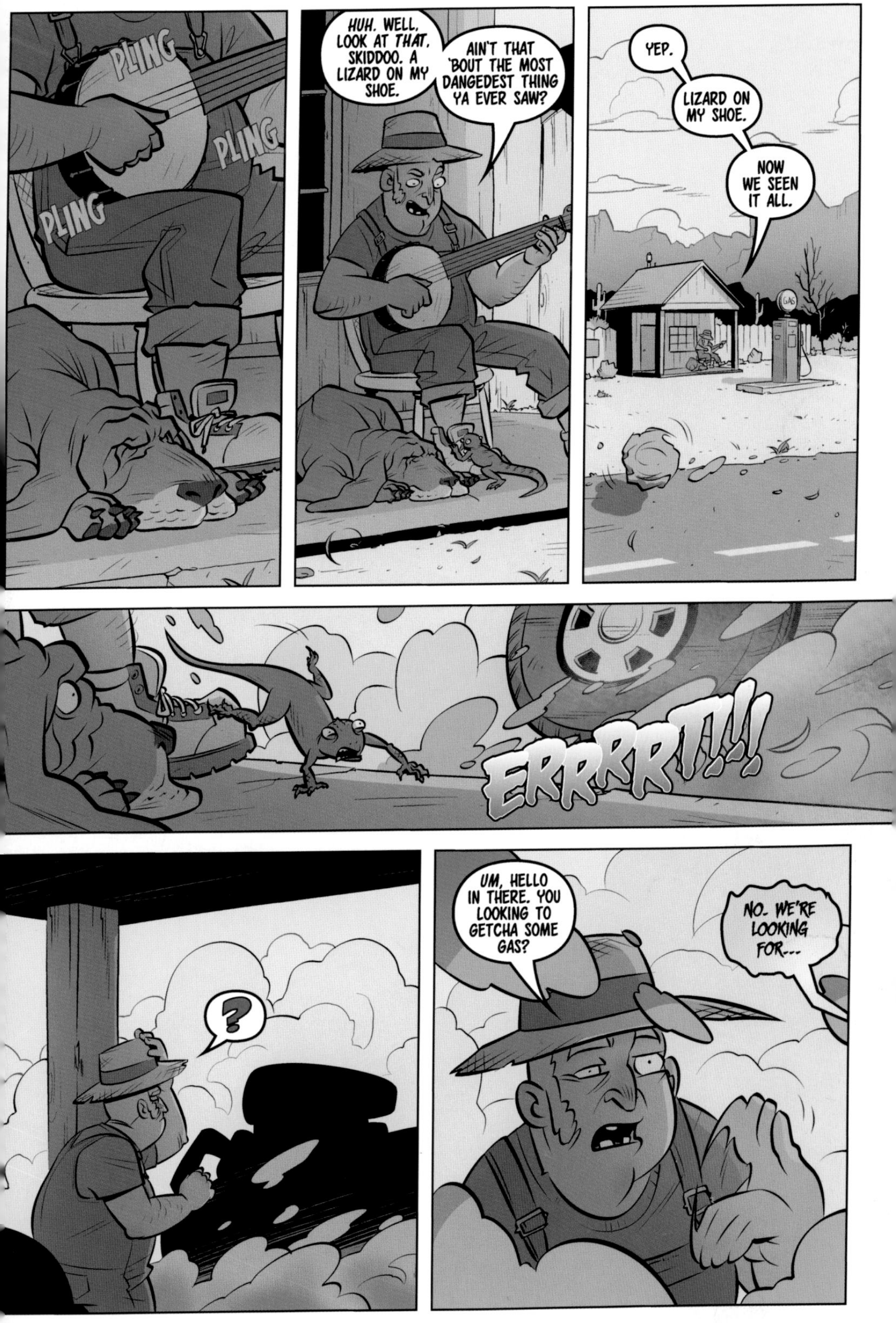
PLING
PLING
PLING
HUH. WELL, LOOK AT THAT, SKIDDOO. A LIZARD ON MY SHOE.
AIN'T THAT 'BOUT THE MOST DANGEDEST THING YA EVER SAW?
YEP.
LIZARD ON MY SHOE.
NOW WE SEEN IT ALL.
GAS
ERRRRT!!!
?
UM, HELLO IN THERE. YOU LOOKING TO GETCHA SOME GAS?
NO. WE'RE LOOKING FOR...

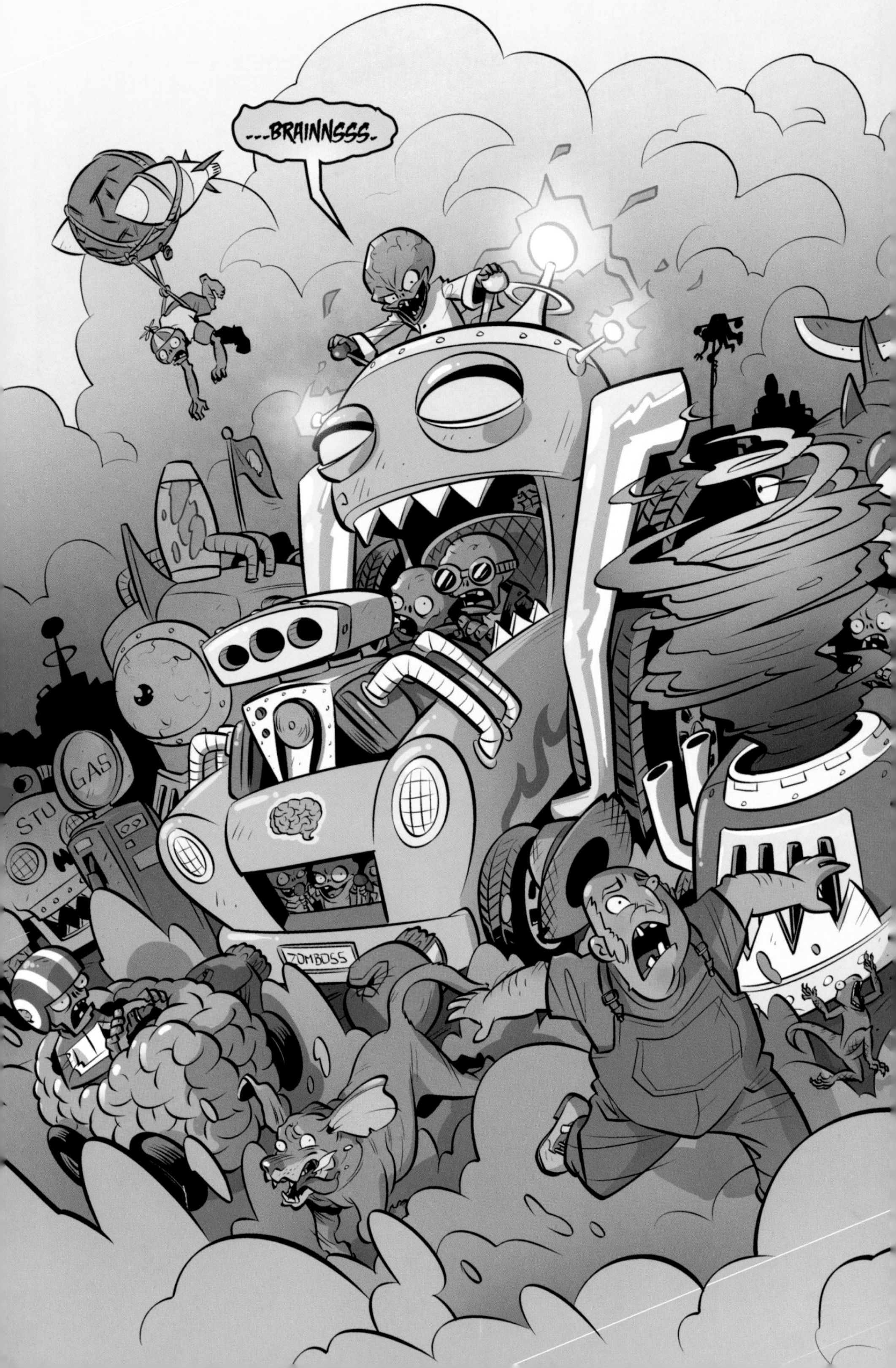
...BRAINNSSS.
GAS
STU
ZOMBOSS

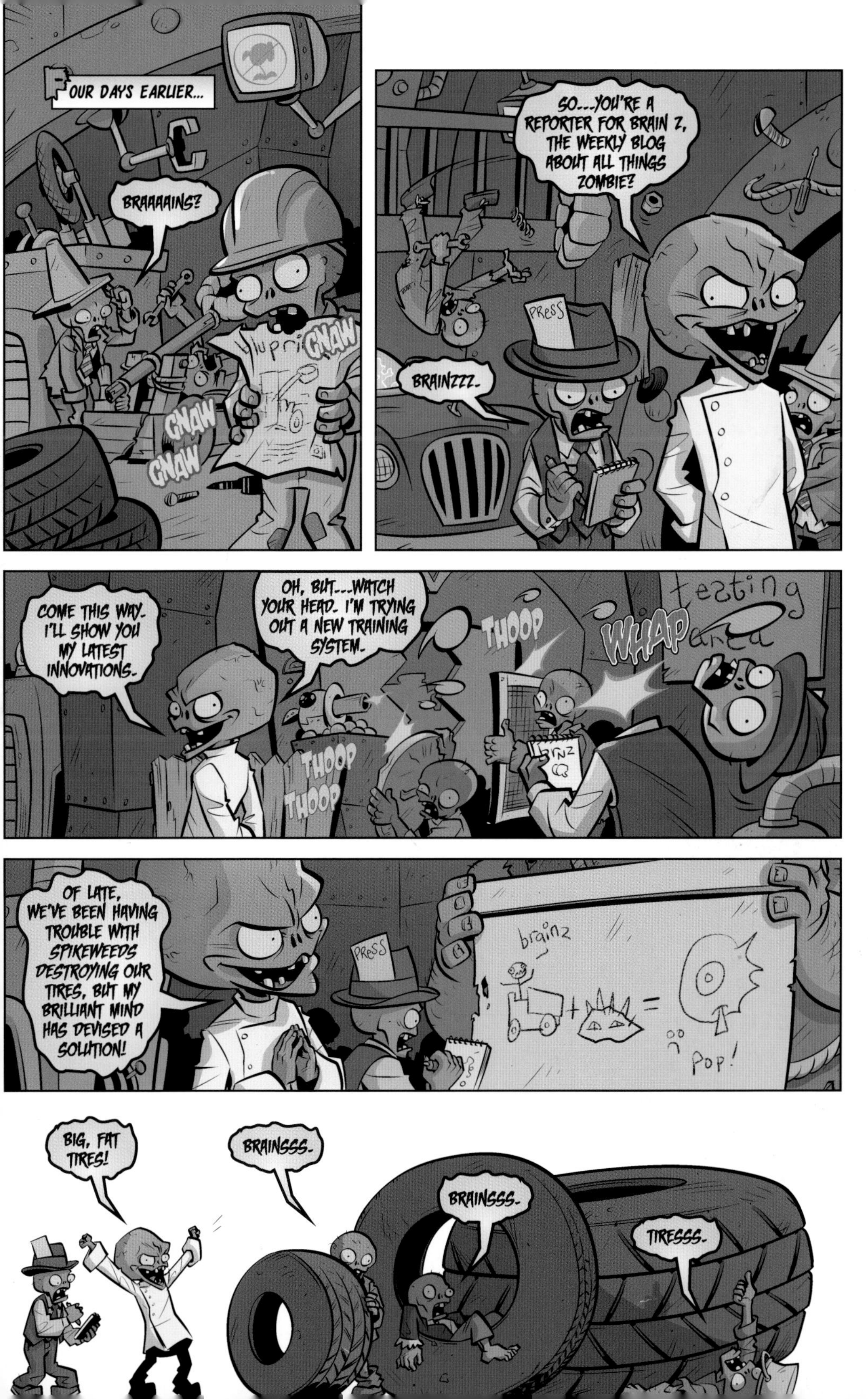
FOUR DAYS EARLIER...
BRAAAAINS?
blupri
GNAW
GNAW
GNAW
SO...YOU'RE A REPORTER FOR BRAIN Z, THE WEEKLY BLOG ABOUT ALL THINGS ZOMBIE?
PRESS
BRAINZZZ.
COME THIS WAY. I'LL SHOW YOU MY LATEST INNOVATIONS.
OH, BUT...WATCH YOUR HEAD. I'M TRYING OUT A NEW TRAINING SYSTEM.
THOOP
testing area
WHAP
THOOP
THOOP
OF LATE, WE'VE BEEN HAVING TROUBLE WITH SPIKEWEEDS DESTROYING OUR TIRES, BUT MY BRILLIANT MIND HAS DEVISED A SOLUTION!
PRESS
brainz
pop!
BIG, FAT TIRES!
BRAINSSS.
BRAINSSS.
TIRESSS.

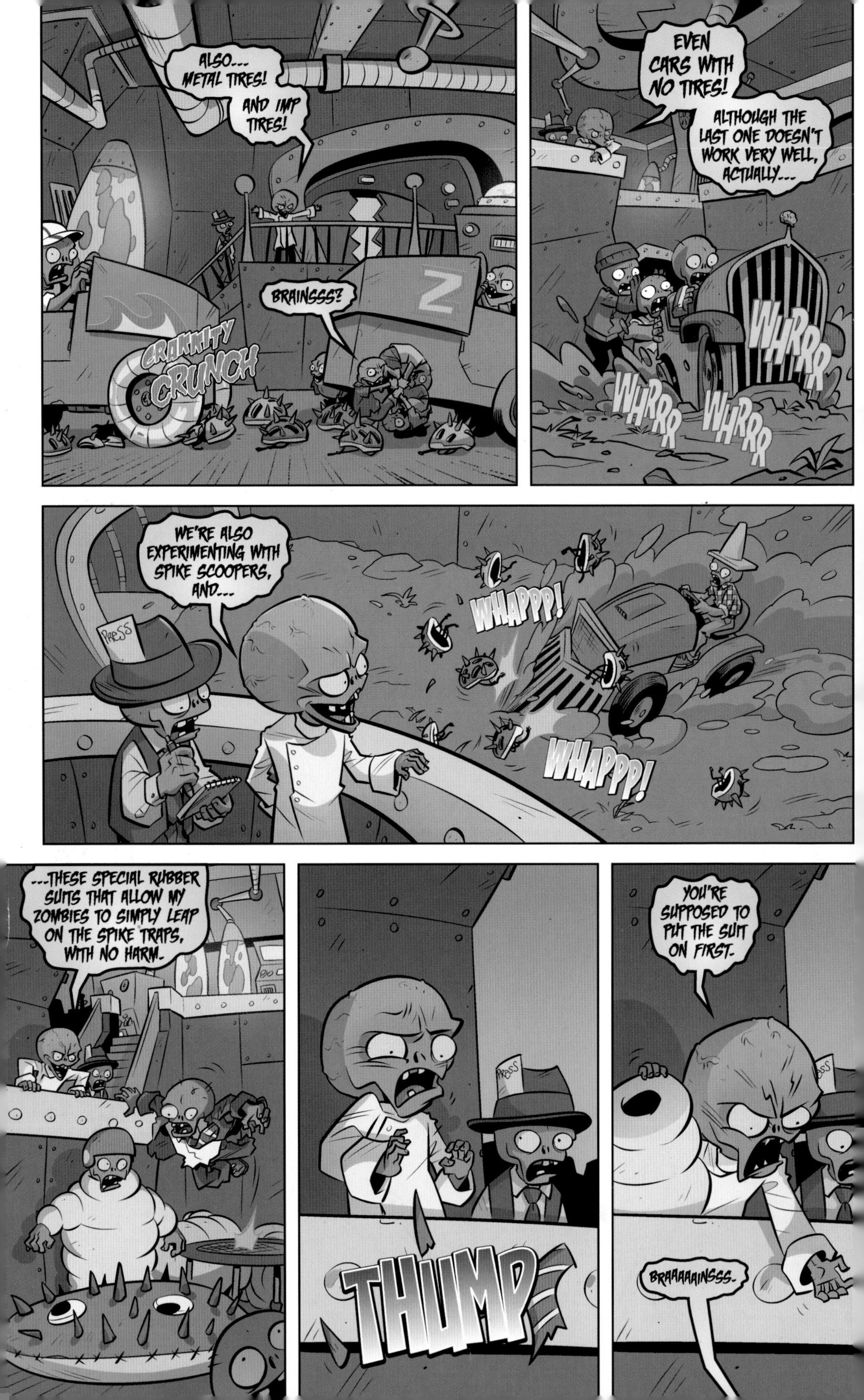
ALSO... METAL TIRES!
AND IMP TIRES!
BRAINSSS?
CRANKITY CRUNCH
EVEN CARS WITH NO TIRES!
ALTHOUGH THE LAST ONE DOESN'T WORK VERY WELL, ACTUALLY...
WHRRRR
WHRRRR
WHRRRR
WE'RE ALSO EXPERIMENTING WITH SPIKE SCOOPERS, AND...
WHAPPP!
WHAPPP!
PRESS
...THESE SPECIAL RUBBER SUITS THAT ALLOW MY ZOMBIES TO SIMPLY LEAP ON THE SPIKE TRAPS, WITH NO HARM.
PRESS
THUMP
YOU'RE SUPPOSED TO PUT THE SUIT ON FIRST.
BRAAAAAINSSS.

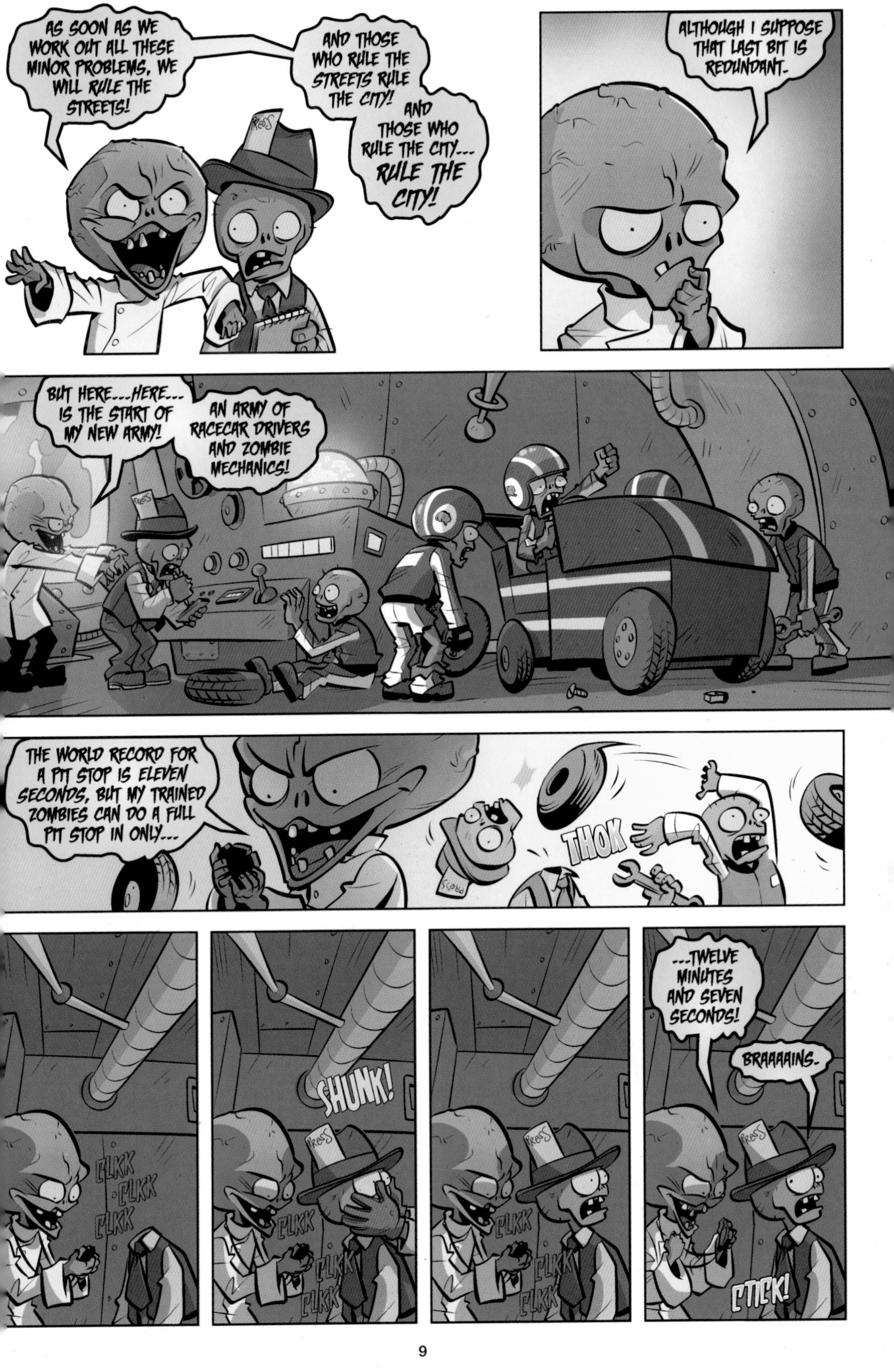
AS SOON AS WE WORK OUT ALL THESE MINOR PROBLEMS, WE WILL RULE THE STREETS!
AND THOSE WHO RULE THE STREETS RULE THE CITY!
AND THOSE WHO RULE THE CITY... RULE THE CITY!
ALTHOUGH I SUPPOSE THAT LAST BIT IS REDUNDANT.
BUT HERE...HERE... IS THE START OF MY NEW ARMY!
AN ARMY OF RACECAR DRIVERS AND ZOMBIE MECHANICS!
THE WORLD RECORD FOR A PIT STOP IS ELEVEN SECONDS, BUT MY TRAINED ZOMBIES CAN DO A FULL PIT STOP IN ONLY...
THOK
CLKK CLKK CLKK
SHUNK!
CLKK CLKK CLKK
CLKK CLKK
...TWELVE MINUTES AND SEVEN SECONDS!
BRAAAAINS.
CTICK!

MEANWHILE...

!

LOOK OUT FOR THAT DUCK!

AAAH!

!!!

OH, NO!

FAILED
FAILED
FAILED

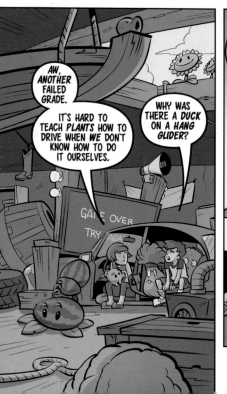

AW, ANOTHER FAILED GRADE.

IT'S HARD TO TEACH PLANTS HOW TO DRIVE WHEN WE DON'T KNOW HOW TO DO IT OURSELVES.

WHY WAS THERE A DUCK ON A HANG GLIDER?

GAME OVER
TRY AGA

I WISH I COULD CONVINCE MY UNCLE TO HELP TEACH THE PLANTS. BUT THAT'S NOT HAPPENING.

"AT LEAST NOT UNTIL HE GETS THE HIGH SCORE ON DON'T BLINK."

DON'T BLINK

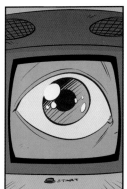

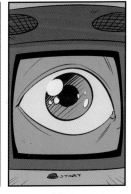

START
START
TREMBLE
START
HE'S BREAKING.
HE'S NOT EVEN CLOSE TO A HIGH SCORE.
START
START
TREMBLE
QUIVER
TREMOR
BLINK
MACHINE WINS!
OM FLONGLE.
C'MON, DAVE, MAYBE YOU CAN COME BACK LATER?
PRACTICE IN THE MEANTIME?
YOU LOSE!

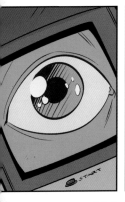

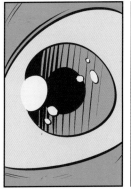

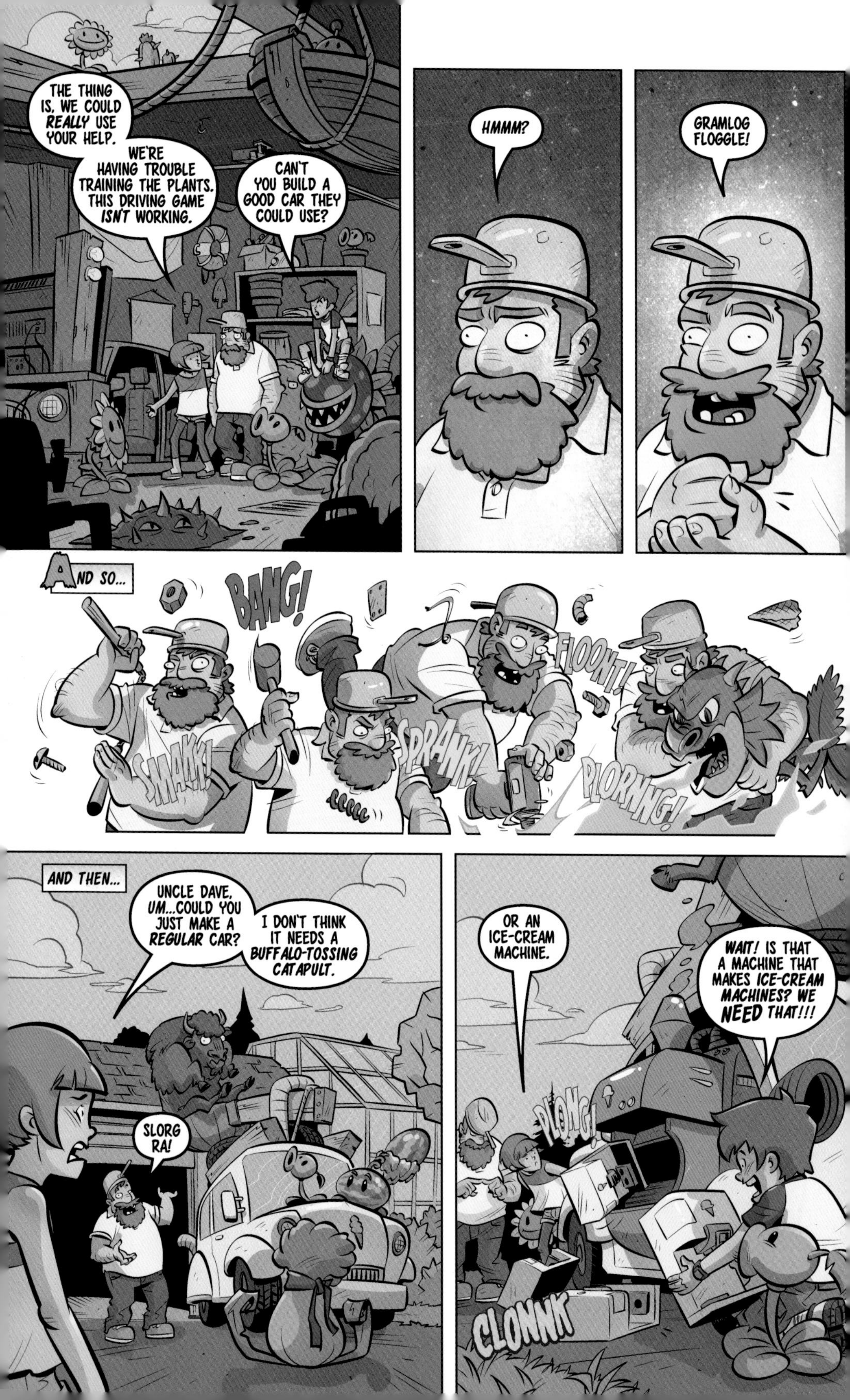
THE THING IS, WE COULD *REALLY* USE YOUR HELP.
WE'RE HAVING TROUBLE TRAINING THE PLANTS. THIS DRIVING GAME *ISN'T* WORKING.
CAN'T YOU BUILD A GOOD CAR THEY COULD USE?
HMMM?
GRAMLOG FLOGGLE!
AND SO...
BANG!
FLOONT!
SMAKK!
SPRANK!
PLORNNG!
AND THEN...
UNCLE DAVE, UM...COULD YOU JUST MAKE A *REGULAR* CAR?
I DON'T THINK IT NEEDS A *BUFFALO-TOSSING CATAPULT.*
SLORG RA!
OR AN ICE-CREAM MACHINE.
WAIT! IS THAT A MACHINE THAT MAKES *ICE-CREAM MACHINES*? WE **NEED** THAT!!!
PLONG!
CLONNK

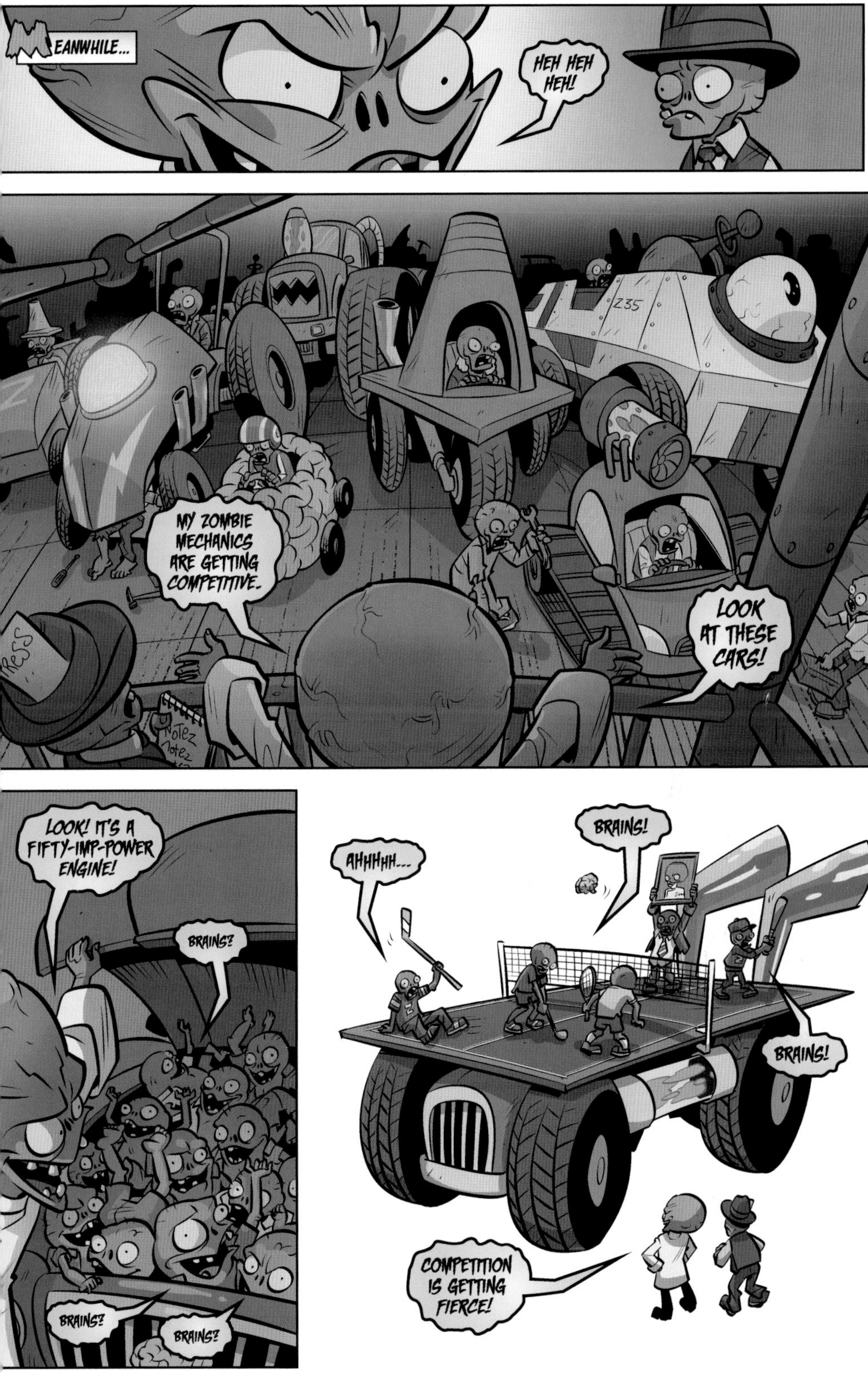
MEANWHILE...
HEH HEH HEH!
MY ZOMBIE MECHANICS ARE GETTING COMPETITIVE.
LOOK AT THESE CARS!
LOOK! IT'S A FIFTY-IMP-POWER ENGINE!
BRAINS?
BRAINS?
BRAINS?
AHHHHH...
BRAINS!
BRAINS!
COMPETITION IS GETTING FIERCE!

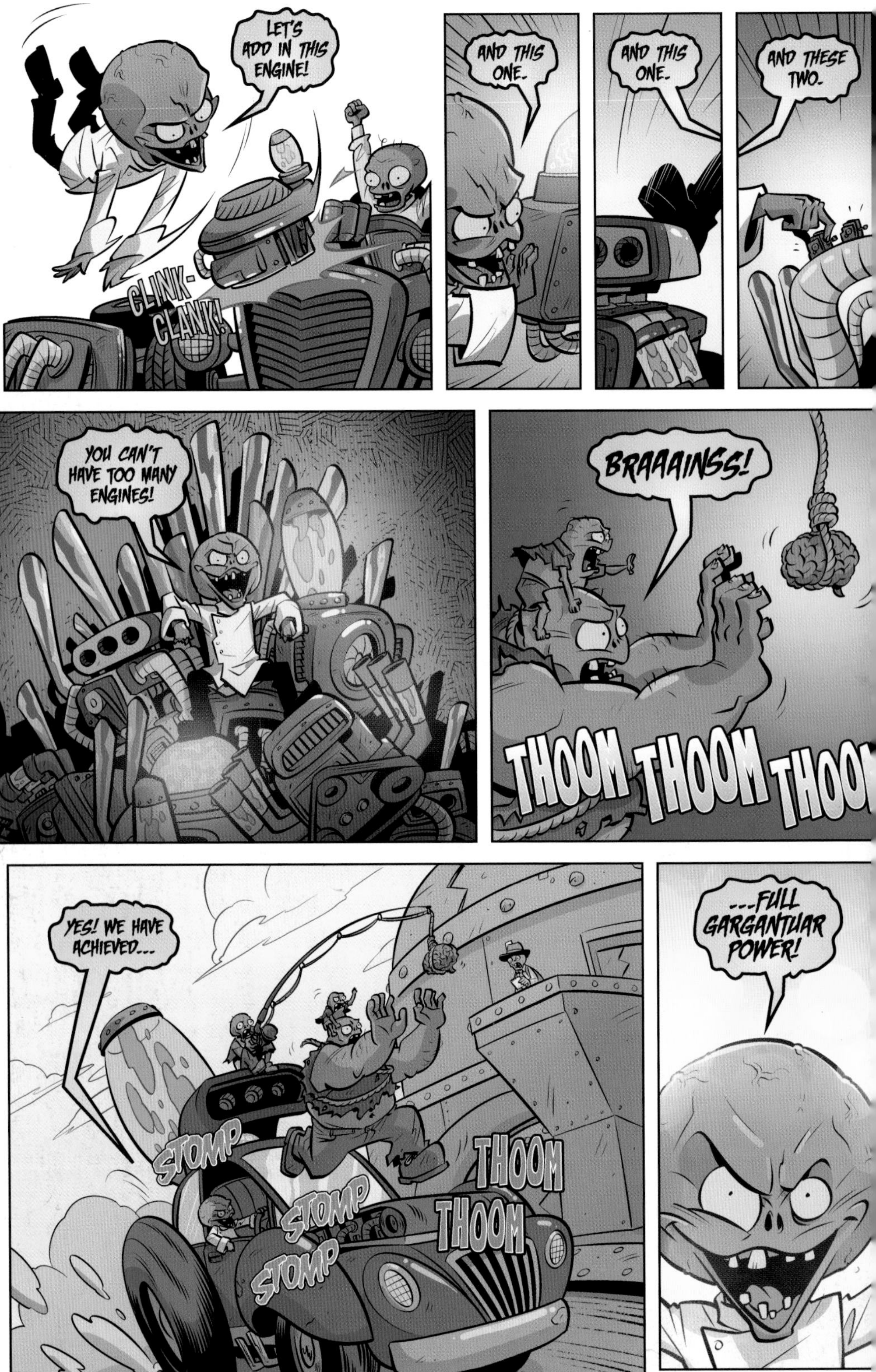
LET'S ADD IN THIS ENGINE!
CLINK-CLANK!
AND THIS ONE.
AND THIS ONE.
AND THESE TWO.
YOU CAN'T HAVE TOO MANY ENGINES!
BRAAAINSS!
THOOM THOOM
YES! WE HAVE ACHIEVED...
STOMP
STOMP
STOMP
THOOM
THOOM
...FULL GARGANTUAR POWER!

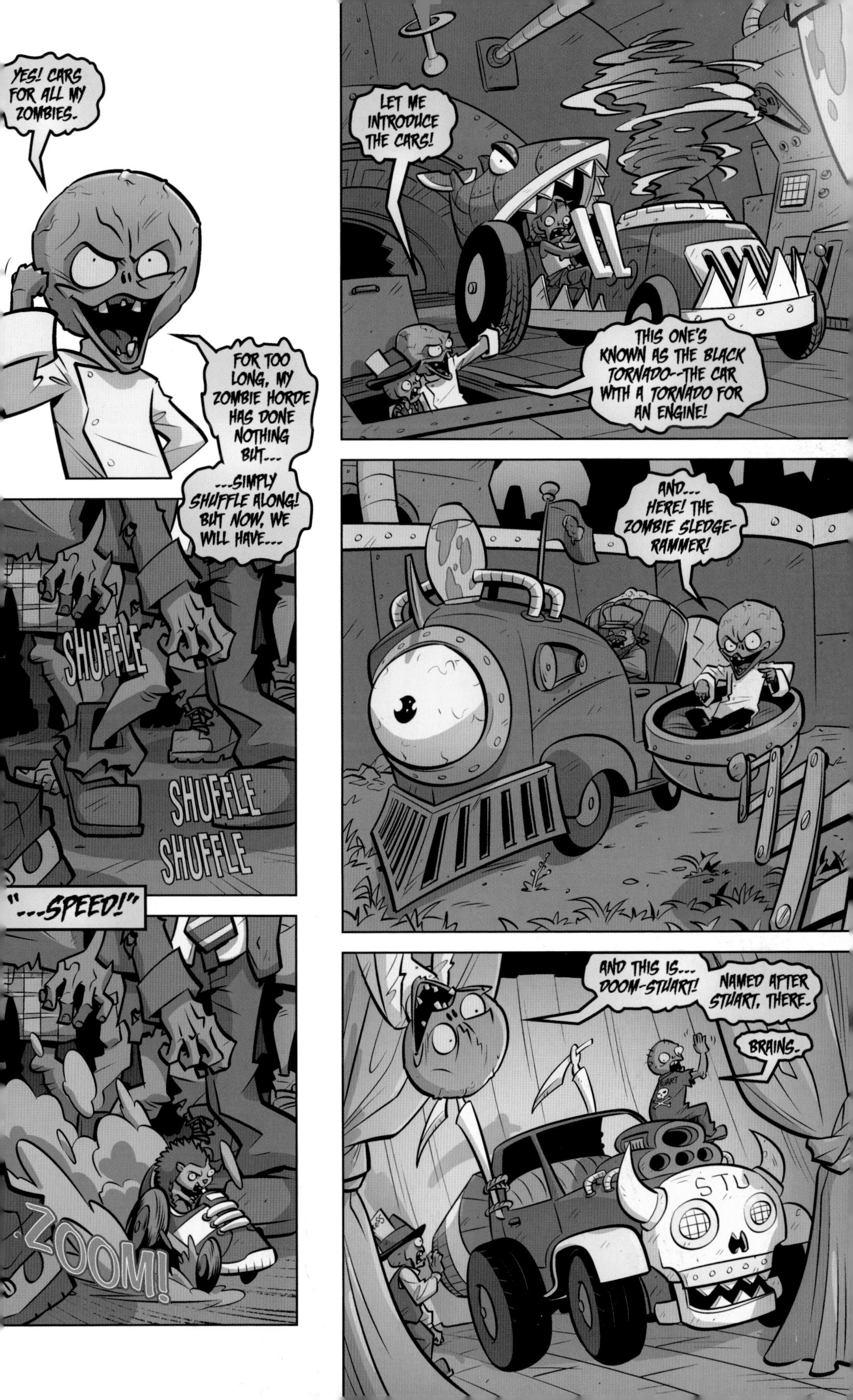
YES! CARS FOR ALL MY ZOMBIES.
FOR TOO LONG, MY ZOMBIE HORDE HAS DONE NOTHING BUT...
...SIMPLY SHUFFLE ALONG! BUT NOW, WE WILL HAVE...
SHUFFLE
SHUFFLE
SHUFFLE
"...SPEED!"
ZOOM!
LET ME INTRODUCE THE CARS!
THIS ONE'S KNOWN AS THE BLACK TORNADO--THE CAR WITH A TORNADO FOR AN ENGINE!
AND... HERE! THE ZOMBIE SLEDGE-RAMMER!
AND THIS IS... DOOM-STUART!
NAMED AFTER STUART, THERE.
BRAINS.
STU

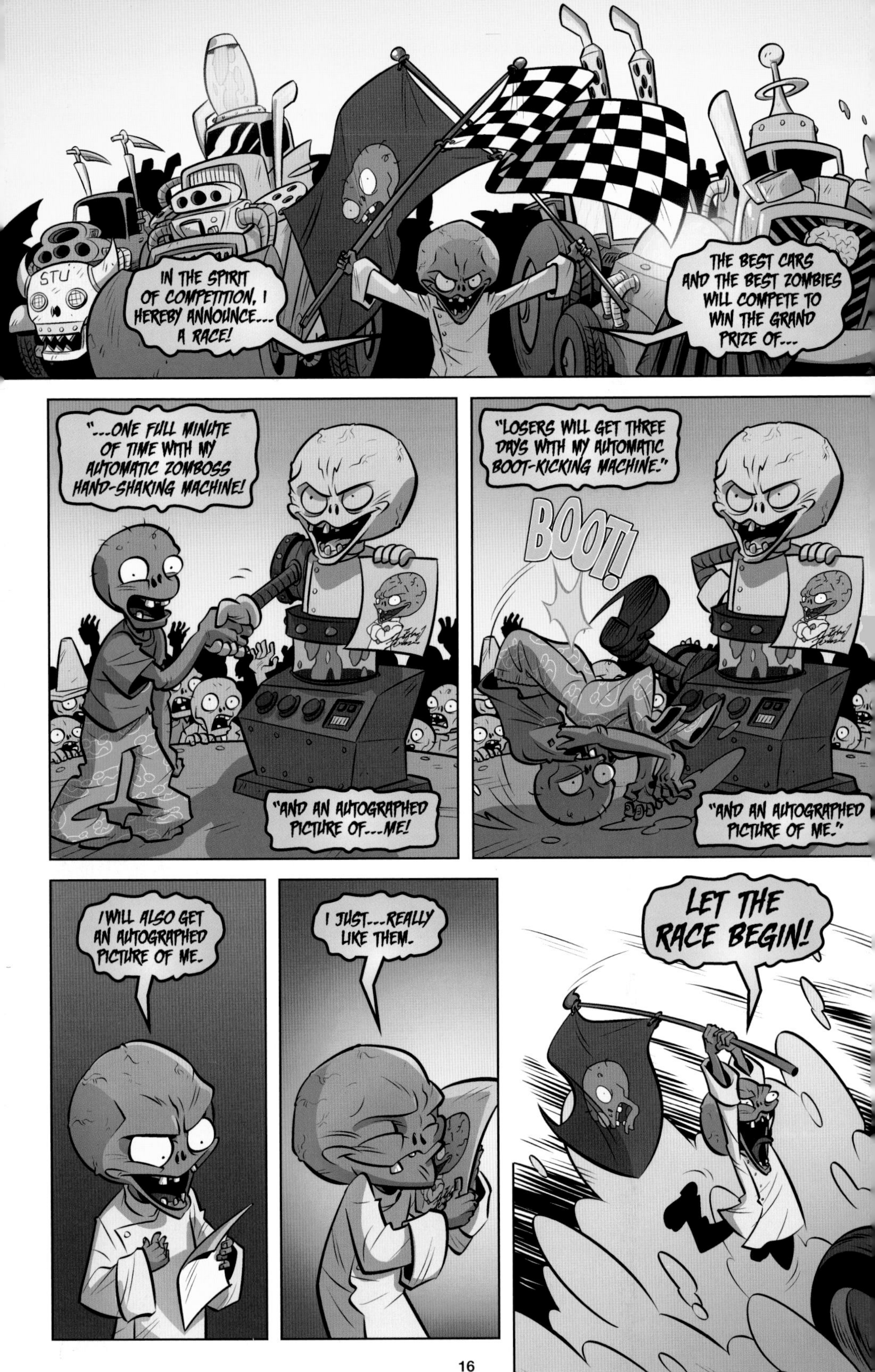
STU
IN THE SPIRIT OF COMPETITION, I HEREBY ANNOUNCE... A RACE!
THE BEST CARS AND THE BEST ZOMBIES WILL COMPETE TO WIN THE GRAND PRIZE OF...
"...ONE FULL MINUTE OF TIME WITH MY AUTOMATIC ZOMBOSS HAND-SHAKING MACHINE!
"AND AN AUTOGRAPHED PICTURE OF...ME!
"LOSERS WILL GET THREE DAYS WITH MY AUTOMATIC BOOT-KICKING MACHINE."
BOOT!
"AND AN AUTOGRAPHED PICTURE OF ME."
I WILL ALSO GET AN AUTOGRAPHED PICTURE OF ME.
I JUST...REALLY LIKE THEM.
LET THE RACE BEGIN!

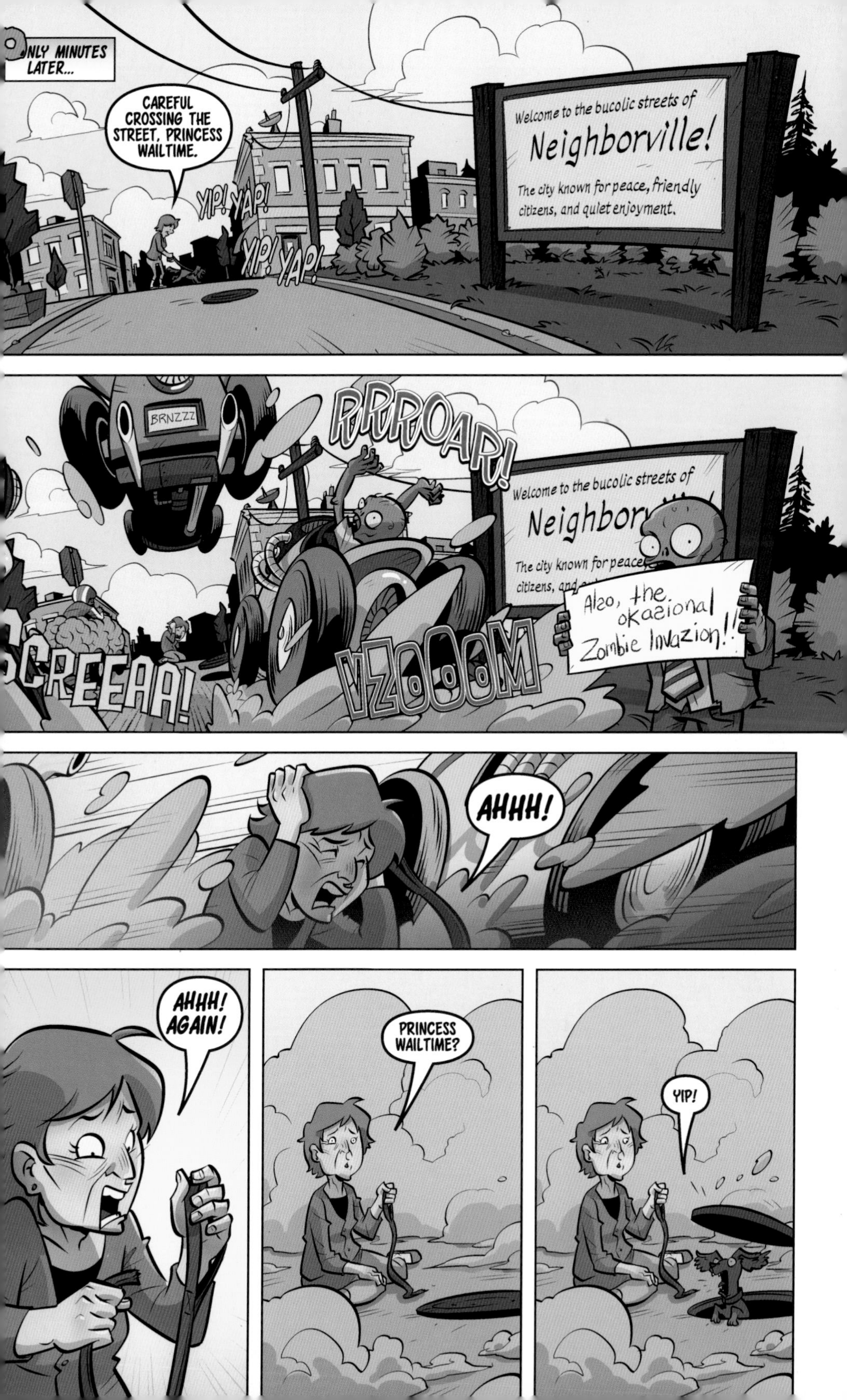

ONLY MINUTES LATER...
CAREFUL CROSSING THE STREET, PRINCESS WAILTIME.
YIP! YAP!
YIP! YAP!
Welcome to the bucolic streets of
Neighborville!
The city known for peace, friendly citizens, and quiet enjoyment.
BRNZZZ
RRROAR!
Alzo, the okazional Zombie Invazion!!
SCREEAA!
VZOOOOM
AHHH!
AHHH! AGAIN!
PRINCESS WAILTIME?
YIP!

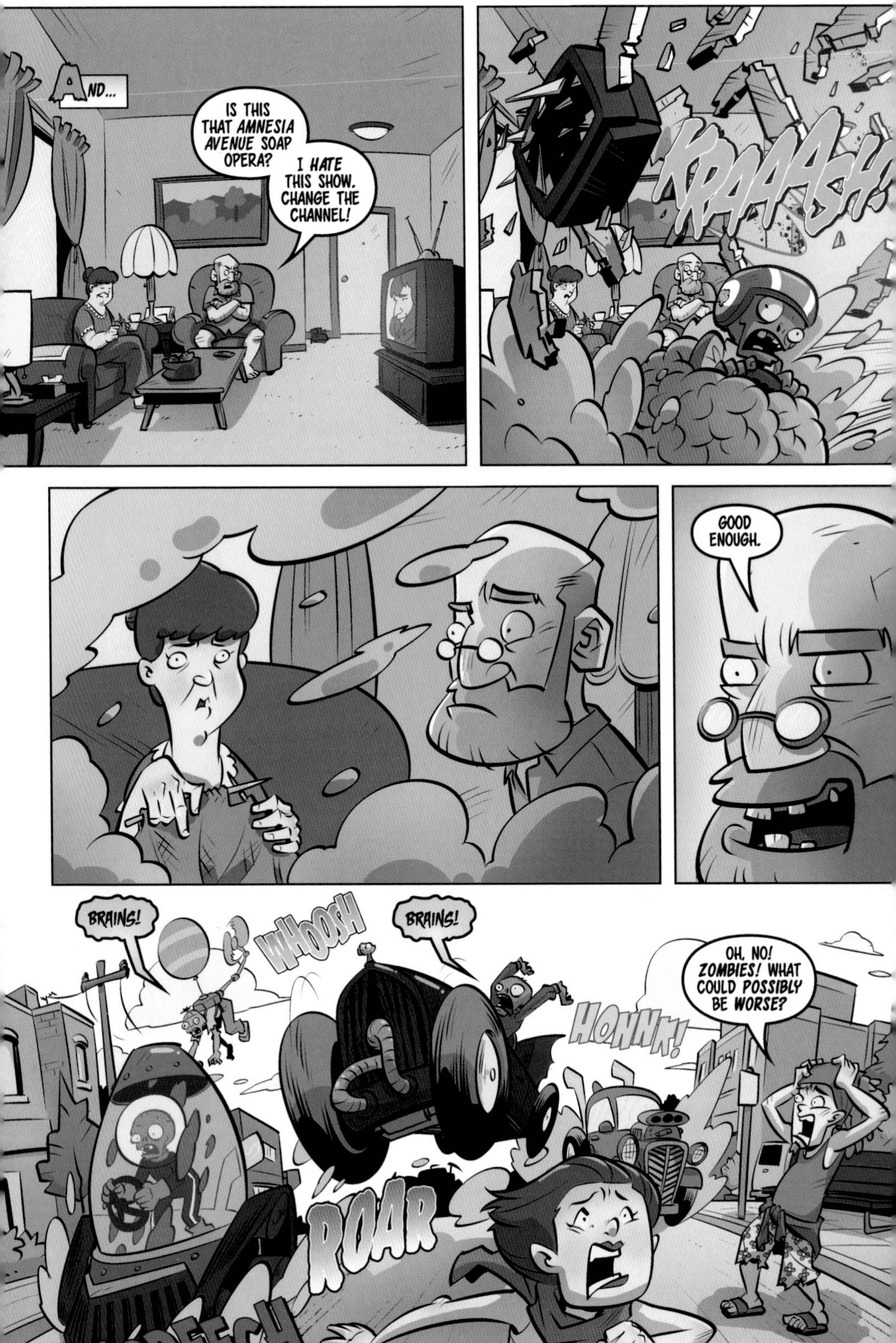
AND...
IS THIS THAT AMNESIA AVENUE SOAP OPERA?
I HATE THIS SHOW. CHANGE THE CHANNEL!
KRAAASH!
GOOD ENOUGH.
BRAINS!
WHOOSH
BRAINS!
HONNK!
OH, NO! ZOMBIES! WHAT COULD POSSIBLY BE WORSE?
ROAR
SCREECH

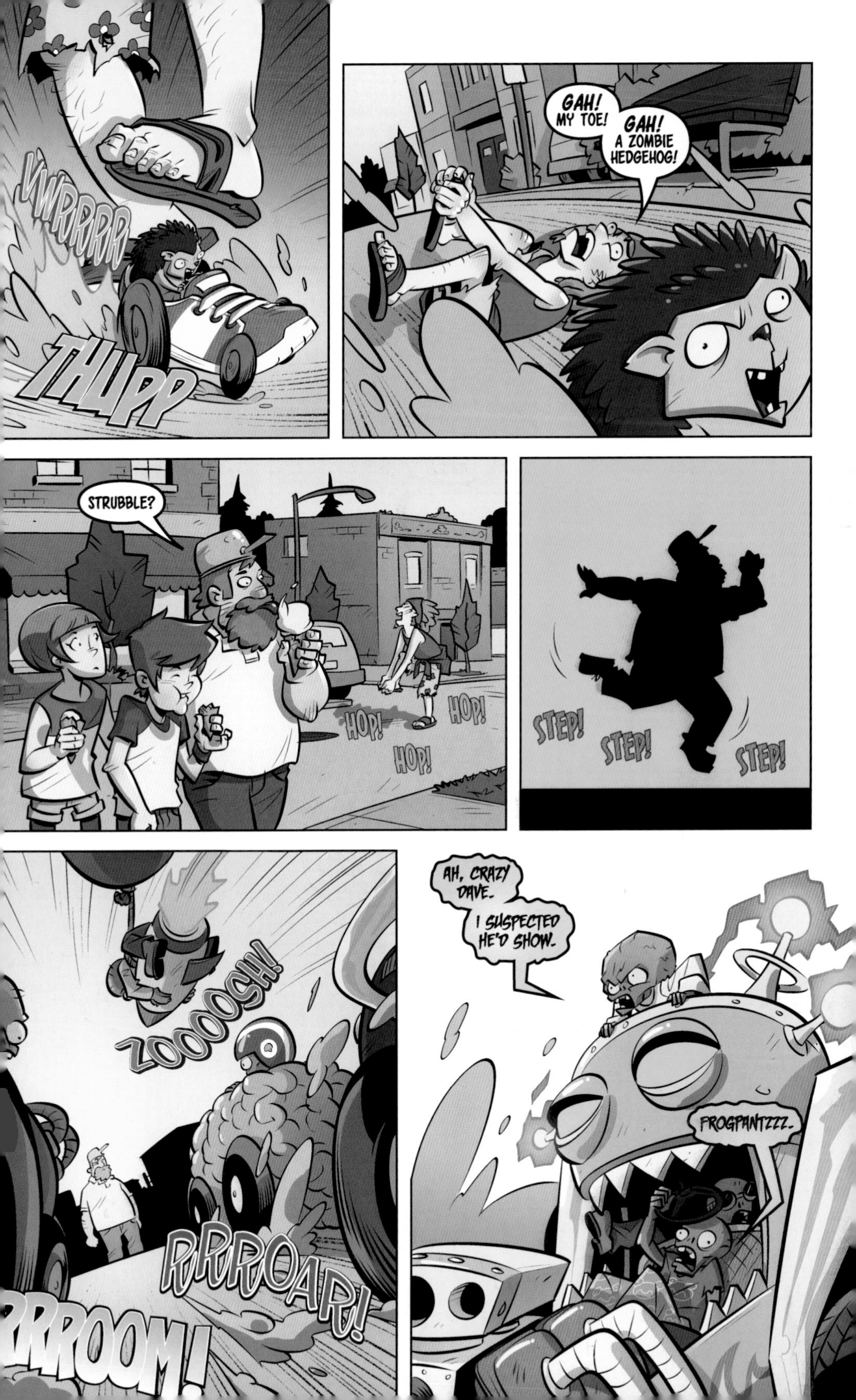
VWRRRRR
THUPP
GAH! MY TOE!
GAH! A ZOMBIE HEDGEHOG!
STRUBBLE?
HOP!
HOP!
HOP!
STEP!
STEP!
STEP!
ZOOOOOSH!
RRRROAR!
RRROOM!
AH, CRAZY DAVE.
I SUSPECTED HE'D SHOW.
FROGPANTZZZ.

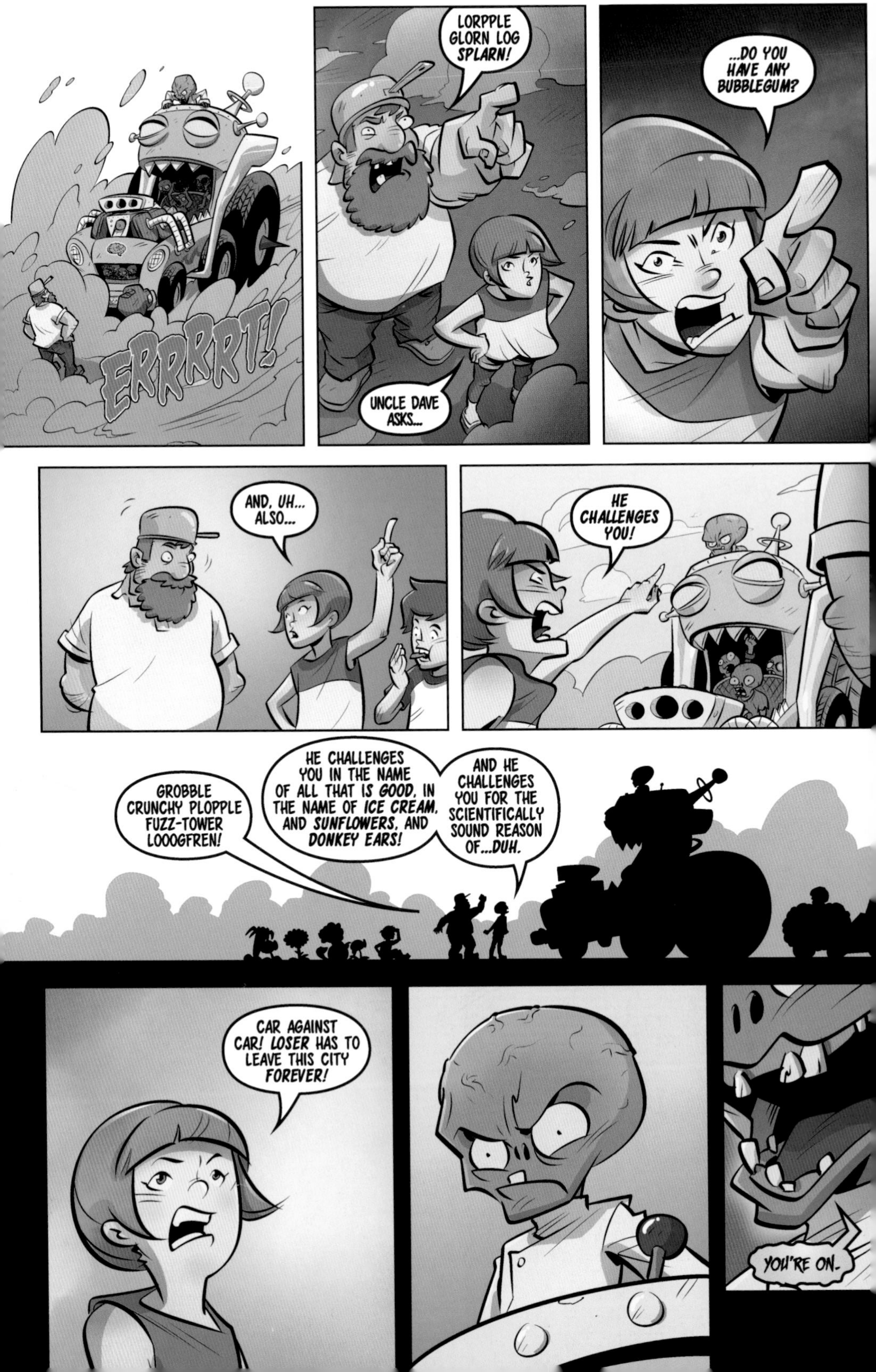
ERRRRT!
LORPPLE GLORN LOG SPLARN!
UNCLE DAVE ASKS...
...DO YOU HAVE ANY BUBBLEGUM?
AND, UH... ALSO...
HE CHALLENGES YOU!
GROBBLE CRUNCHY PLOPPLE FUZZ-TOWER LOOOGFREN!
HE CHALLENGES YOU IN THE NAME OF ALL THAT IS GOOD, IN THE NAME OF ICE CREAM, AND SUNFLOWERS, AND DONKEY EARS!
AND HE CHALLENGES YOU FOR THE SCIENTIFICALLY SOUND REASON OF...DUH.
CAR AGAINST CAR! LOSER HAS TO LEAVE THIS CITY FOREVER!
YOU'RE ON.

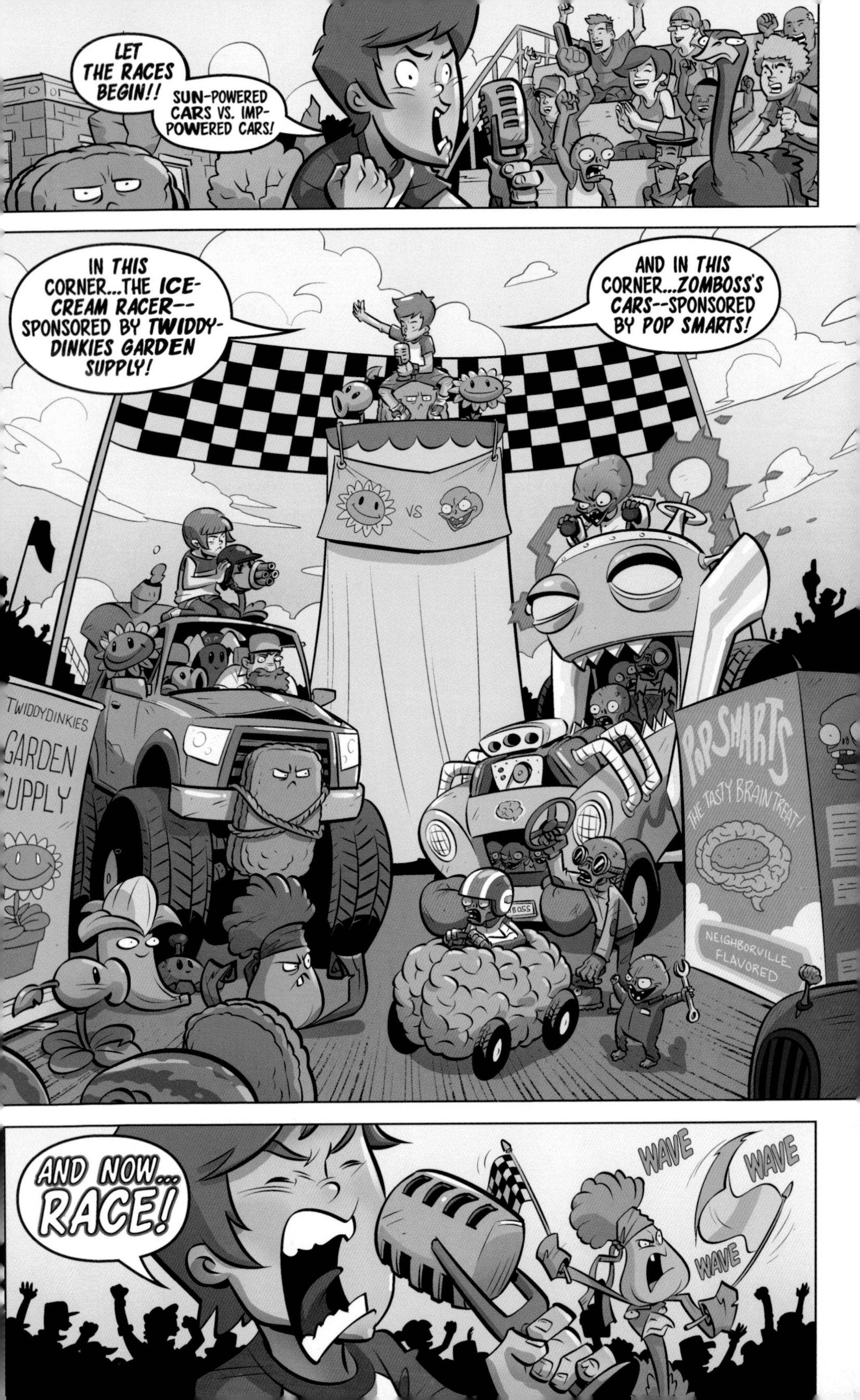
LET THE RACES BEGIN!!
SUN-POWERED CARS VS. IMP-POWERED CARS!
IN THIS CORNER...THE ICE-CREAM RACER--SPONSORED BY TWIDDYDINKIES GARDEN SUPPLY!
AND IN THIS CORNER...ZOMBOSS'S CARS--SPONSORED BY POP SMARTS!
VS
TWIDDYDINKIES GARDEN SUPPLY
POP SMARTS
THE TASTY BRAIN TREAT!
NEIGHBORVILLE FLAVORED
AND NOW... RACE!
WAVE
WAVE
WAVE

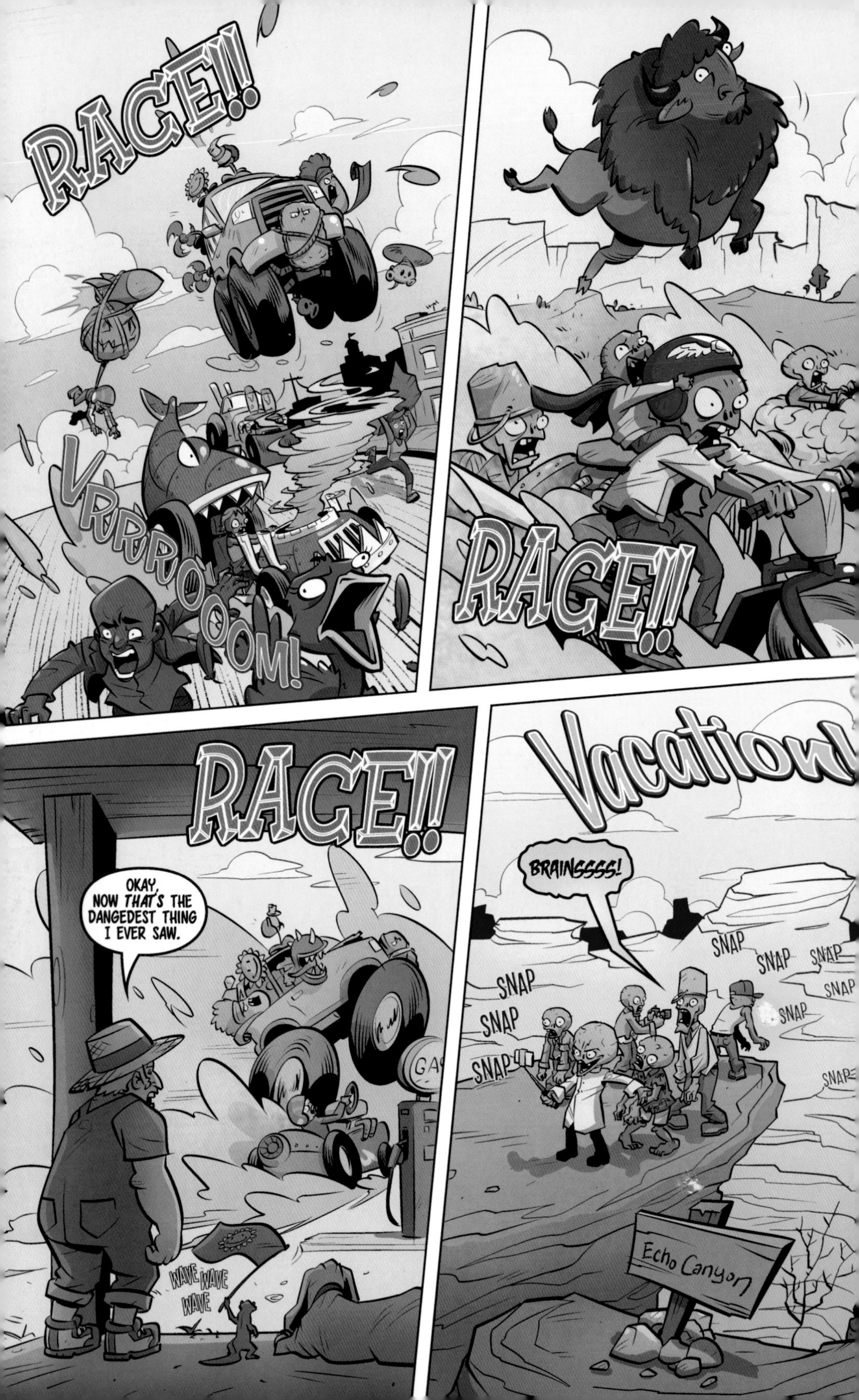
RACE!!
VRRRROOOOM!
RACE!!
RACE!!
OKAY, NOW THAT'S THE DANGEDEST THING I EVER SAW.
GAS
WAVE WAVE
WAVE
Vacation!
BRAINSSSS!
SNAP
SNAP
SNAP
SNAP
SNAP
SNAP
SNAP
SNAP
SNAP
SNAP
Echo Canyon

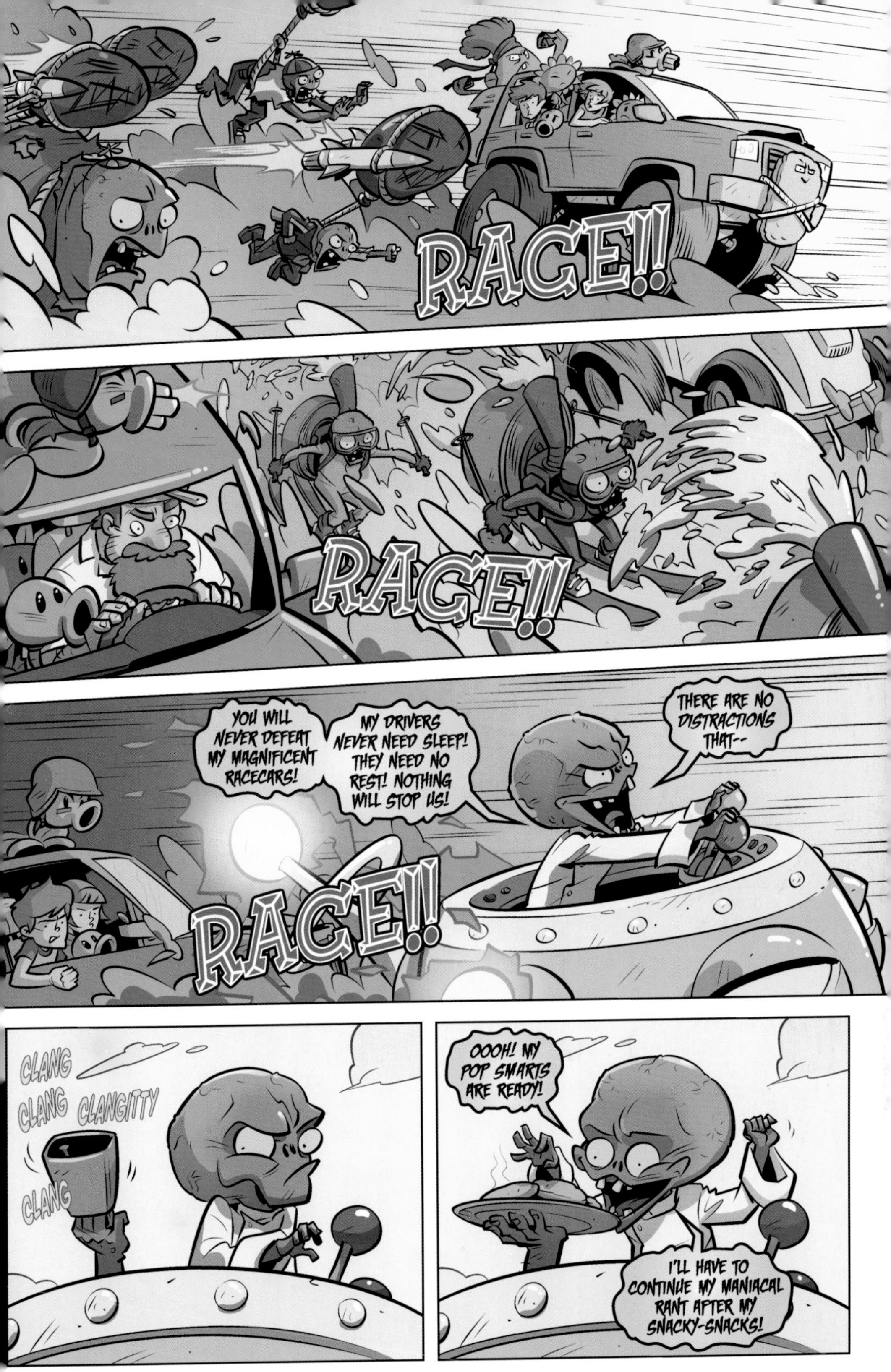
RACE!!
RACE!!
YOU WILL NEVER DEFEAT MY MAGNIFICENT RACECARS!
MY DRIVERS NEVER NEED SLEEP! THEY NEED NO REST! NOTHING WILL STOP US!
THERE ARE NO DISTRACTIONS THAT--
RACE!!
CLANG
CLANG CLANGITTY
CLANG
OOOH! MY POP SMARTS ARE READY!
I'LL HAVE TO CONTINUE MY MANIACAL RANT AFTER MY SNACKY-SNACKS!

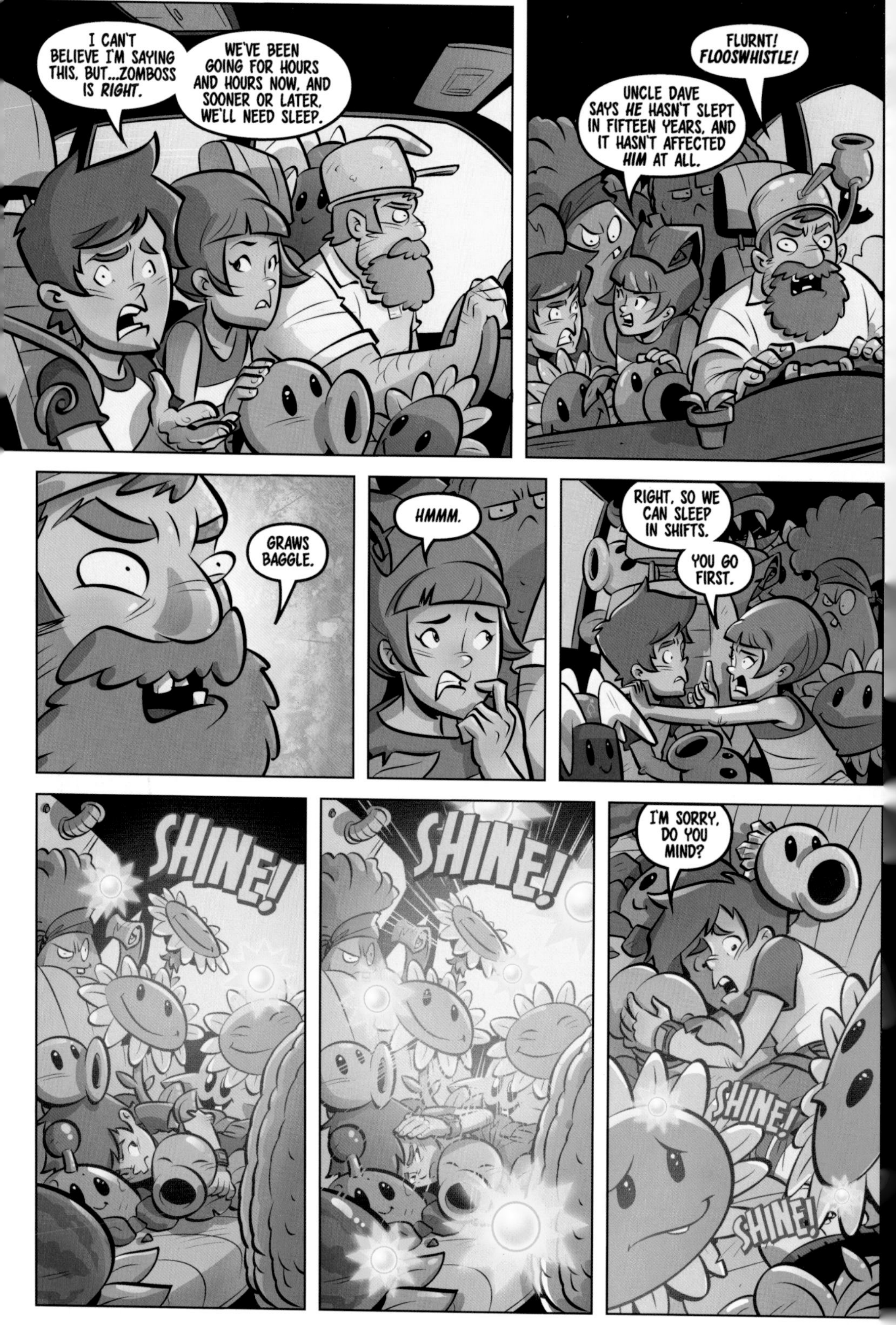

I CAN'T BELIEVE I'M SAYING THIS, BUT...ZOMBOSS IS *RIGHT*.
WE'VE BEEN GOING FOR HOURS AND HOURS NOW, AND SOONER OR LATER, WE'LL NEED SLEEP.
FLURNT! *FLOOSWHISTLE!*
UNCLE DAVE SAYS *HE* HASN'T SLEPT IN FIFTEEN YEARS, AND IT HASN'T AFFECTED *HIM* AT ALL.
GRAWS BAGGLE.
HMMM.
RIGHT, SO WE CAN SLEEP IN SHIFTS.
YOU GO FIRST.
SHINE!
SHINE!
I'M SORRY, DO YOU MIND?
SHINE!
SHINE!

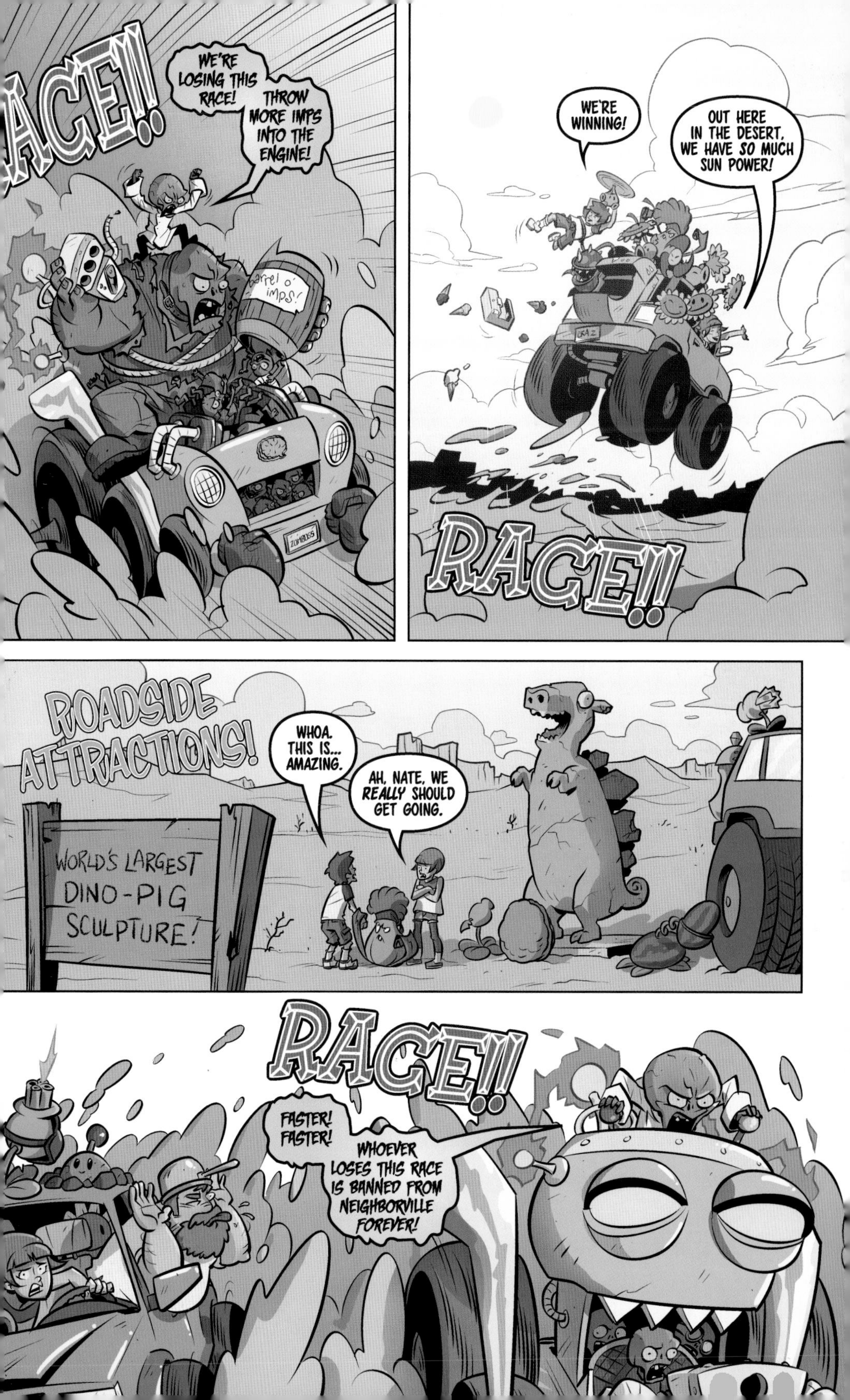
RACE!!
WE'RE LOSING THIS RACE!
THROW MORE IMPS INTO THE ENGINE!
barrel o' imps!
ZOMBOSS
WE'RE WINNING!
OUT HERE IN THE DESERT, WE HAVE SO MUCH SUN POWER!
RACE!!
ROADSIDE ATTRACTIONS!
WHOA. THIS IS... AMAZING.
AH, NATE, WE REALLY SHOULD GET GOING.
WORLD'S LARGEST DINO-PIG SCULPTURE!
RACE!!
FASTER! FASTER!
WHOEVER LOSES THIS RACE IS BANNED FROM NEIGHBORVILLE FOREVER!

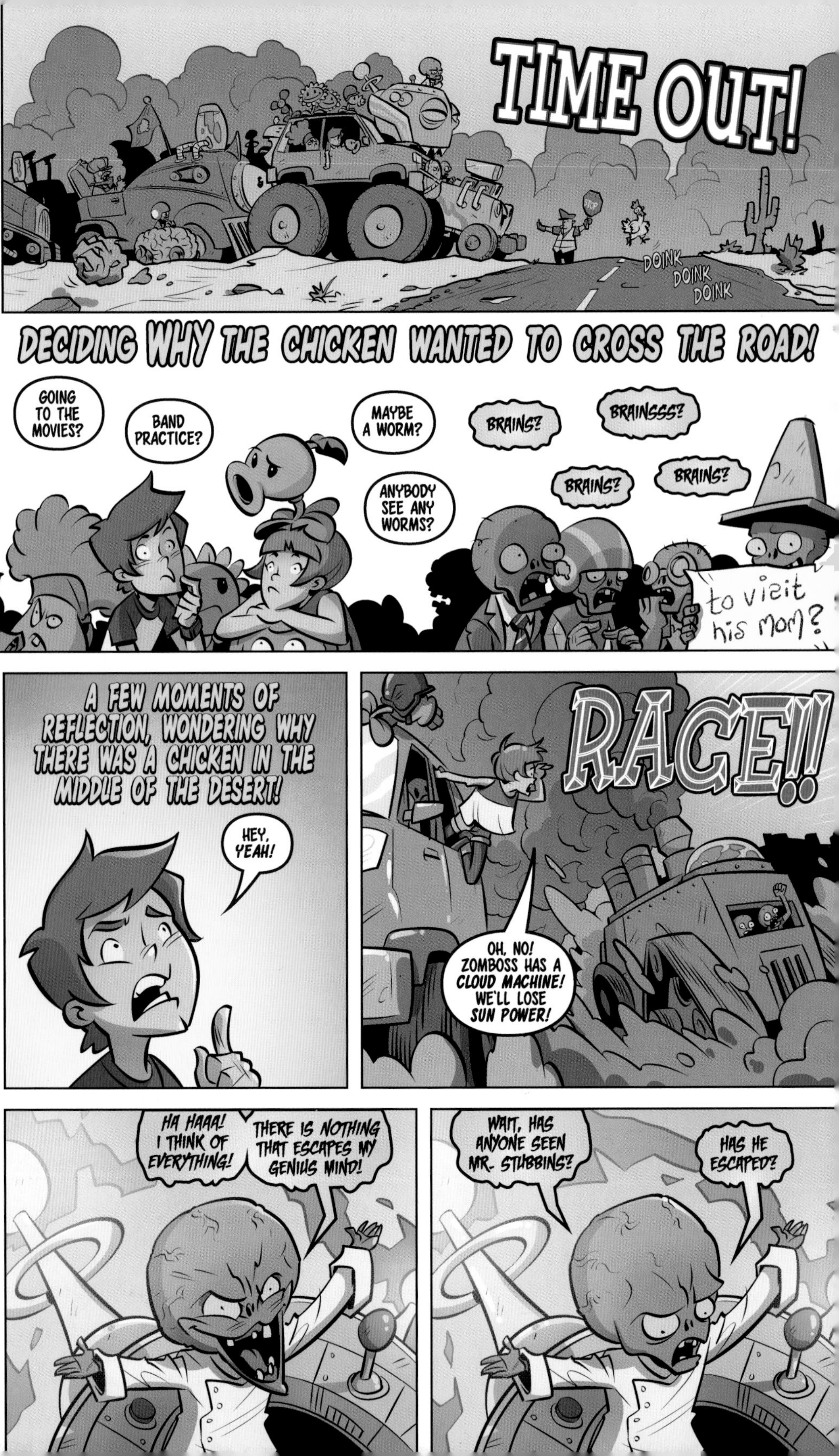
TIME OUT!
DOINK DOINK DOINK
DECIDING WHY THE CHICKEN WANTED TO CROSS THE ROAD!
GOING TO THE MOVIES?
BAND PRACTICE?
MAYBE A WORM?
ANYBODY SEE ANY WORMS?
BRAINS?
BRAINSSS?
BRAINS?
BRAINS?
to visit his mom?
A FEW MOMENTS OF REFLECTION, WONDERING WHY THERE WAS A CHICKEN IN THE MIDDLE OF THE DESERT!
HEY, YEAH!
RACE!!
OH, NO! ZOMBOSS HAS A CLOUD MACHINE! WE'LL LOSE SUN POWER!
HA HAAA! I THINK OF EVERYTHING!
THERE IS NOTHING THAT ESCAPES MY GENIUS MIND!
WAIT, HAS ANYONE SEEN MR. STUBBINS?
HAS HE ESCAPED?

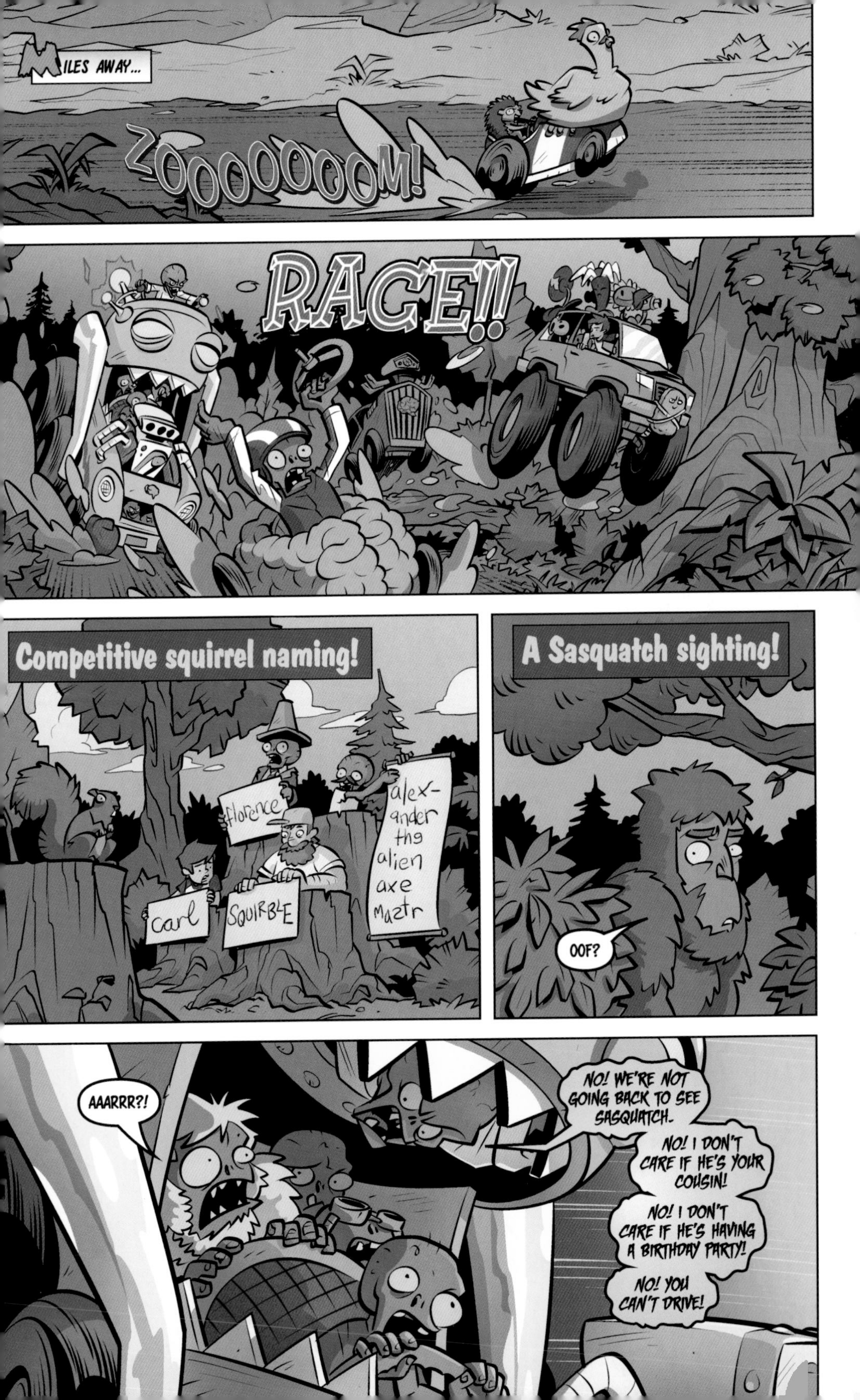
MILES AWAY...
ZOOOOOOOOM!
RACE!!
Competitive squirrel naming!
florence
alex-ander the alien axe maztr
carl
SQUIRBLE
A Sasquatch sighting!
OOF?
AAARRR?!
NO! WE'RE NOT GOING BACK TO SEE SASQUATCH.
NO! I DON'T CARE IF HE'S YOUR COUSIN!
NO! I DON'T CARE IF HE'S HAVING A BIRTHDAY PARTY!
NO! YOU CAN'T DRIVE!

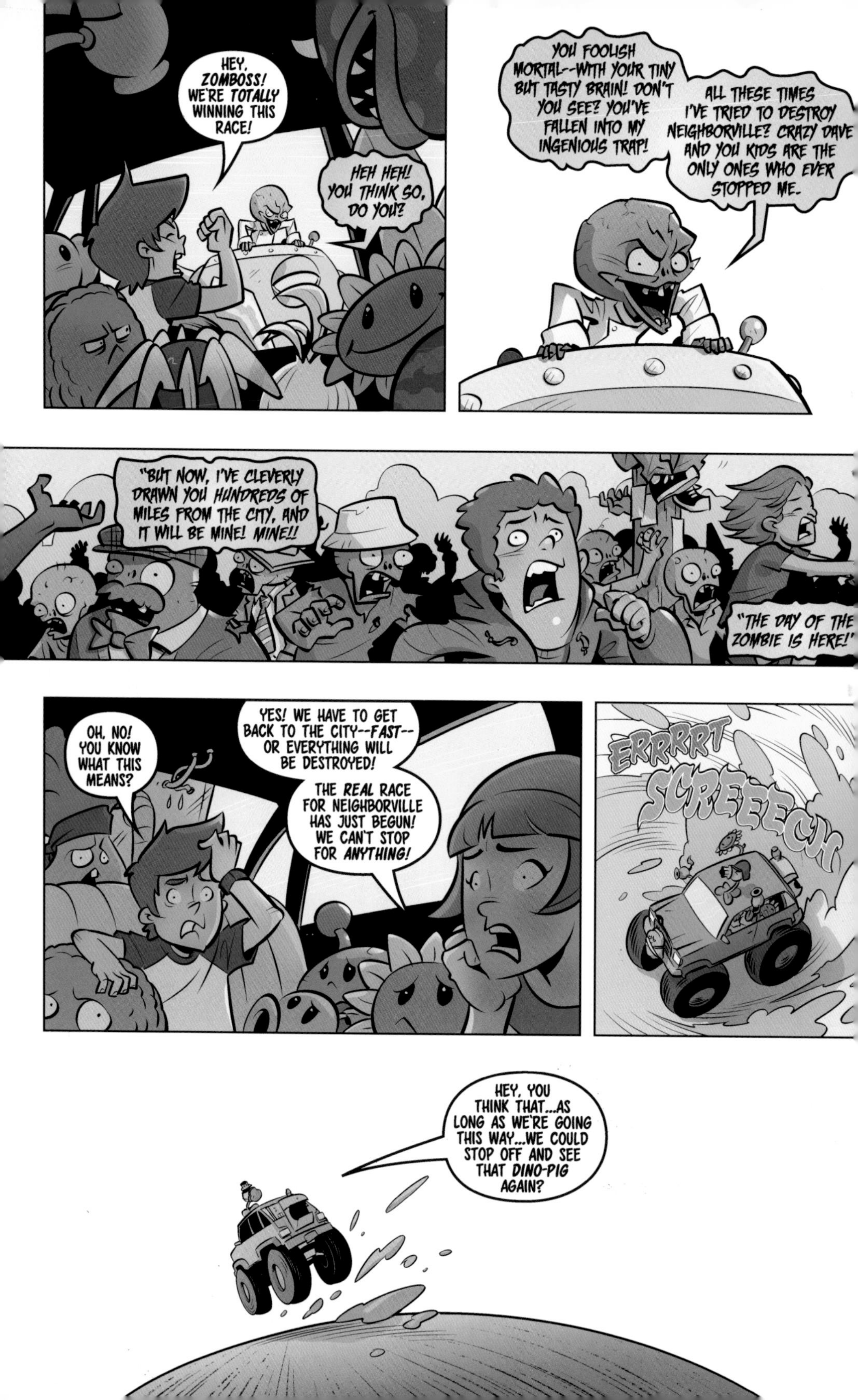

HEY, ZOMBOSS! WE'RE TOTALLY WINNING THIS RACE!
HEH HEH! YOU THINK SO, DO YOU?
YOU FOOLISH MORTAL--WITH YOUR TINY BUT TASTY BRAIN! DON'T YOU SEE? YOU'VE FALLEN INTO MY INGENIOUS TRAP!
ALL THESE TIMES I'VE TRIED TO DESTROY NEIGHBORVILLE? CRAZY DAVE AND YOU KIDS ARE THE ONLY ONES WHO EVER STOPPED ME.
"BUT NOW, I'VE CLEVERLY DRAWN YOU HUNDREDS OF MILES FROM THE CITY, AND IT WILL BE MINE! MINE!!
"THE DAY OF THE ZOMBIE IS HERE!"
OH, NO! YOU KNOW WHAT THIS MEANS?
YES! WE HAVE TO GET BACK TO THE CITY--FAST--OR EVERYTHING WILL BE DESTROYED!
THE REAL RACE FOR NEIGHBORVILLE HAS JUST BEGUN! WE CAN'T STOP FOR ANYTHING!
ERRRRT
SCREEECH
HEY, YOU THINK THAT...AS LONG AS WE'RE GOING THIS WAY...WE COULD STOP OFF AND SEE THAT DINO-PIG AGAIN?

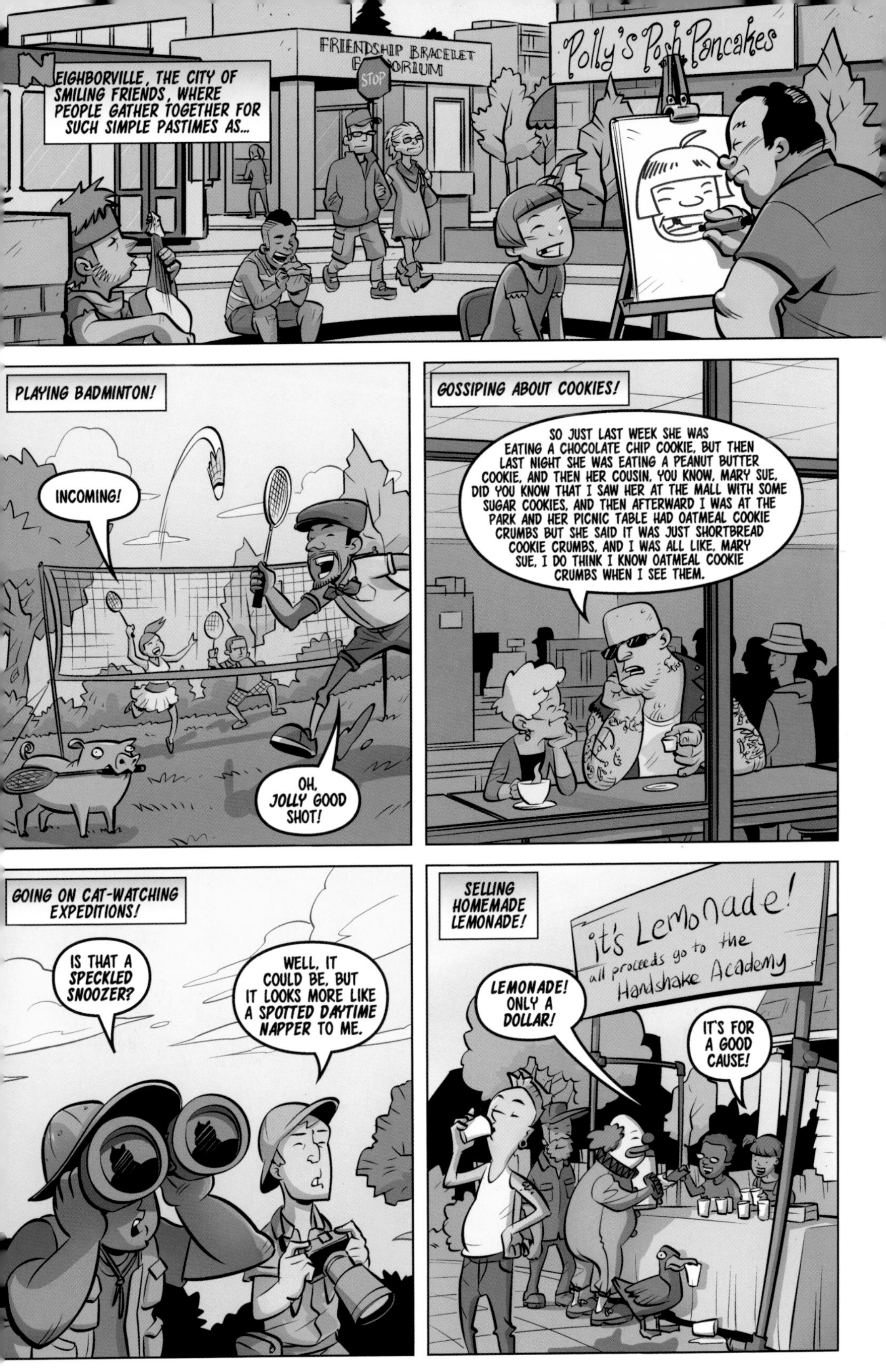
FRIENDSHIP BRACELET
STOP
Polly's Posh Pancakes
NEIGHBORVILLE, THE CITY OF SMILING FRIENDS, WHERE PEOPLE GATHER TOGETHER FOR SUCH SIMPLE PASTIMES AS...
PLAYING BADMINTON!
INCOMING!
OH, JOLLY GOOD SHOT!
GOSSIPING ABOUT COOKIES!
SO JUST LAST WEEK SHE WAS EATING A CHOCOLATE CHIP COOKIE, BUT THEN LAST NIGHT SHE WAS EATING A PEANUT BUTTER COOKIE, AND THEN HER COUSIN, YOU KNOW, MARY SUE, DID YOU KNOW THAT I SAW HER AT THE MALL WITH SOME SUGAR COOKIES, AND THEN AFTERWARD I WAS AT THE PARK AND HER PICNIC TABLE HAD OATMEAL COOKIE CRUMBS BUT SHE SAID IT WAS JUST SHORTBREAD COOKIE CRUMBS, AND I WAS ALL LIKE, MARY SUE, I DO THINK I KNOW OATMEAL COOKIE CRUMBS WHEN I SEE THEM.
GOING ON CAT-WATCHING EXPEDITIONS!
IS THAT A SPECKLED SNOOZER?
WELL, IT COULD BE, BUT IT LOOKS MORE LIKE A SPOTTED DAYTIME NAPPER TO ME.
SELLING HOMEMADE LEMONADE!
it's Lemonade!
all proceeds go to the Handshake Academy
LEMONADE! ONLY A DOLLAR!
IT'S FOR A GOOD CAUSE!

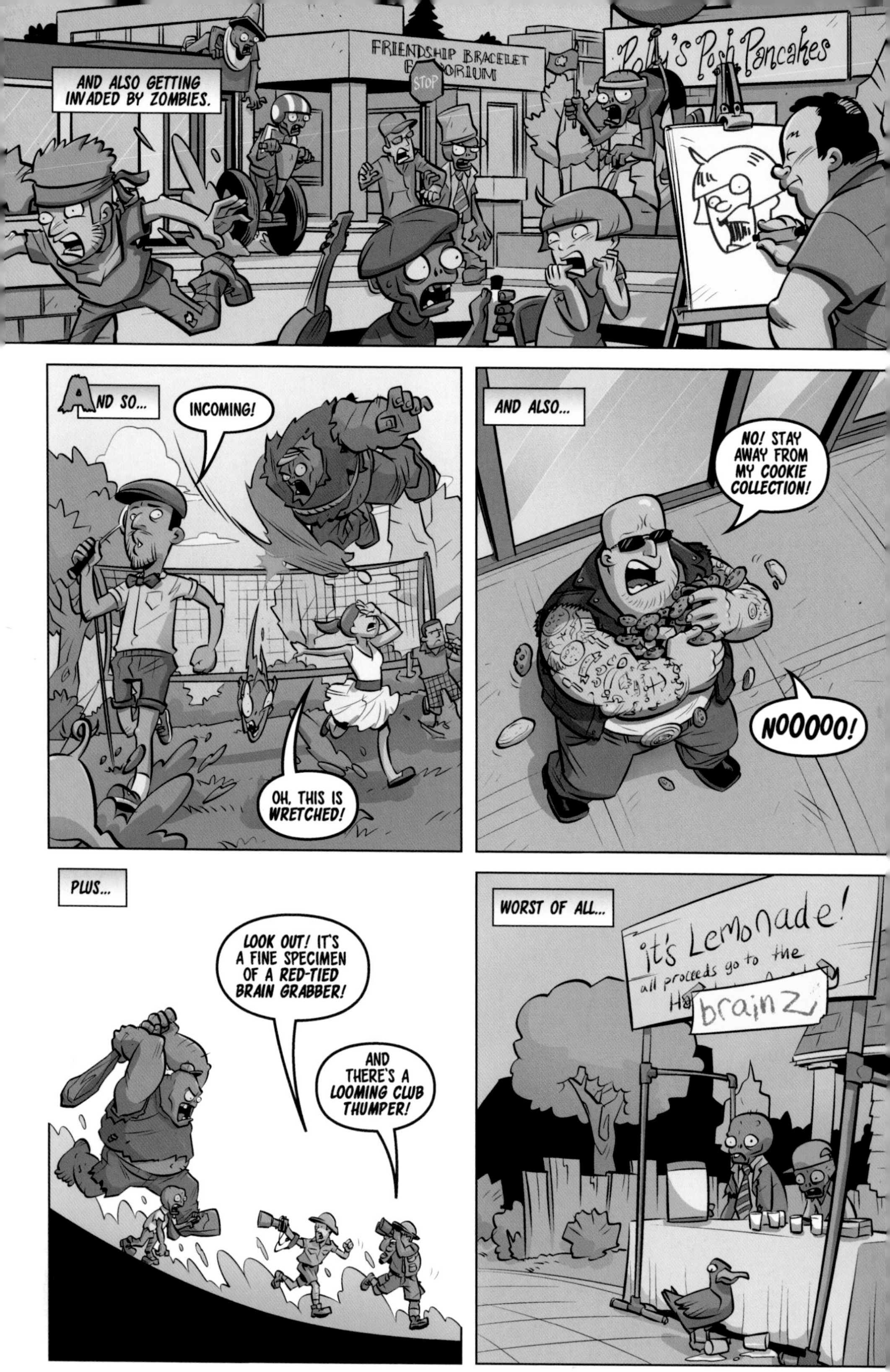
AND ALSO GETTING INVADED BY ZOMBIES.
FRIENDSHIP BRACELET
STOP
Posh Pancakes
AND SO...
INCOMING!
OH, THIS IS WRETCHED!
AND ALSO...
NO! STAY AWAY FROM MY COOKIE COLLECTION!
NOOOOO!
PLUS...
LOOK OUT! IT'S A FINE SPECIMEN OF A RED-TIED BRAIN GRABBER!
AND THERE'S A LOOMING CLUB THUMPER!
WORST OF ALL...
it's Lemonade!
all proceeds go to the
brainz

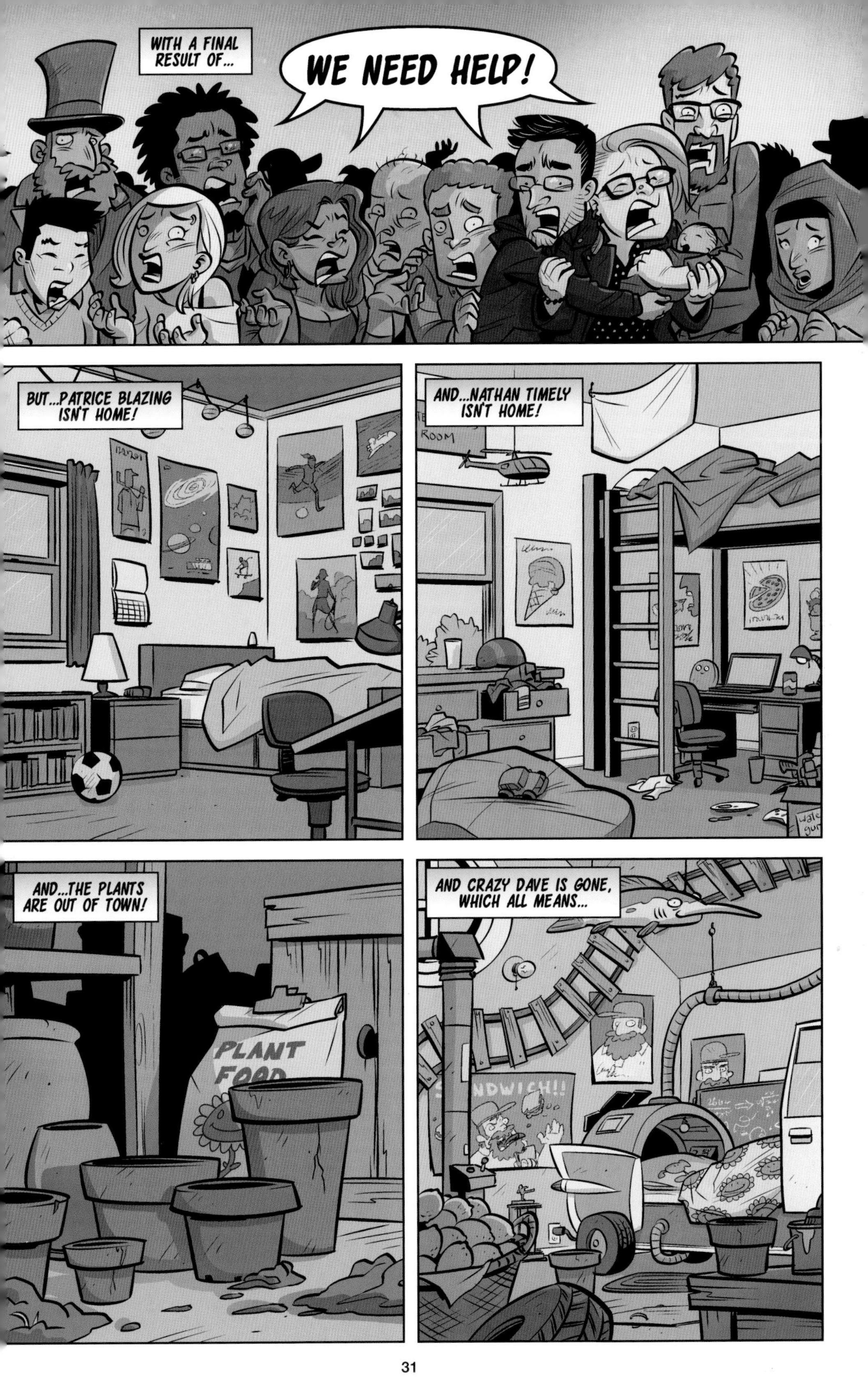
WITH A FINAL RESULT OF...
WE NEED HELP!
BUT...PATRICE BLAZING ISN'T HOME!
AND...NATHAN TIMELY ISN'T HOME!
AND...THE PLANTS ARE OUT OF TOWN!
PLANT FOOD
AND CRAZY DAVE IS GONE, WHICH ALL MEANS...
SANDWICH!!

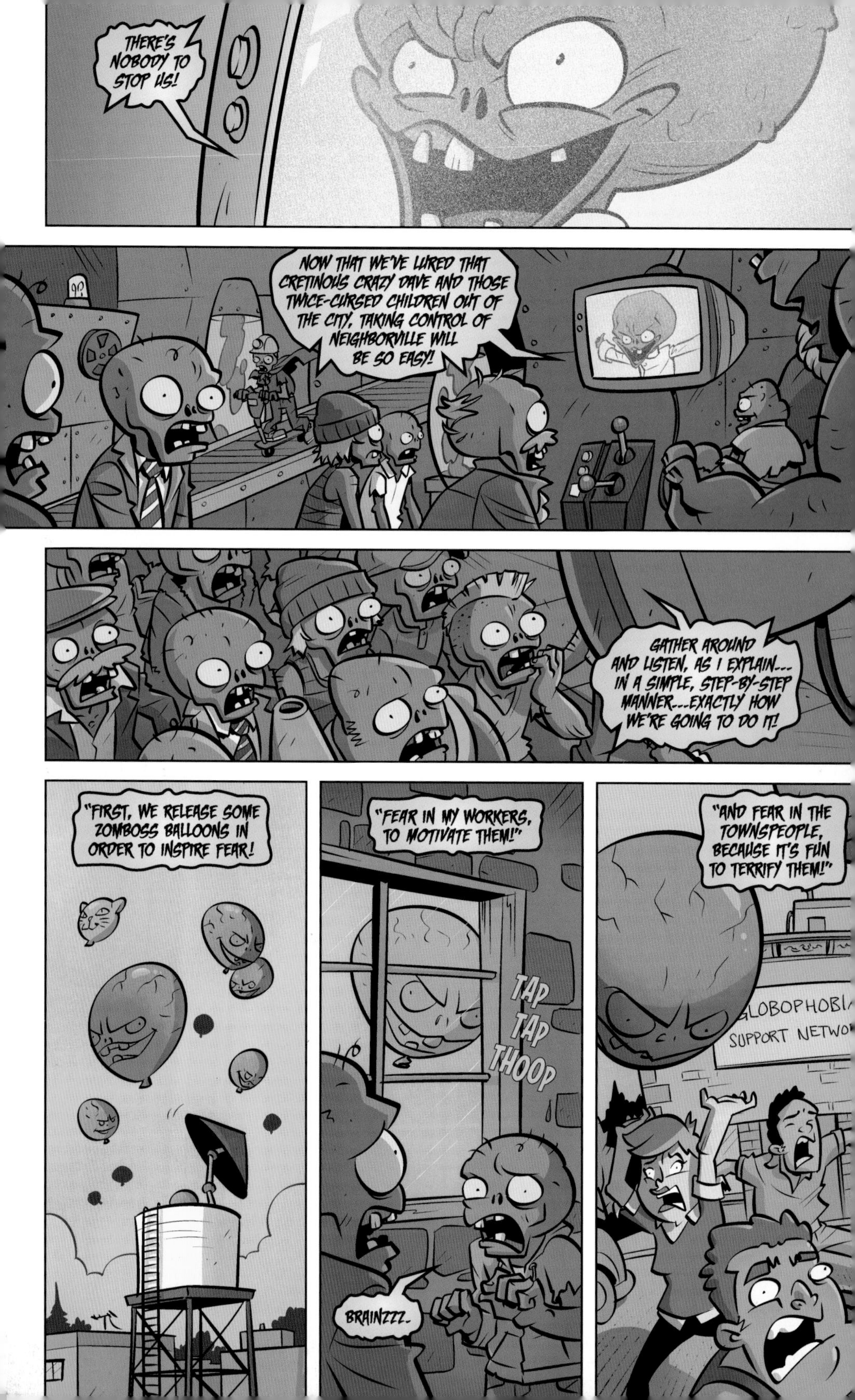
THERE'S NOBODY TO STOP US!
NOW THAT WE'VE LURED THAT CRETINOUS CRAZY DAVE AND THOSE TWICE-CURSED CHILDREN OUT OF THE CITY, TAKING CONTROL OF NEIGHBORVILLE WILL BE SO EASY!
GATHER AROUND AND LISTEN, AS I EXPLAIN... IN A SIMPLE, STEP-BY-STEP MANNER...EXACTLY HOW WE'RE GOING TO DO IT!
"FIRST, WE RELEASE SOME ZOMBOSS BALLOONS IN ORDER TO INSPIRE FEAR!
"FEAR IN MY WORKERS, TO MOTIVATE THEM!"
TAP
TAP
THOOP
BRAINZZZ.
"AND FEAR IN THE TOWNSPEOPLE, BECAUSE IT'S FUN TO TERRIFY THEM!"
GLOBOPHOBI
SUPPORT NETWO

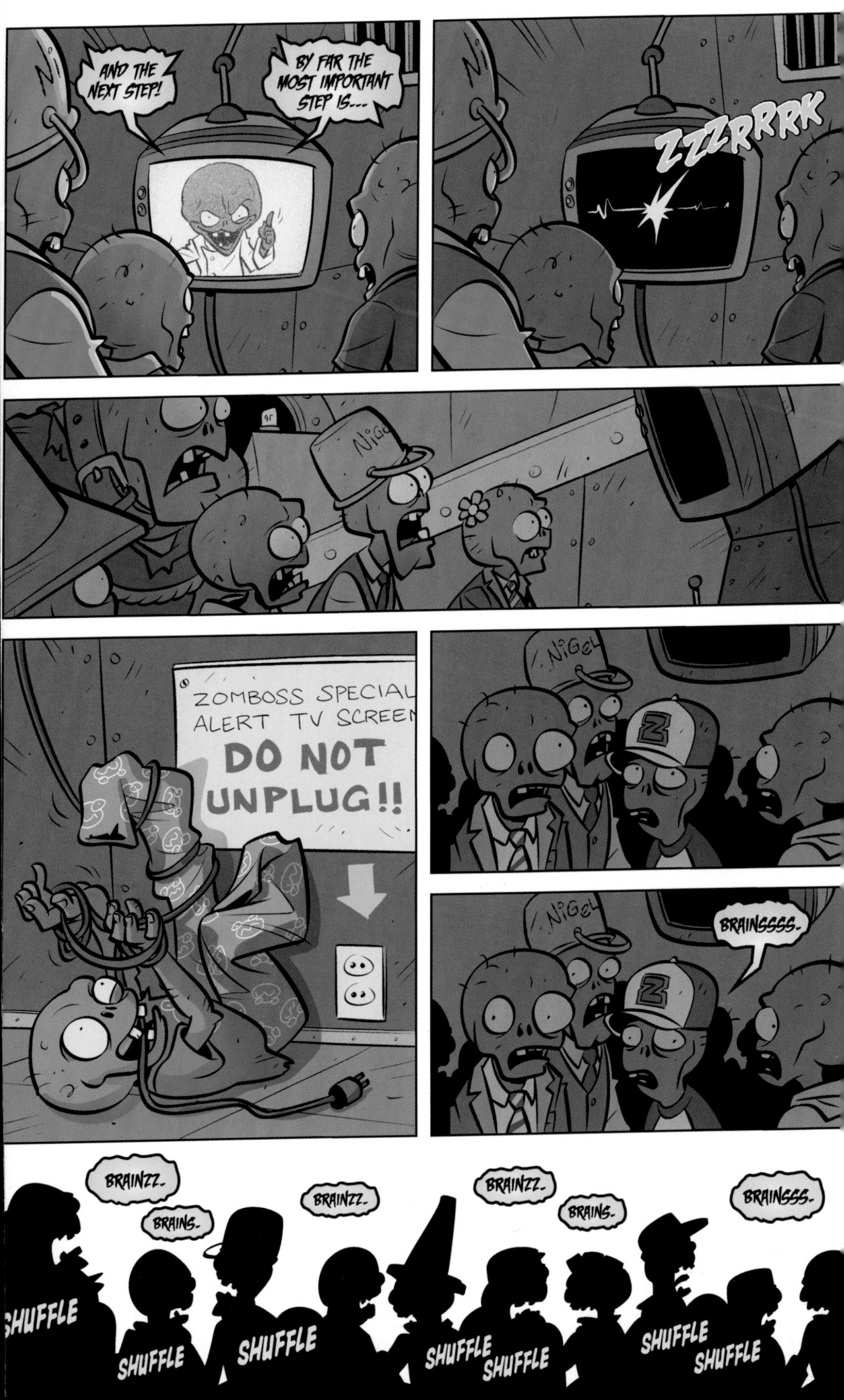
AND THE NEXT STEP!
BY FAR THE MOST IMPORTANT STEP IS...
ZZZRRRK
ZOMBOSS SPECIAL ALERT TV SCREEN
DO NOT UNPLUG!!
BRAINSSSS.
BRAINZZ.
BRAINS.
BRAINZZ.
BRAINZZ.
BRAINS.
BRAINSSS.
SHUFFLE
SHUFFLE
SHUFFLE
SHUFFLE
SHUFFLE
SHUFFLE
SHUFFLE

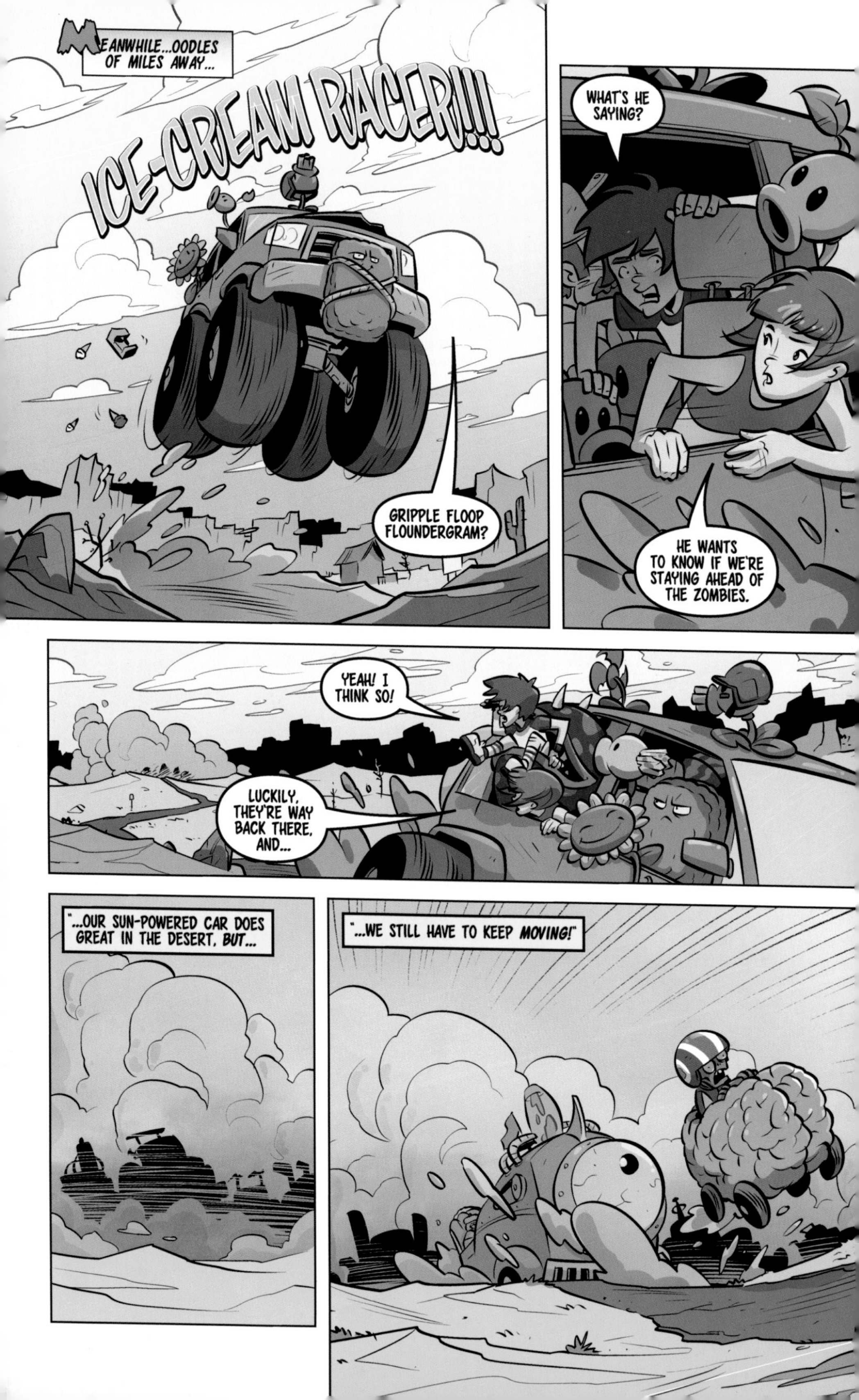
MEANWHILE...OODLES OF MILES AWAY...
ICE-CREAM RACER!!!
GRIPPLE FLOOP FLOUNDERGRAM?
WHAT'S HE SAYING?
HE WANTS TO KNOW IF WE'RE STAYING AHEAD OF THE ZOMBIES.
YEAH! I THINK SO!
LUCKILY, THEY'RE WAY BACK THERE, AND...
"...OUR SUN-POWERED CAR DOES GREAT IN THE DESERT, BUT...
"...WE STILL HAVE TO KEEP MOVING!"

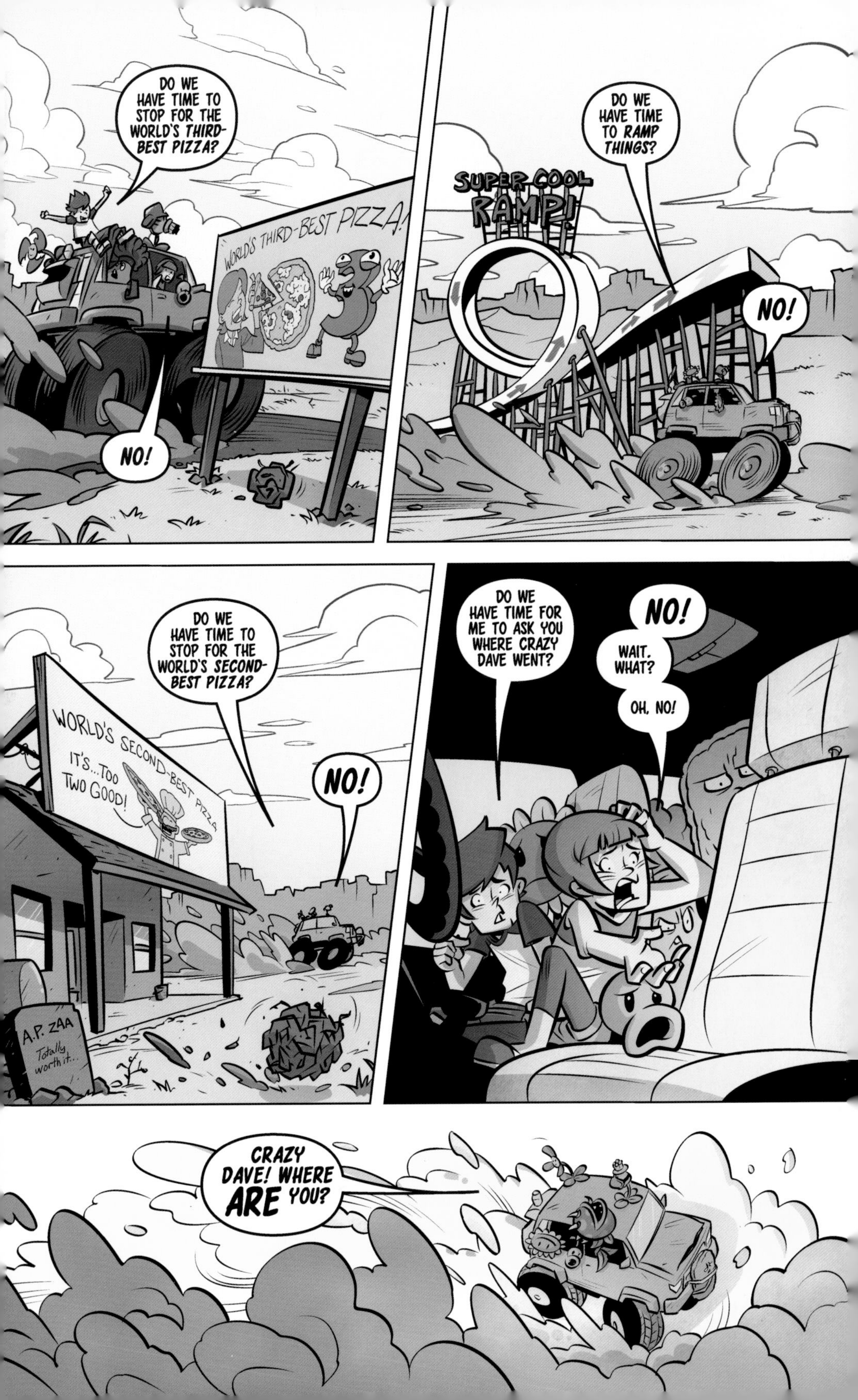
DO WE HAVE TIME TO STOP FOR THE WORLD'S THIRD-BEST PIZZA?
WORLD'S THIRD-BEST PIZZA!
NO!
SUPER COOL RAMP!
DO WE HAVE TIME TO RAMP THINGS?
NO!
DO WE HAVE TIME TO STOP FOR THE WORLD'S SECOND-BEST PIZZA?
WORLD'S SECOND-BEST PIZZA
IT'S...TOO TWO GOOD!
A.P. ZAA
Totally worth it...
NO!
DO WE HAVE TIME FOR ME TO ASK YOU WHERE CRAZY DAVE WENT?
NO!
WAIT. WHAT?
OH, NO!
CRAZY DAVE! WHERE ARE YOU?

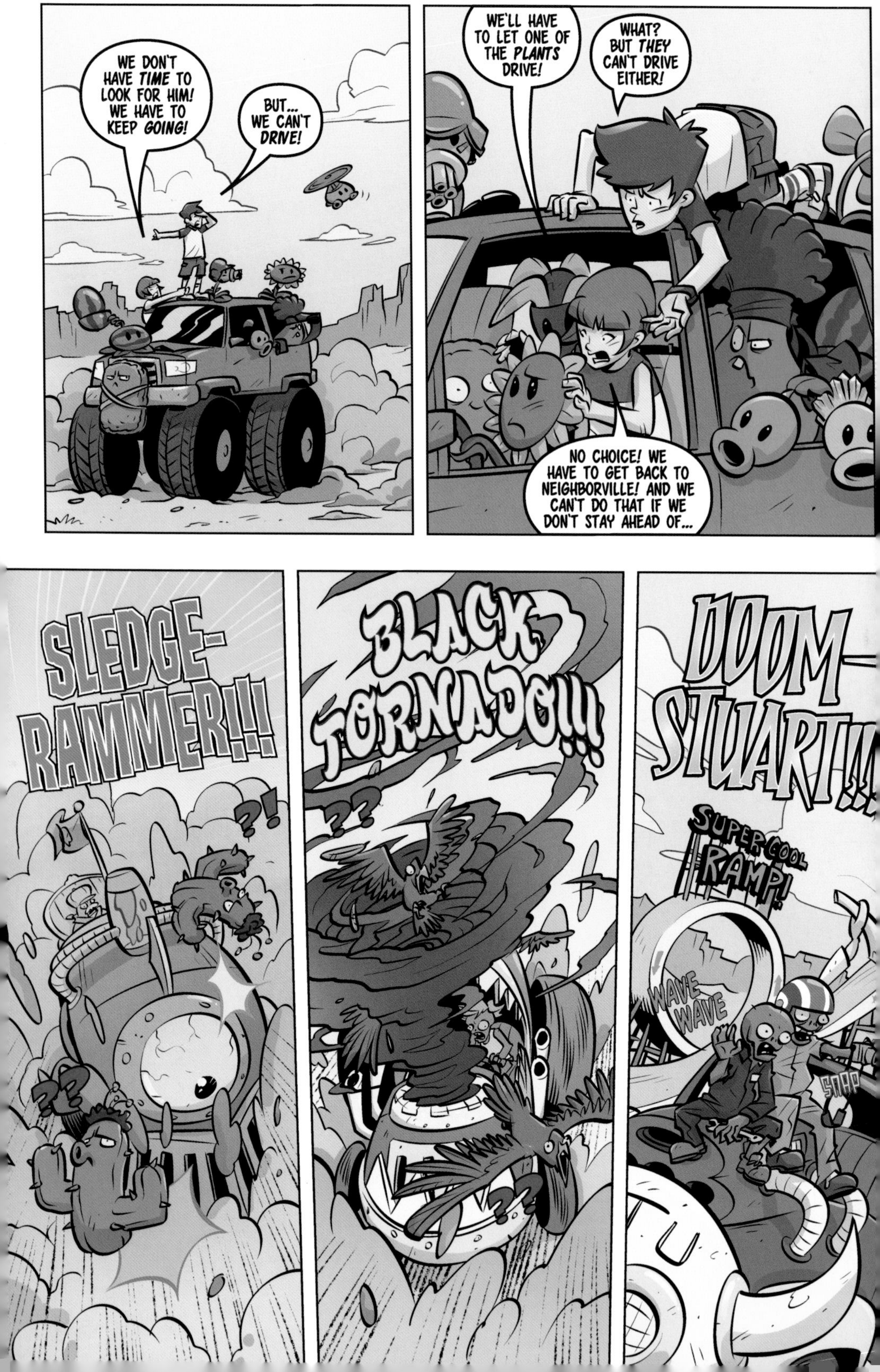

WE DON'T HAVE TIME TO LOOK FOR HIM! WE HAVE TO KEEP GOING!
BUT... WE CAN'T DRIVE!
WE'LL HAVE TO LET ONE OF THE PLANTS DRIVE!
WHAT? BUT THEY CAN'T DRIVE EITHER!
NO CHOICE! WE HAVE TO GET BACK TO NEIGHBORVILLE! AND WE CAN'T DO THAT IF WE DON'T STAY AHEAD OF...
SLEDGE-RAMMER!!!
?!
BLACK TORNADO!!!
??
DOOM-STUART!!!
SUPER COOL RAMP!
WAVE WAVE

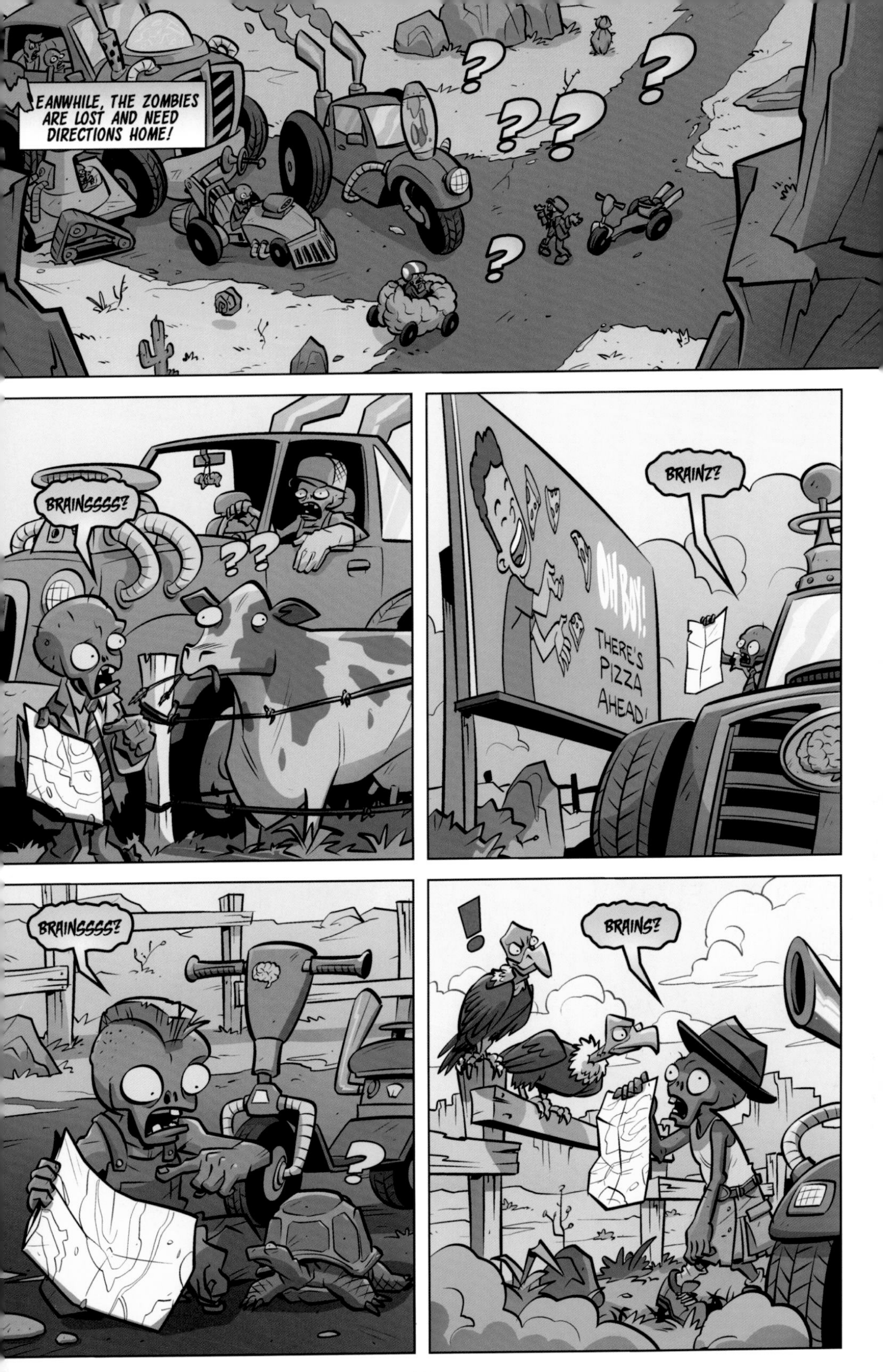
EANWHILE, THE ZOMBIES ARE LOST AND NEED DIRECTIONS HOME!
BRAINSSSS?
BRAINZ?
OH BOY! THERE'S PIZZA AHEAD!
BRAINSSSS?
BRAINS?

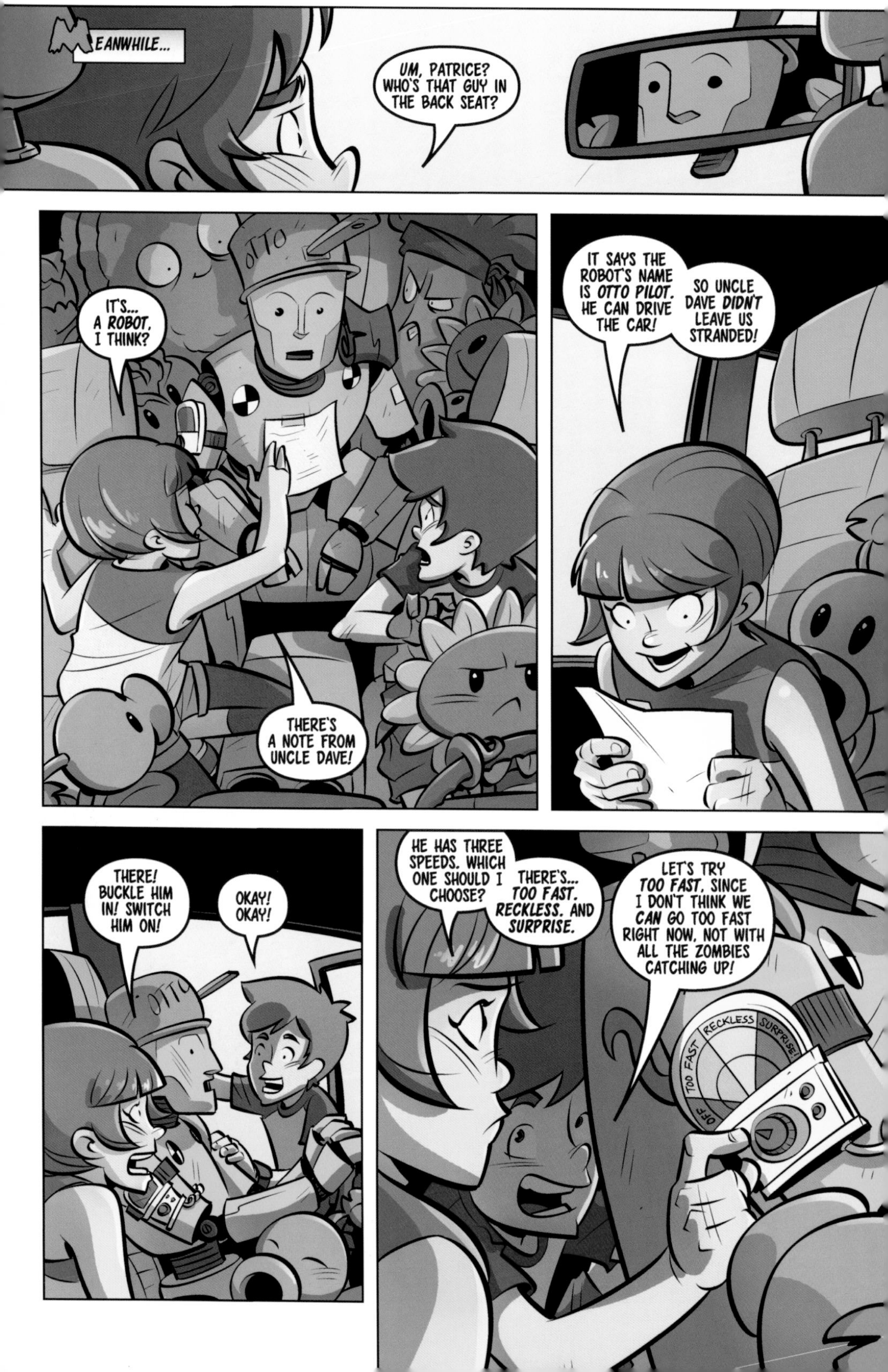
MEANWHILE...
UM, PATRICE? WHO'S THAT GUY IN THE BACK SEAT?
IT'S... A ROBOT, I THINK?
THERE'S A NOTE FROM UNCLE DAVE!
IT SAYS THE ROBOT'S NAME IS OTTO PILOT. HE CAN DRIVE THE CAR!
SO UNCLE DAVE DIDN'T LEAVE US STRANDED!
OTTO
THERE! BUCKLE HIM IN! SWITCH HIM ON!
OKAY! OKAY!
HE HAS THREE SPEEDS. WHICH ONE SHOULD I CHOOSE?
THERE'S... TOO FAST, RECKLESS, AND SURPRISE.
LET'S TRY TOO FAST, SINCE I DON'T THINK WE CAN GO TOO FAST RIGHT NOW, NOT WITH ALL THE ZOMBIES CATCHING UP!
OFF
TOO FAST
RECKLESS
SURPRISE!

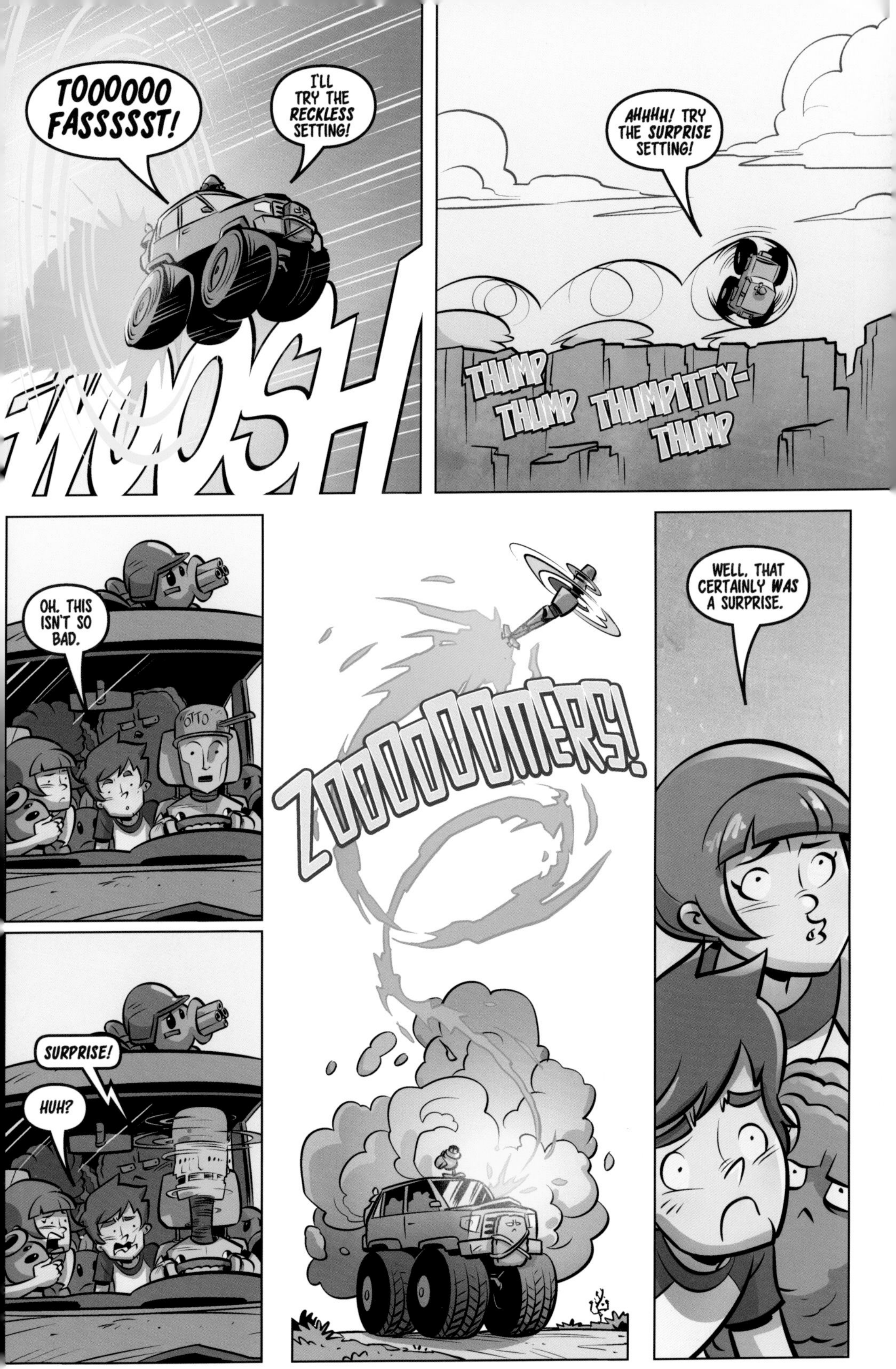
TOOOOOO FASSSSST!
I'LL TRY THE RECKLESS SETTING!
FWOOSH
AHHHH! TRY THE SURPRISE SETTING!
THUMP THUMP THUMPITTY-THUMP
OH. THIS ISN'T SO BAD.
OTTO
SURPRISE!
HUH?
ZOOOOOOOMERS!
WELL, THAT CERTAINLY WAS A SURPRISE.

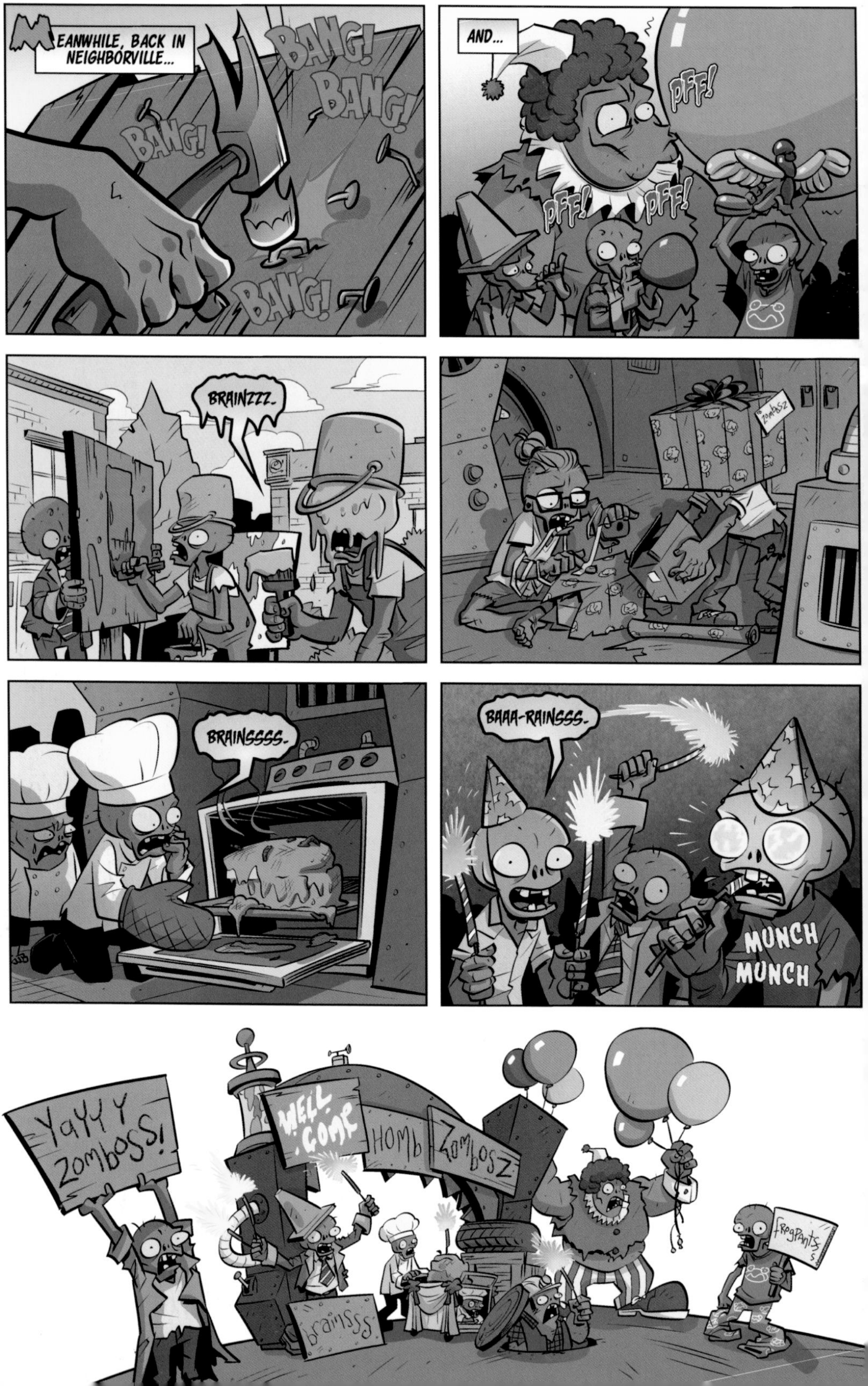
MEANWHILE, BACK IN NEIGHBORVILLE...
BANG!
BANG!
BANG!
BANG!
AND...
PFF!
PFF!
PFF!
BRAINZZZ...
BRAINSSSS...
BAAA-RAINSSS...
MUNCH
MUNCH
YaYYY Zomboss!
WELL COME
HOMb
Zombosz
brainsss
frogpants

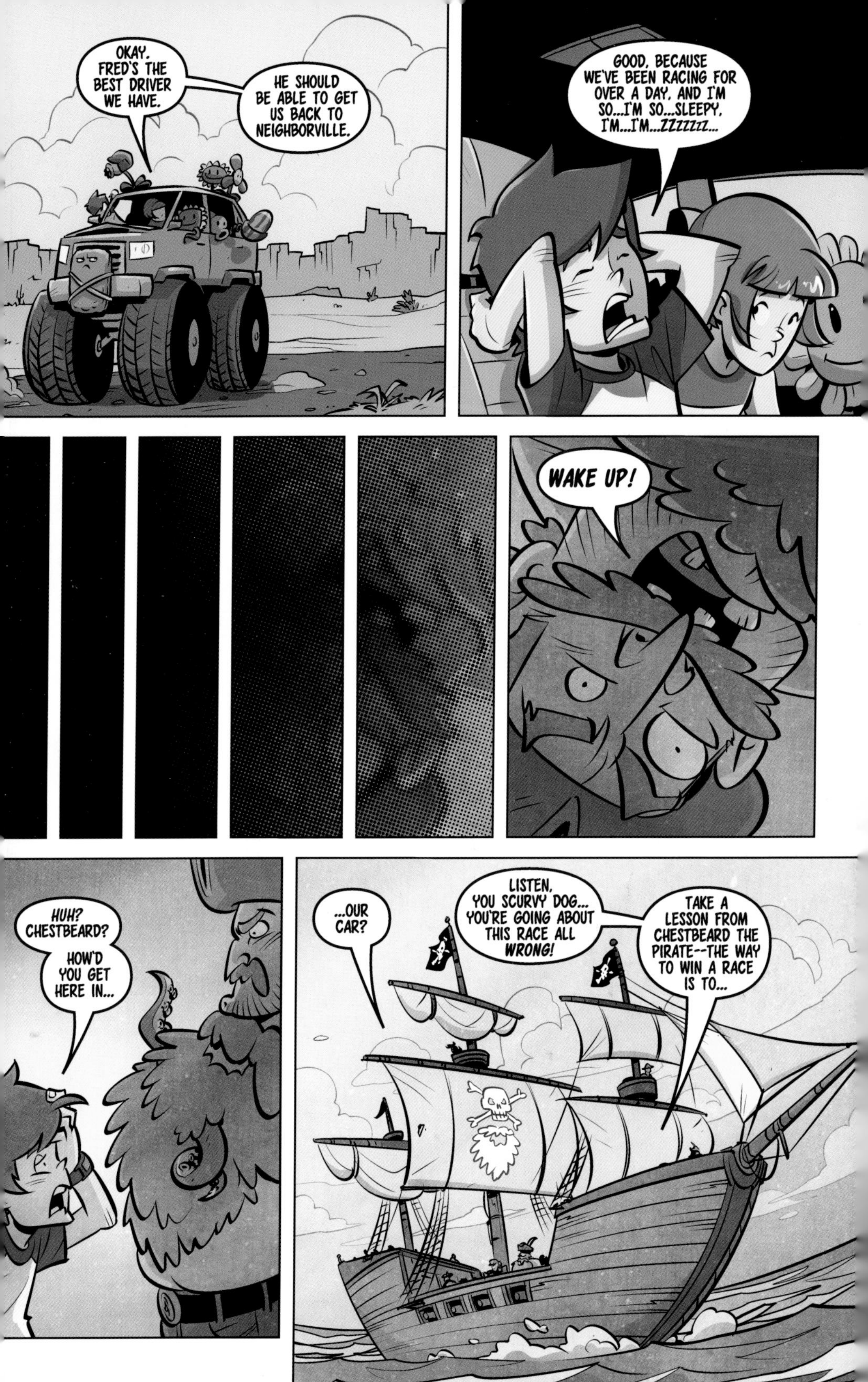
OKAY. FRED'S THE BEST DRIVER WE HAVE.
HE SHOULD BE ABLE TO GET US BACK TO NEIGHBORVILLE.
GOOD, BECAUSE WE'VE BEEN RACING FOR OVER A DAY, AND I'M SO...I'M SO...SLEEPY, I'M...I'M...ZZZZZZZ...
WAKE UP!
HUH? CHESTBEARD?
HOW'D YOU GET HERE IN...
...OUR CAR?
LISTEN, YOU SCURVY DOG... YOU'RE GOING ABOUT THIS RACE ALL WRONG!
TAKE A LESSON FROM CHESTBEARD THE PIRATE--THE WAY TO WIN A RACE IS TO...

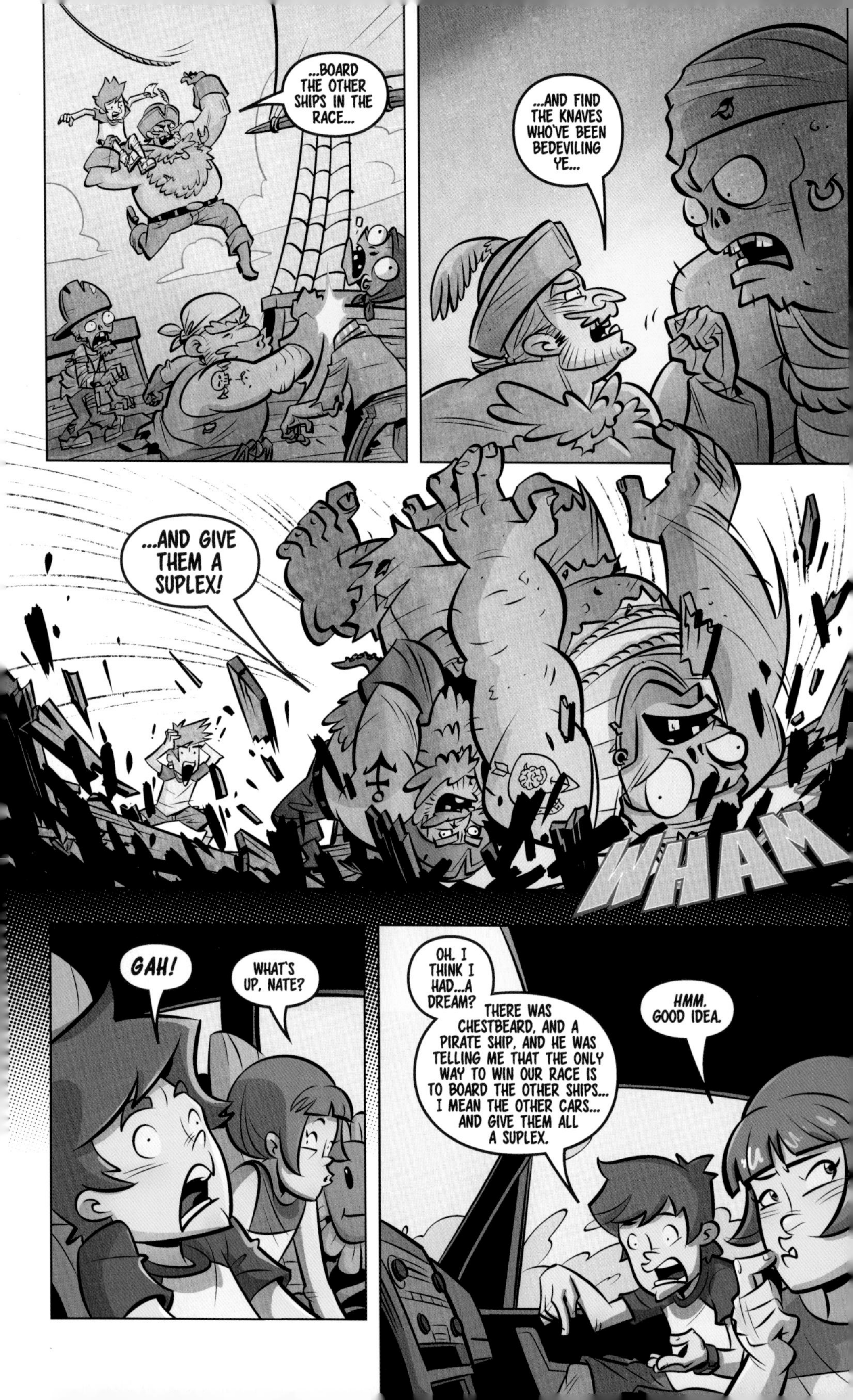

...BOARD THE OTHER SHIPS IN THE RACE...
...AND FIND THE KNAVES WHO'VE BEEN BEDEVILING YE...
...AND GIVE THEM A SUPLEX!
WHAM
GAH!
WHAT'S UP, NATE?
OH. I THINK I HAD...A DREAM?
THERE WAS CHESTBEARD, AND A PIRATE SHIP, AND HE WAS TELLING ME THAT THE ONLY WAY TO WIN OUR RACE IS TO BOARD THE OTHER SHIPS... I MEAN THE OTHER CARS... AND GIVE THEM ALL A SUPLEX.
HMM. GOOD IDEA.

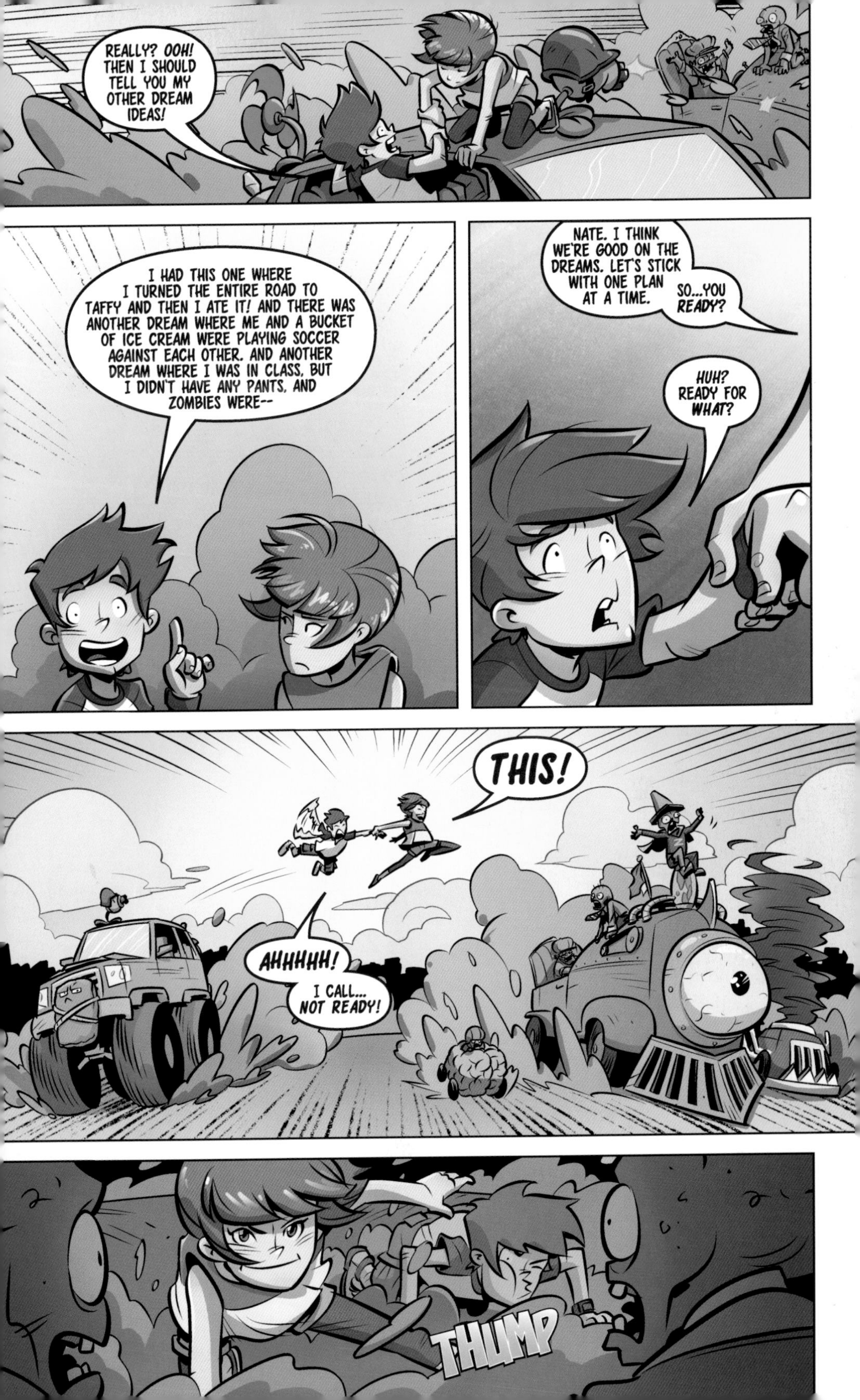
REALLY? OOH! THEN I SHOULD TELL YOU MY OTHER DREAM IDEAS!
I HAD THIS ONE WHERE I TURNED THE ENTIRE ROAD TO TAFFY AND THEN I ATE IT! AND THERE WAS ANOTHER DREAM WHERE ME AND A BUCKET OF ICE CREAM WERE PLAYING SOCCER AGAINST EACH OTHER. AND ANOTHER DREAM WHERE I WAS IN CLASS, BUT I DIDN'T HAVE ANY PANTS, AND ZOMBIES WERE--
NATE. I THINK WE'RE GOOD ON THE DREAMS. LET'S STICK WITH ONE PLAN AT A TIME.
SO...YOU READY?
HUH? READY FOR WHAT?
THIS!
AHHHHH!
I CALL... NOT READY!
THUMP

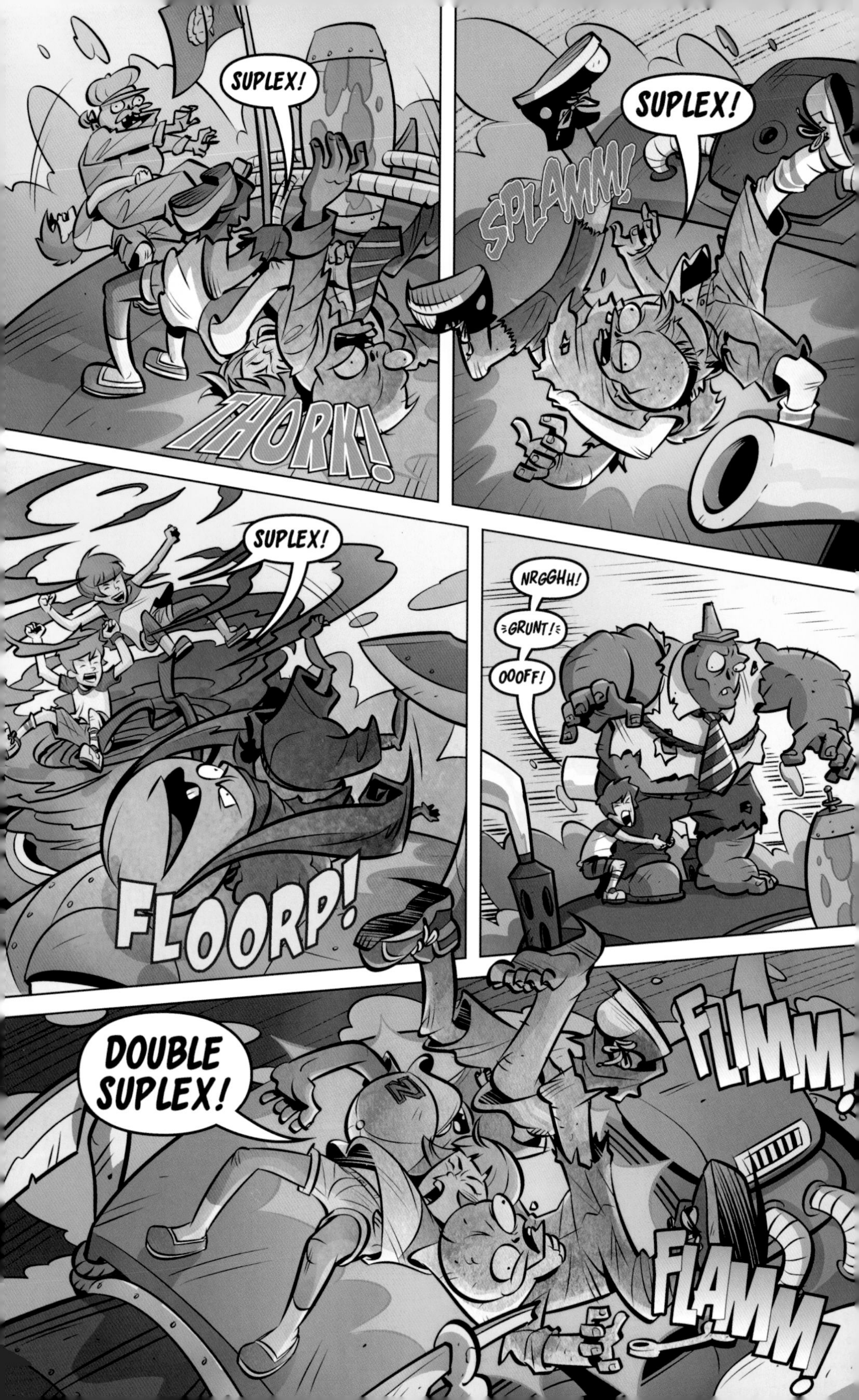
SUPLEX!
THORK!
SUPLEX!
SPLAMM!
SUPLEX!
FLOORP!
NRGGHH!
GRUNT!
OOOFF!
DOUBLE SUPLEX!
FLIMM!
FLAMM!

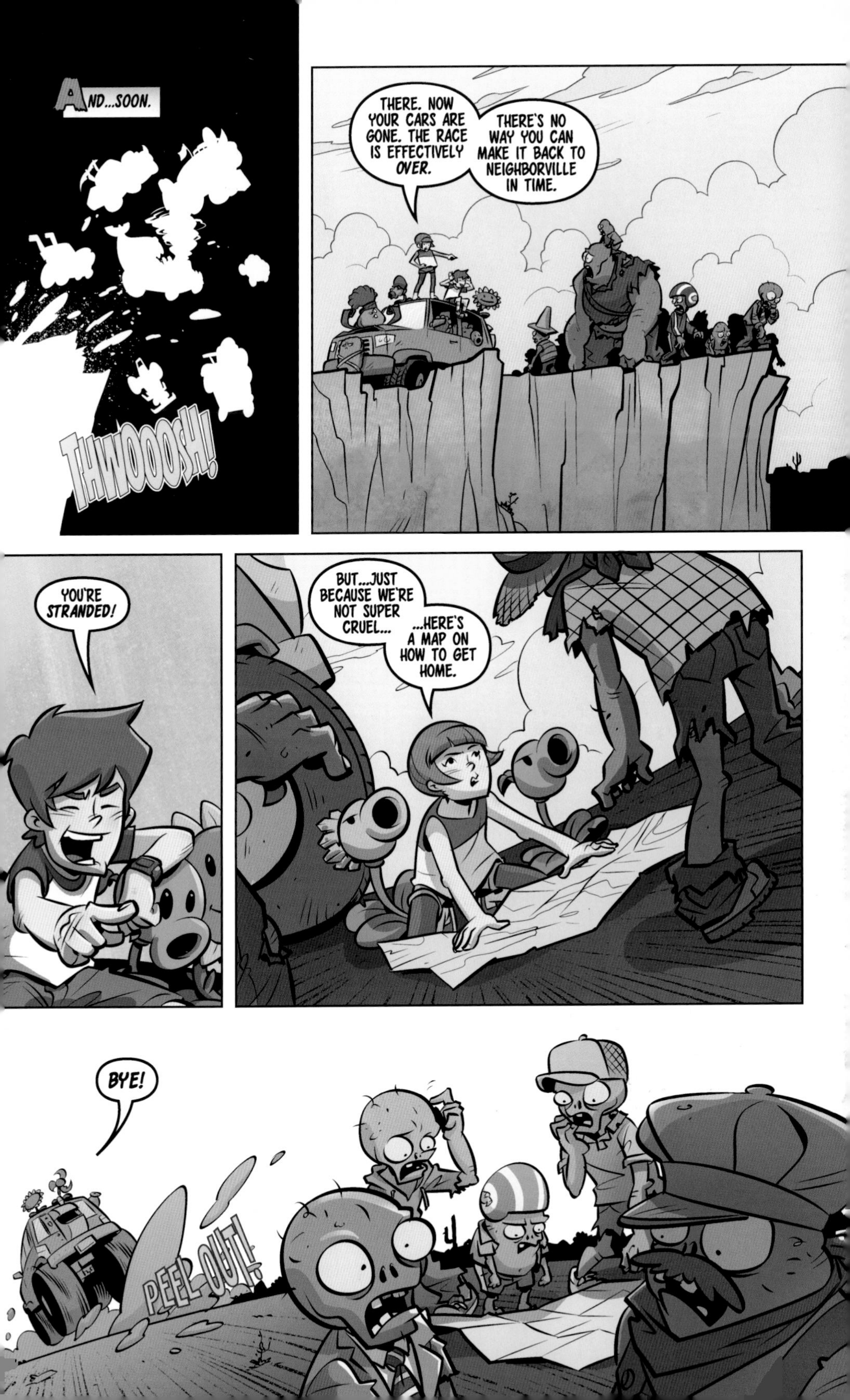
AND...SOON.
THWOOOSH!
THERE. NOW YOUR CARS ARE GONE. THE RACE IS EFFECTIVELY OVER.
THERE'S NO WAY YOU CAN MAKE IT BACK TO NEIGHBORVILLE IN TIME.
YOU'RE STRANDED!
BUT...JUST BECAUSE WE'RE NOT SUPER CRUEL...
...HERE'S A MAP ON HOW TO GET HOME.
BYE!
PEEL OUT!

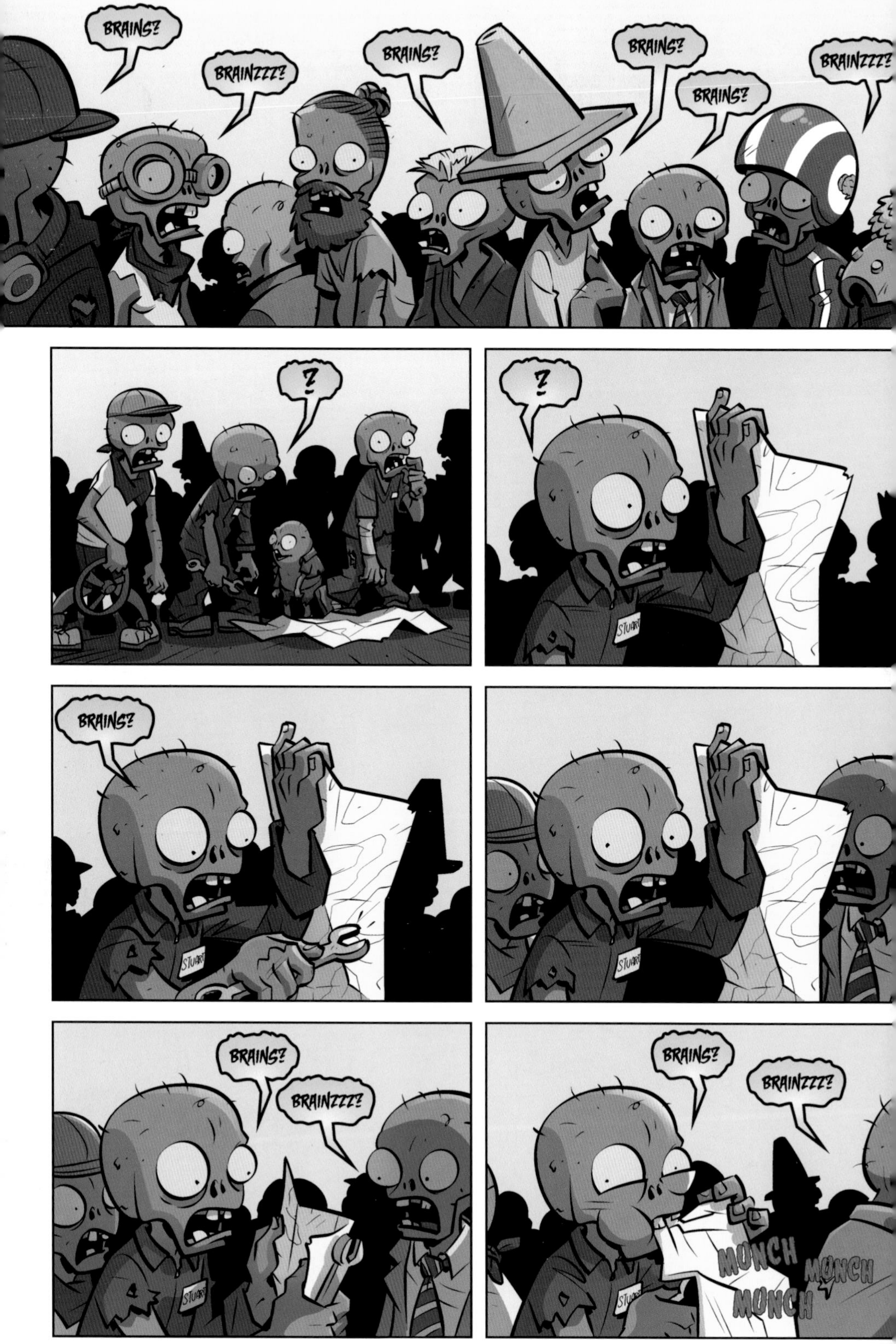

BRAINS?
BRAINZZZ?
BRAINS?
BRAINS?
BRAINS?
BRAINZZZ?
?
?
BRAINS?
BRAINS?
BRAINZZZ?
BRAINS?
BRAINZZZ?
MUNCH
MUNCH
MUNCH
STUART

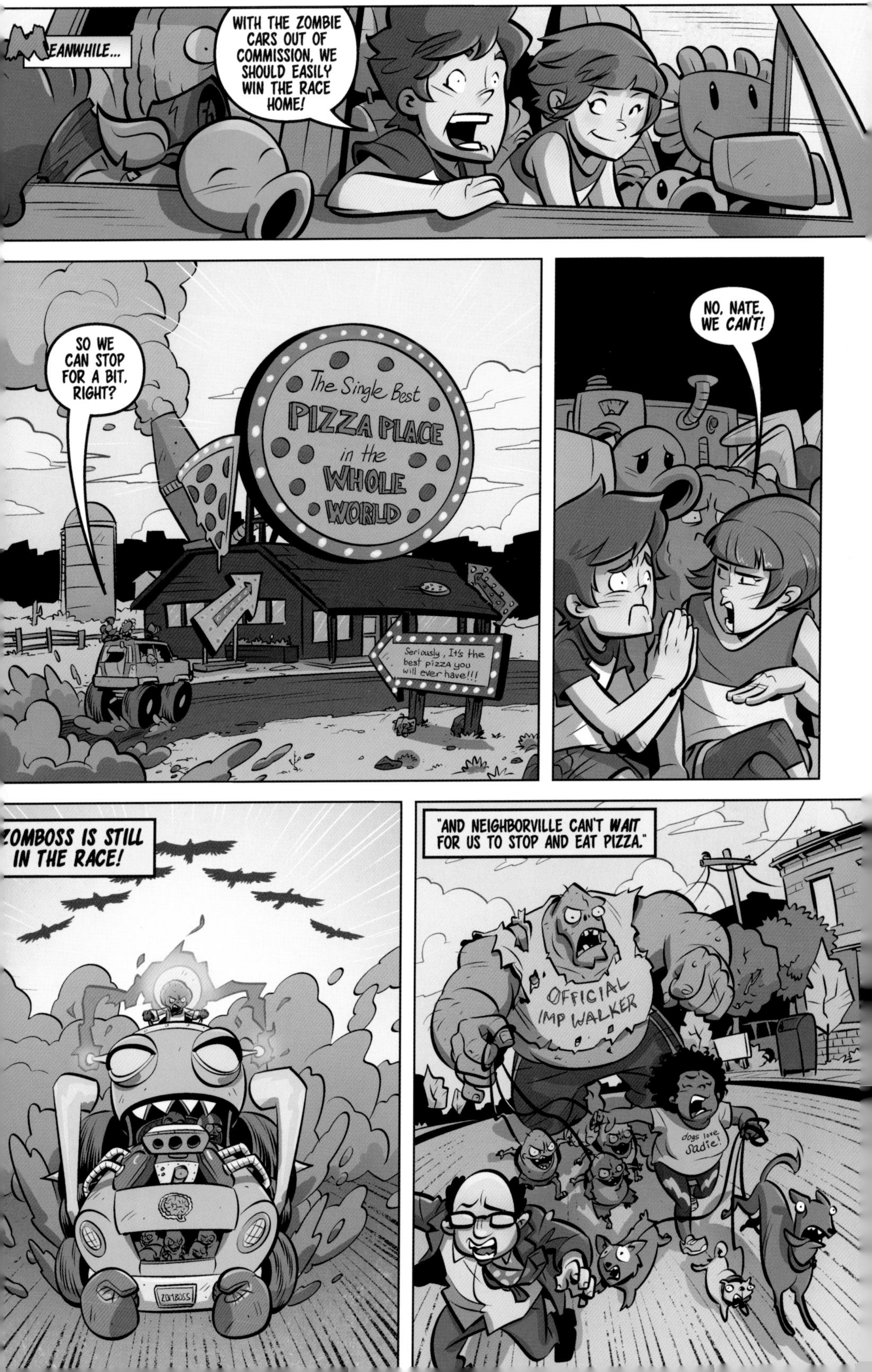
MEANWHILE...
WITH THE ZOMBIE CARS OUT OF COMMISSION, WE SHOULD EASILY WIN THE RACE HOME!
SO WE CAN STOP FOR A BIT, RIGHT?
The Single Best PIZZA PLACE in the WHOLE WORLD
Seriously, It's the best pizza you will ever have!!!
NO, NATE. WE CAN'T!
ZOMBOSS IS STILL IN THE RACE!
ZOMBOSS
"AND NEIGHBORVILLE CAN'T WAIT FOR US TO STOP AND EAT PIZZA."
OFFICIAL IMP WALKER
dogs love Sadie!

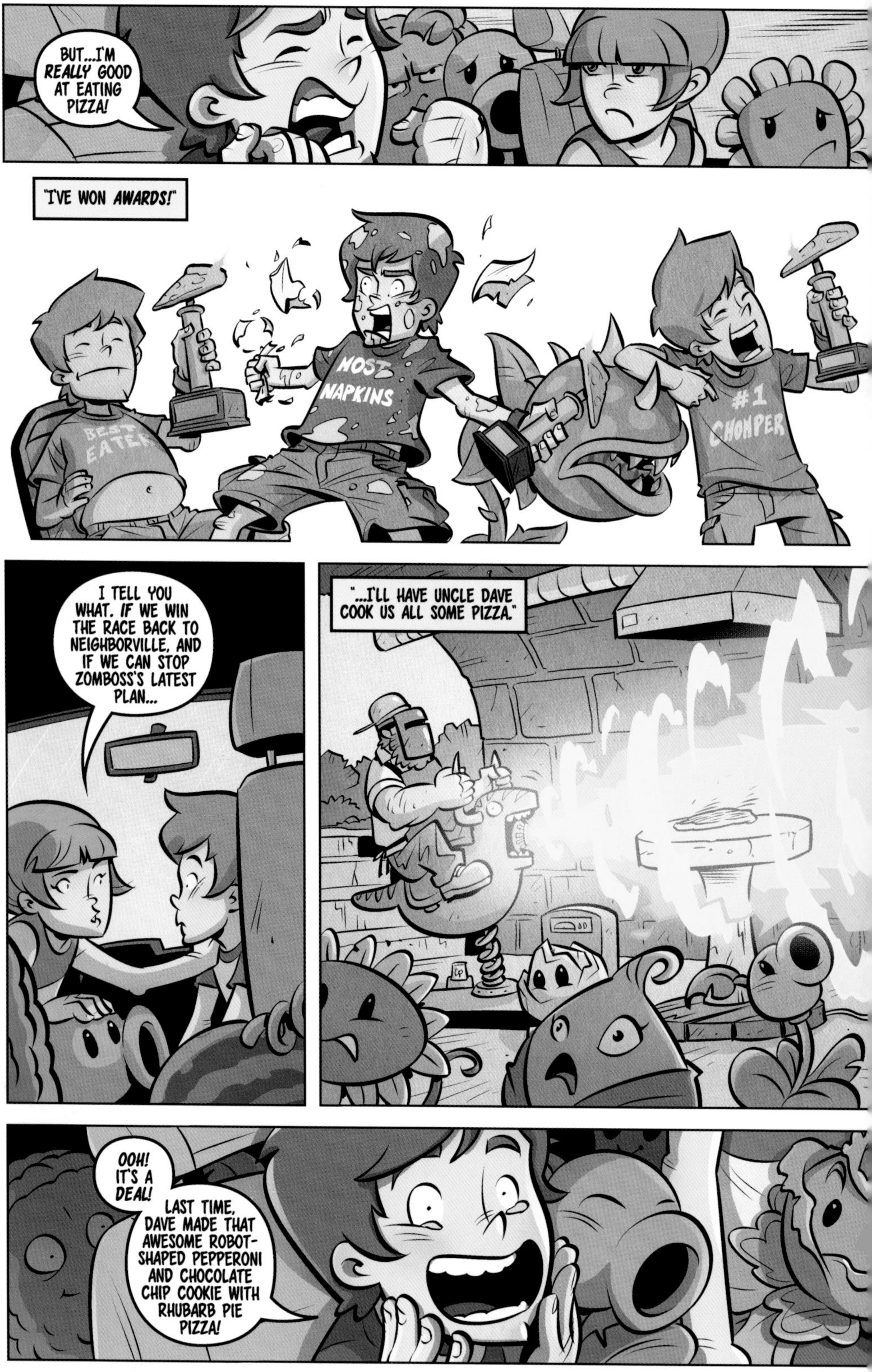
BUT...I'M REALLY GOOD AT EATING PIZZA!
"I'VE WON AWARDS!"
BEST EATER
MOST NAPKINS
#1 CHOMPER
I TELL YOU WHAT. IF WE WIN THE RACE BACK TO NEIGHBORVILLE, AND IF WE CAN STOP ZOMBOSS'S LATEST PLAN...
"...I'LL HAVE UNCLE DAVE COOK US ALL SOME PIZZA."
OOH! IT'S A DEAL!
LAST TIME, DAVE MADE THAT AWESOME ROBOT-SHAPED PEPPERONI AND CHOCOLATE CHIP COOKIE WITH RHUBARB PIE PIZZA!

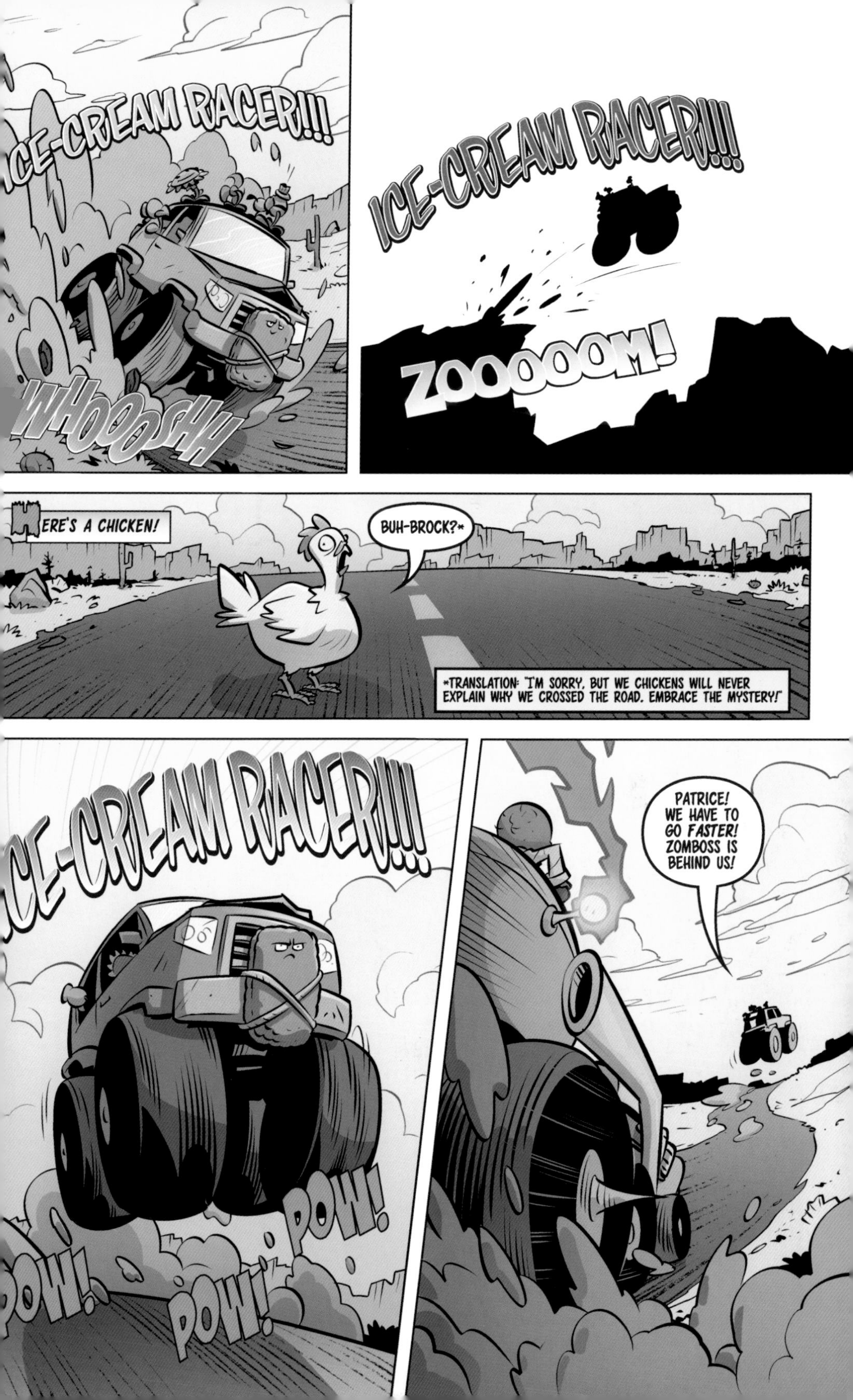
ICE-CREAM RACER!!!
WHOOOOSHH
ICE-CREAM RACER!!!
ZOOOOOOM!
HERE'S A CHICKEN!
BUH-BROCK?*
*TRANSLATION: "I'M SORRY, BUT WE CHICKENS WILL NEVER EXPLAIN WHY WE CROSSED THE ROAD. EMBRACE THE MYSTERY!"
ICE-CREAM RACER!!!
POW!
POW!
POW!
PATRICE! WE HAVE TO GO FASTER! ZOMBOSS IS BEHIND US!

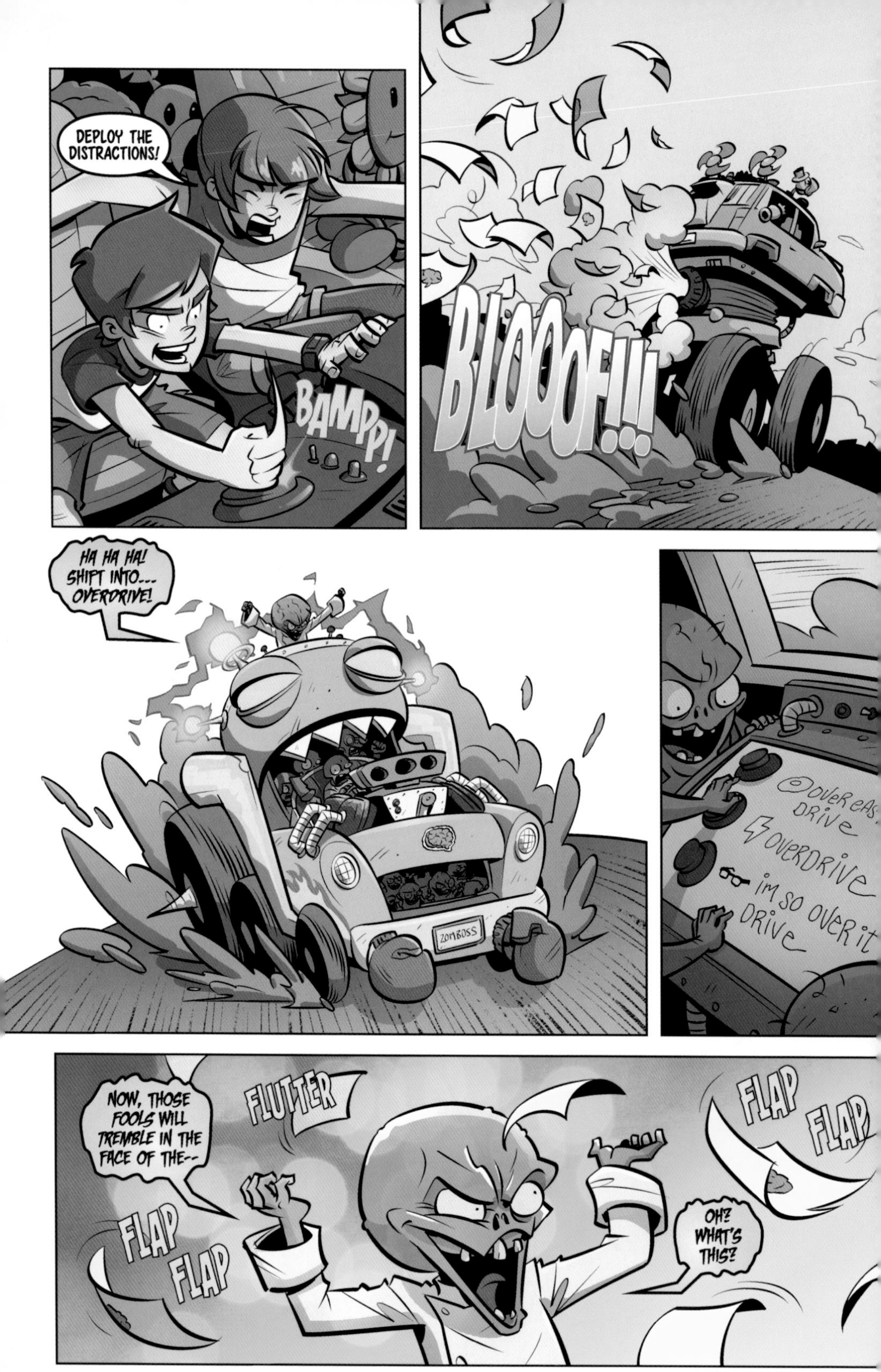
DEPLOY THE DISTRACTIONS!
BAMPP!
BLOOOF!!!
HA HA HA! SHIFT INTO... OVERDRIVE!
ZOMBOSS
OVER EASY DRIVE
OVERDRIVE
im SO OVER it DRIVE
NOW, THOSE FOOLS WILL TREMBLE IN THE FACE OF THE--
FLUTTER
FLAP
FLAP
FLAP
FLAP
OH? WHAT'S THIS?

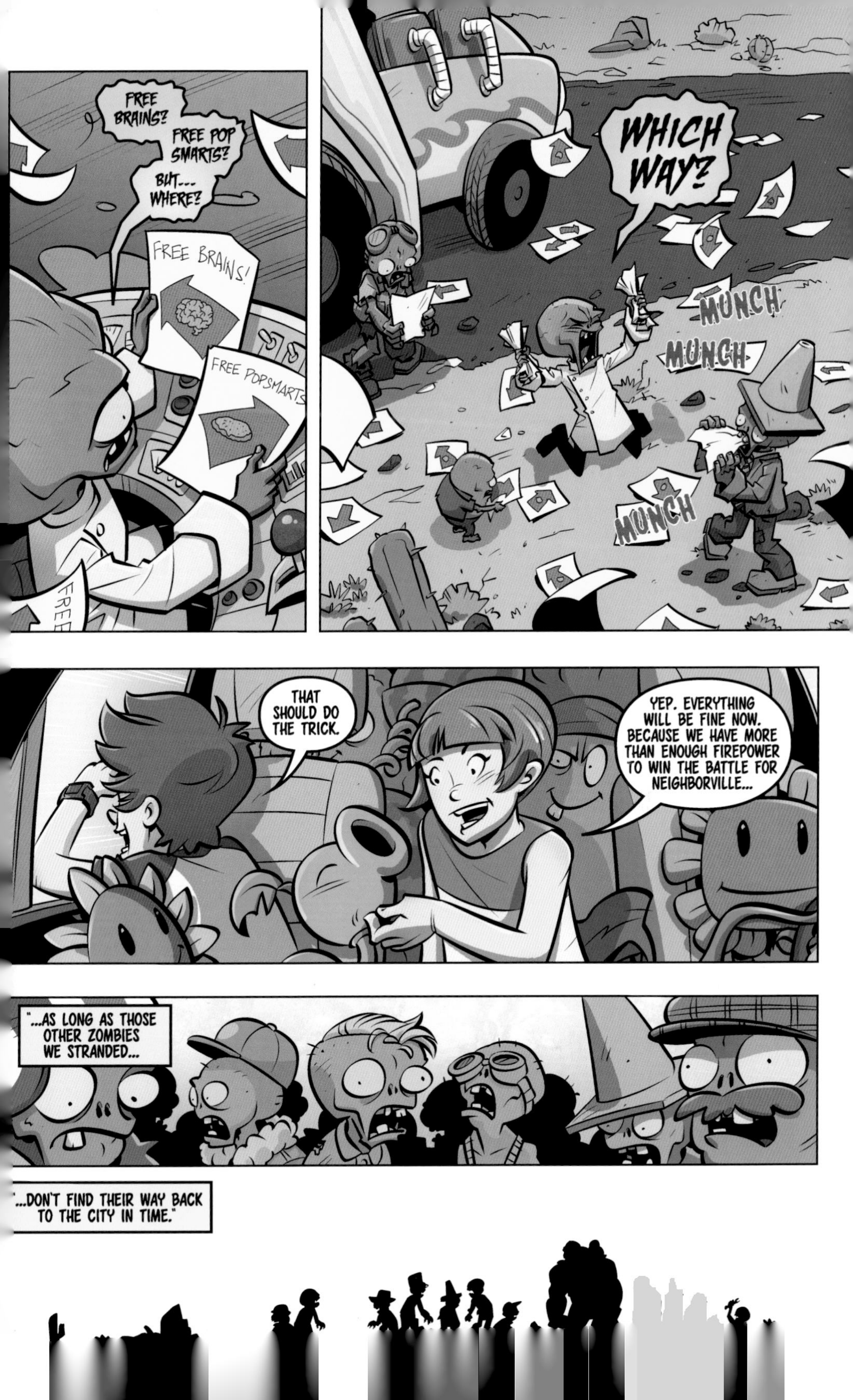
FREE BRAINS?
FREE POP SMARTS?
BUT... WHERE?
FREE BRAINS!
FREE POPSMARTS
WHICH WAY?
MUNCH
MUNCH
MUNCH
THAT SHOULD DO THE TRICK.
YEP. EVERYTHING WILL BE FINE NOW. BECAUSE WE HAVE MORE THAN ENOUGH FIREPOWER TO WIN THE BATTLE FOR NEIGHBORVILLE...
"...AS LONG AS THOSE OTHER ZOMBIES WE STRANDED...
"...DON'T FIND THEIR WAY BACK TO THE CITY IN TIME."

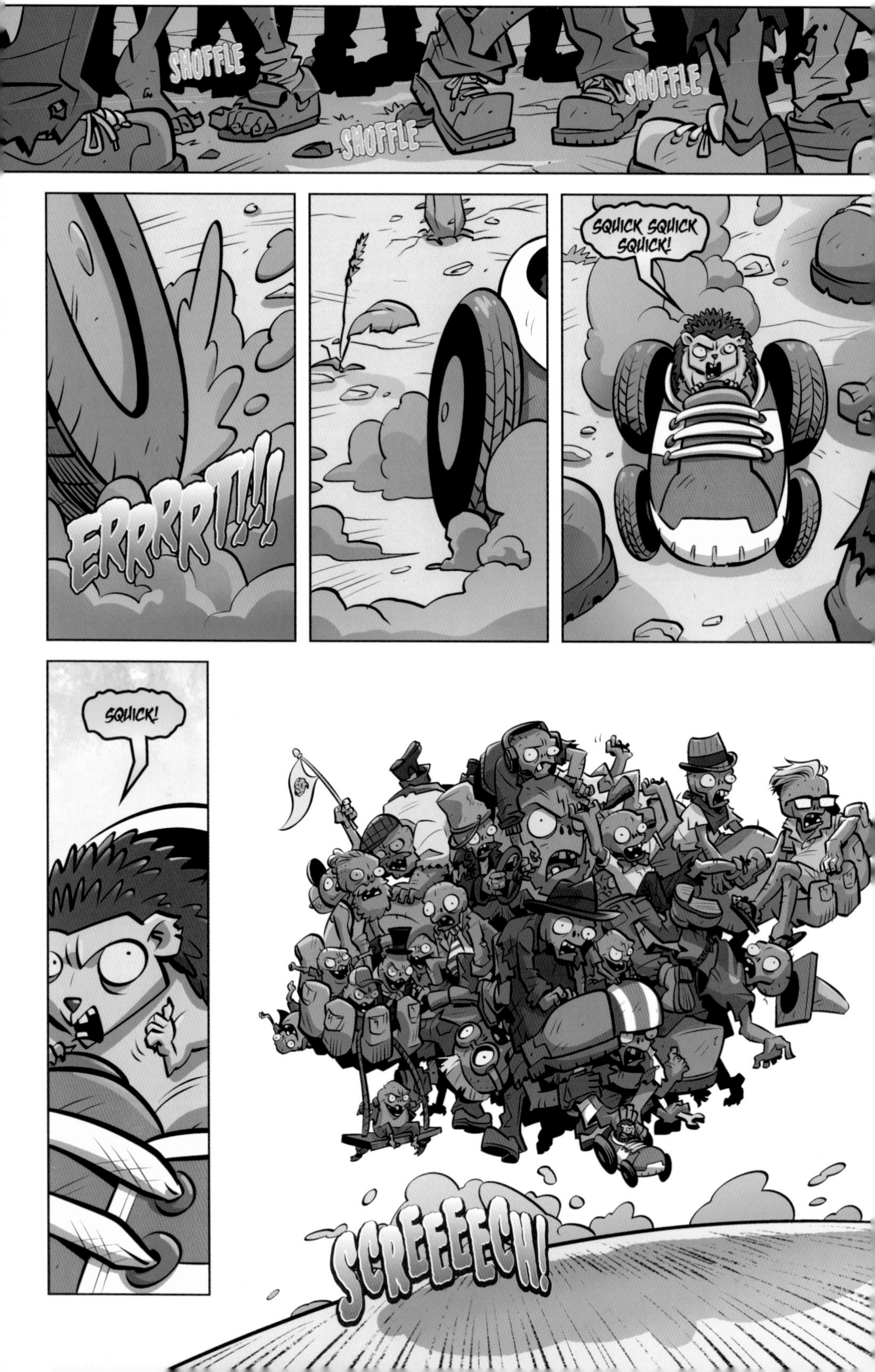
SHOFFLE
SHOFFLE
SHOFFLE
ERRRRT!!!
SQUICK SQUICK SQUICK!
SQUICK!
SCREEEECH!

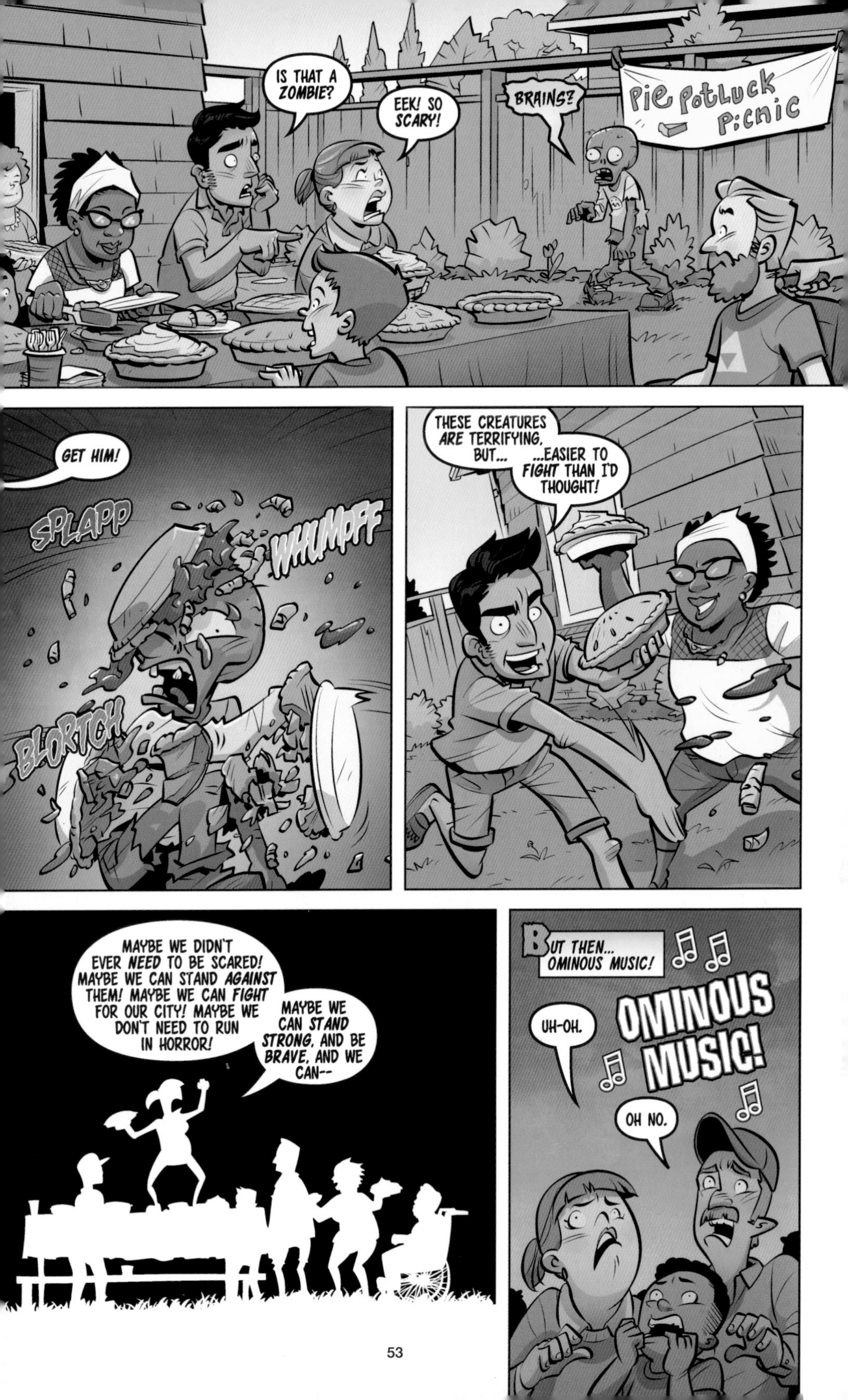

IS THAT A ZOMBIE?
EEK! SO SCARY!
BRAINS?
Pie Potluck Picnic
GET HIM!
SPLAPP
WHUMPFF
BLORTCH
THESE CREATURES ARE TERRIFYING, BUT...
...EASIER TO FIGHT THAN I'D THOUGHT!
MAYBE WE DIDN'T EVER NEED TO BE SCARED! MAYBE WE CAN STAND AGAINST THEM! MAYBE WE CAN FIGHT FOR OUR CITY! MAYBE WE DON'T NEED TO RUN IN HORROR!
MAYBE WE CAN STAND STRONG, AND BE BRAVE, AND WE CAN--
BUT THEN... OMINOUS MUSIC!
UH-OH.
OMINOUS MUSIC!
OH NO.

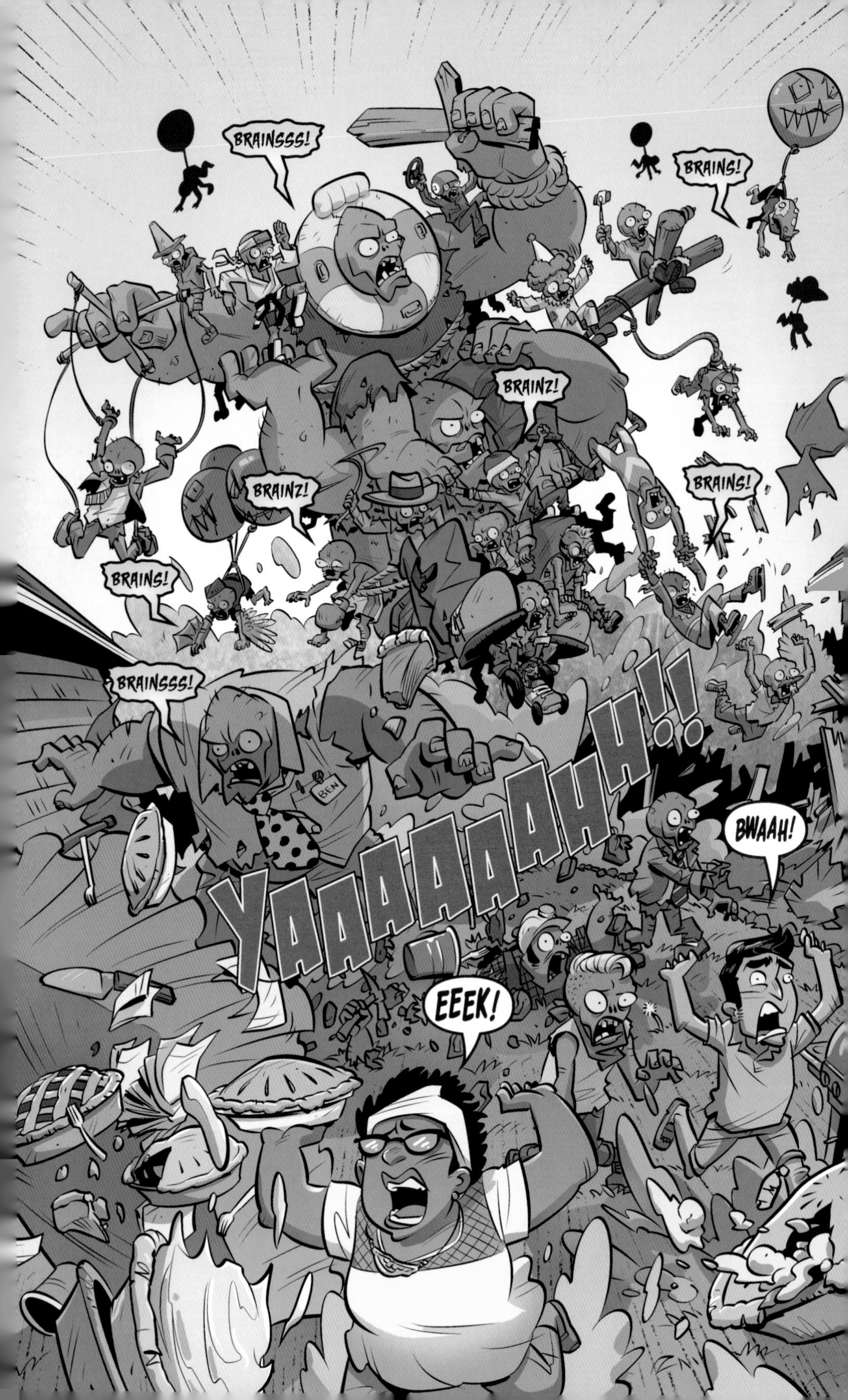
BRAINSSS!
BRAINS!
BRAINZ!
BRAINZ!
BRAINS!
BRAINS!
BRAINSSS!
BEN
YAAAAAAAHH!!
BWAAH!
EEEK!

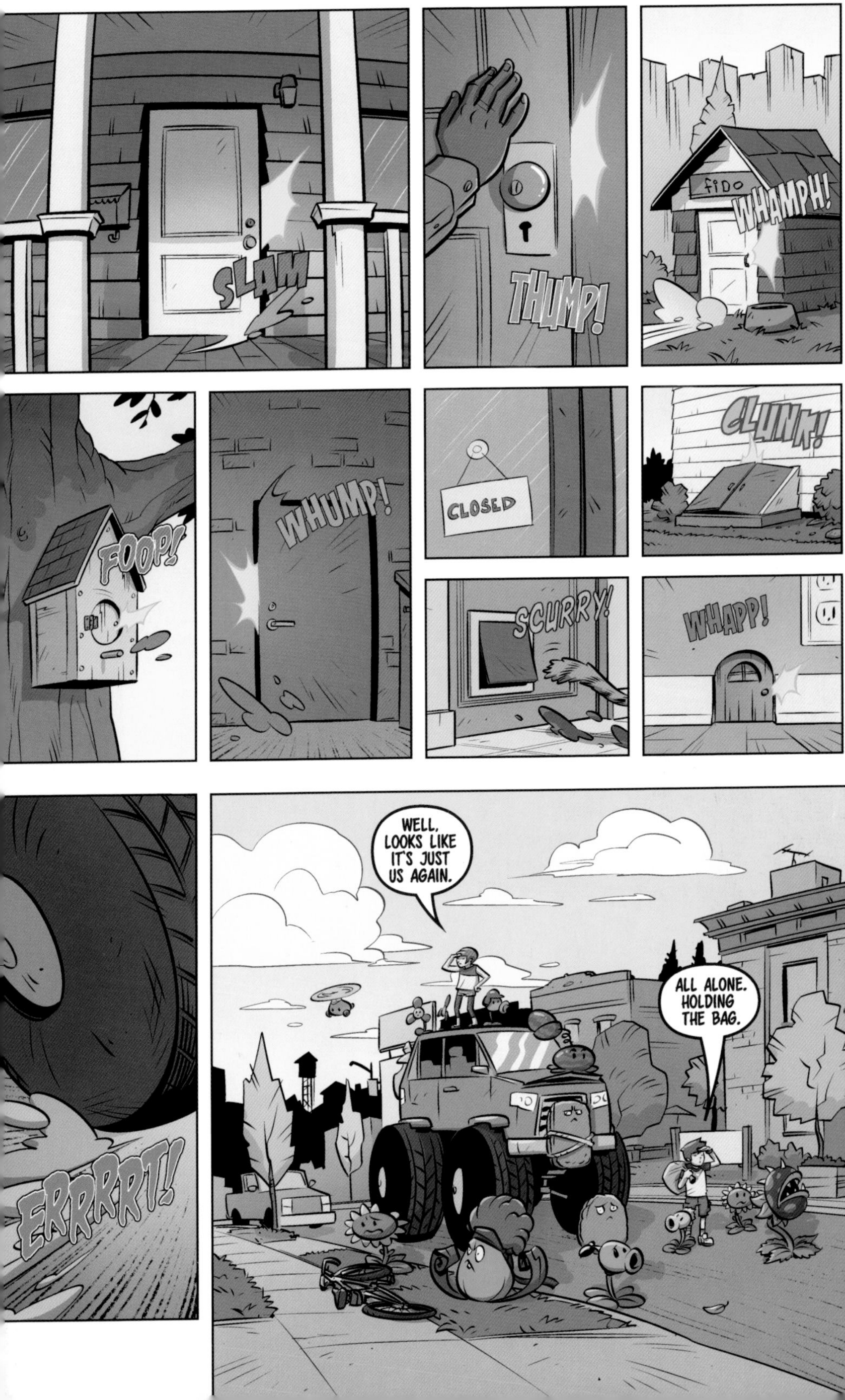
SLAM
THUMP!
fido
WHAMPH!
FOOP!
WHUMP!
CLOSED
CLUNK!
SCURRY!
WHAPP!
ERRRRT!
WELL, LOOKS LIKE IT'S JUST US AGAIN.
ALL ALONE. HOLDING THE BAG.

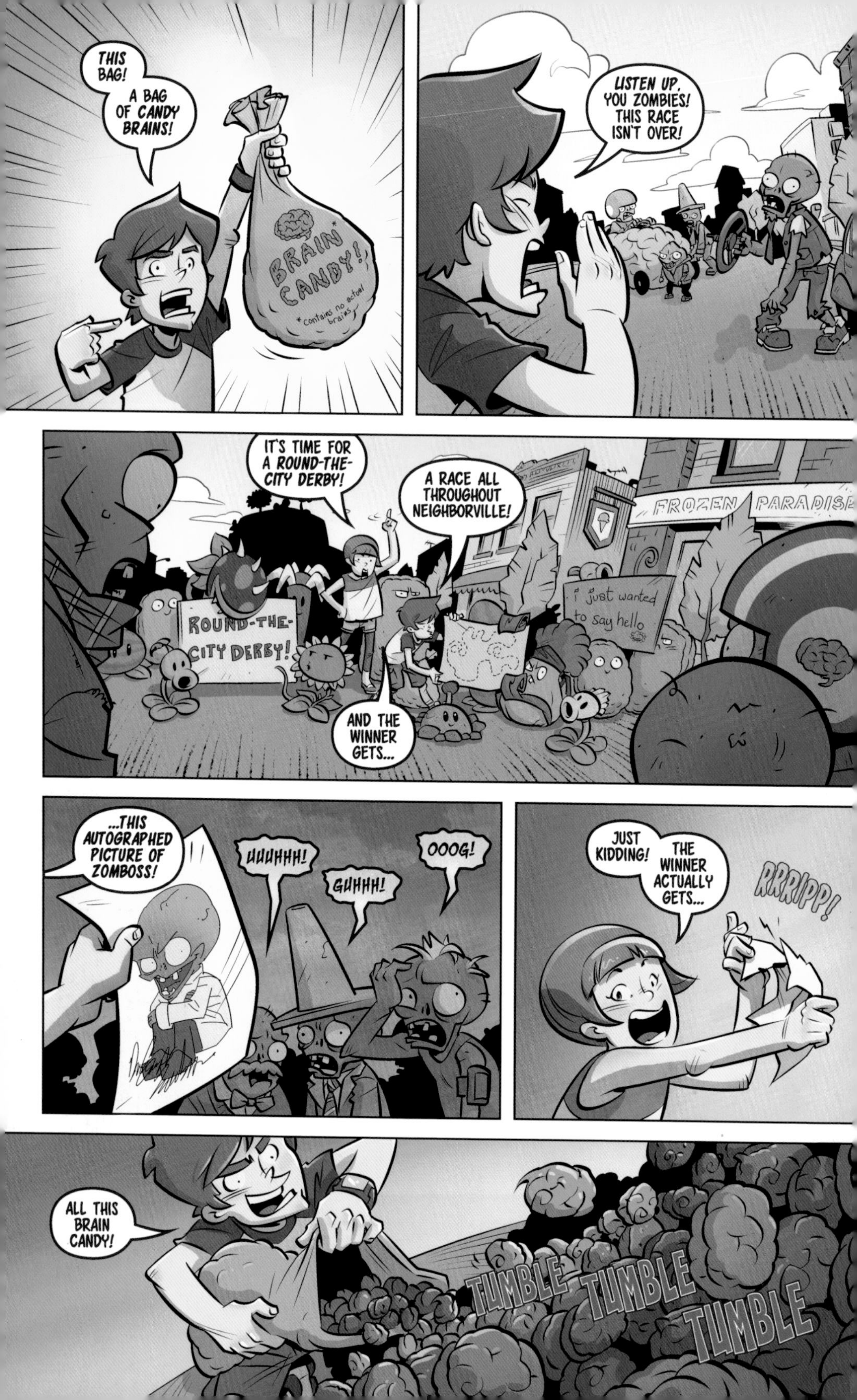
THIS BAG!
A BAG OF CANDY BRAINS!
BRAIN CANDY!*
*contains no actual brains
LISTEN UP, YOU ZOMBIES! THIS RACE ISN'T OVER!
IT'S TIME FOR A ROUND-THE-CITY DERBY!
A RACE ALL THROUGHOUT NEIGHBORVILLE!
FROZEN PARADISE
ROUND-THE-CITY DERBY!
i just wanted to say hello
AND THE WINNER GETS...
...THIS AUTOGRAPHED PICTURE OF ZOMBOSS!
UUUHHH!
GUHHH!
OOOG!
JUST KIDDING!
THE WINNER ACTUALLY GETS...
RRRIPP!
ALL THIS BRAIN CANDY!
TUMBLE TUMBLE TUMBLE

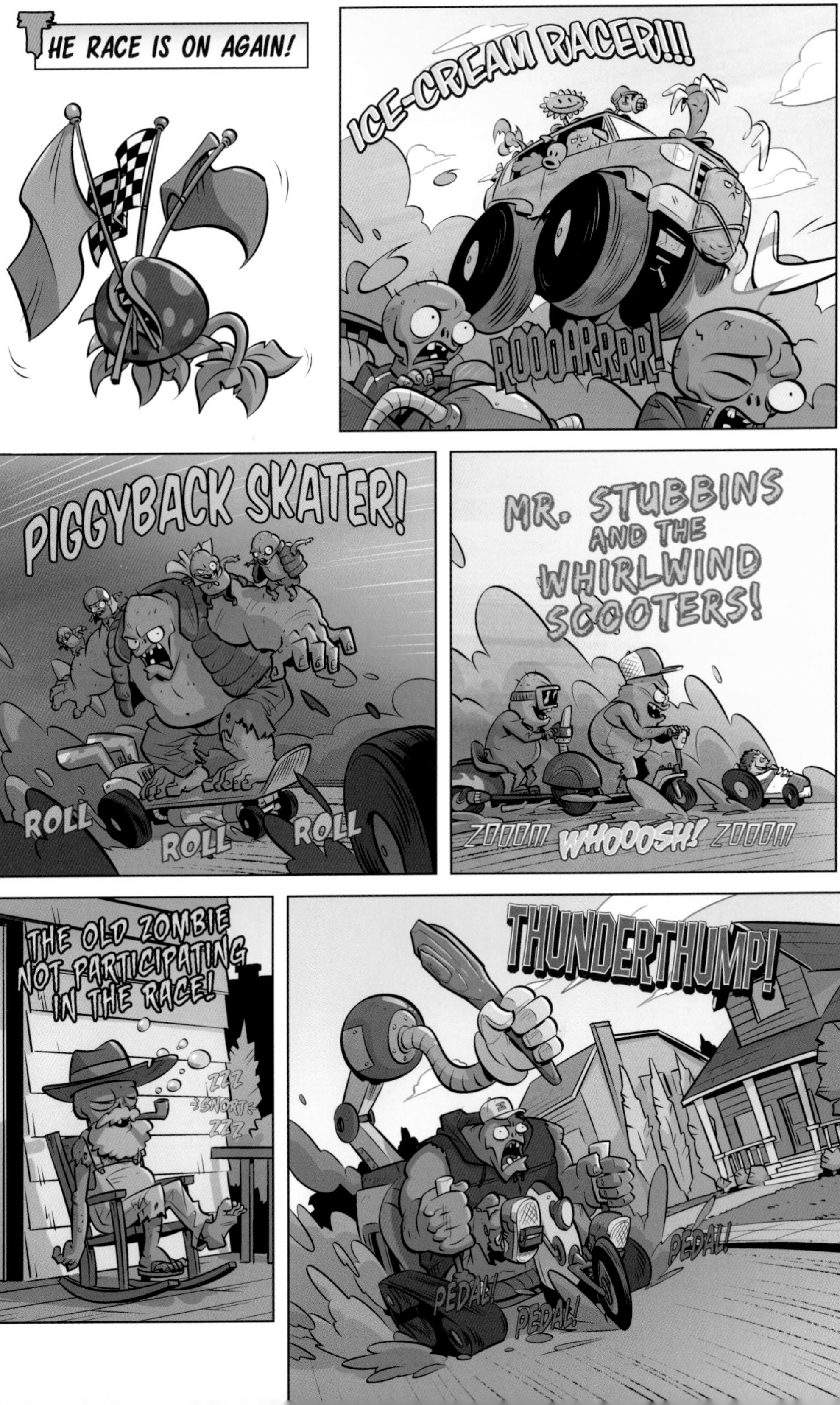
THE RACE IS ON AGAIN!
ICE-CREAM RACER!!!
ROOOARRRR!
PIGGYBACK SKATER!
ROLL
ROLL
ROLL
MR. STUBBINS AND THE WHIRLWIND SCOOTERS!
ZOOOM
WHOOOSH!
ZOOOM
THE OLD ZOMBIE NOT PARTICIPATING IN THE RACE!
ZZZ
SNORT
ZZZ
THUNDERTHUMP!
PEDAL!
PEDAL!
PEDAL!

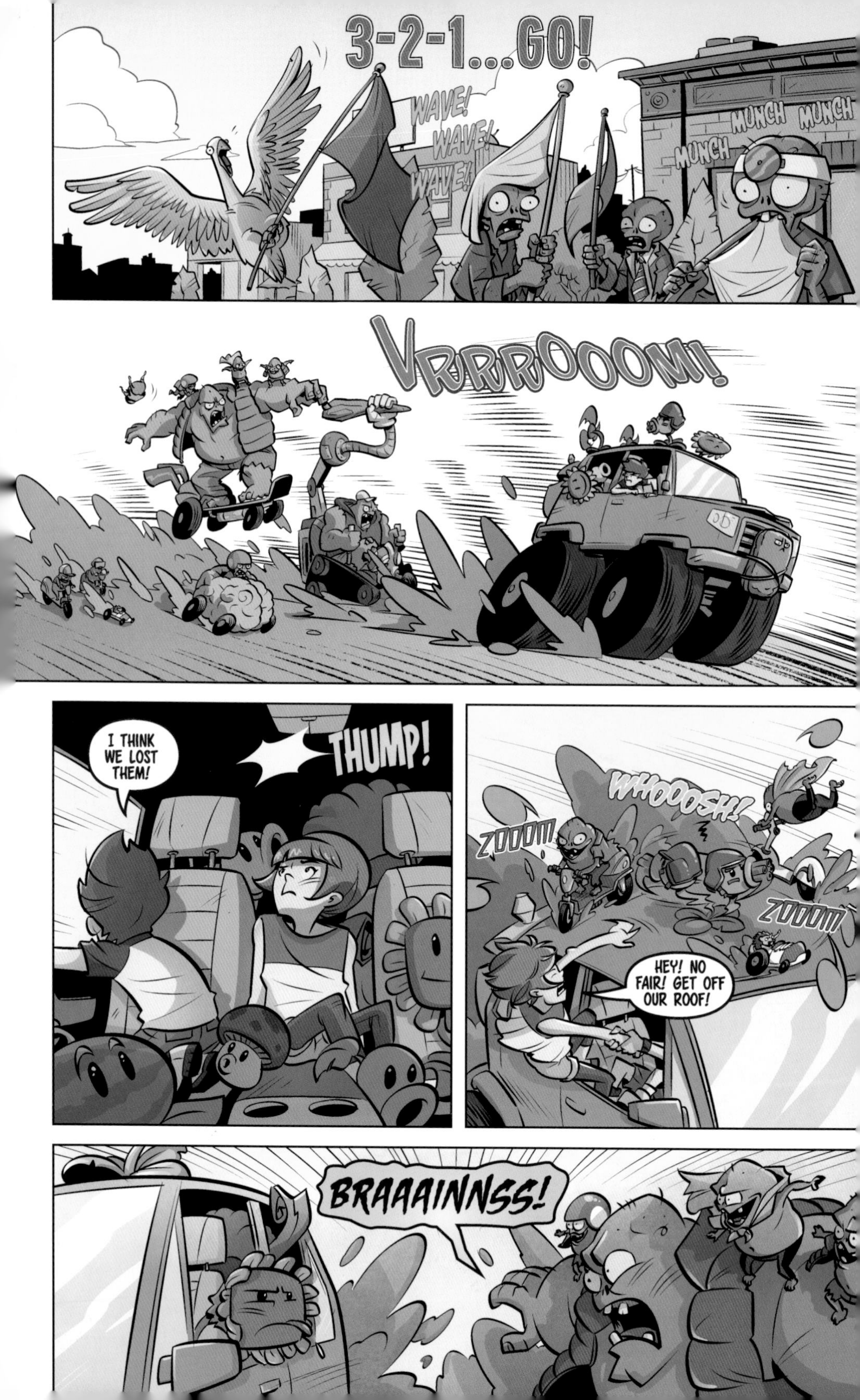
3-2-1...GO!
WAVE!
WAVE!
WAVE!
MUNCH
MUNCH
MUNCH
VRRROOOM!
I THINK WE LOST THEM!
THUMP!
WHOOOSH!
ZOOOM
ZOOOM
HEY! NO FAIR! GET OFF OUR ROOF!
BRAAAINNSS!

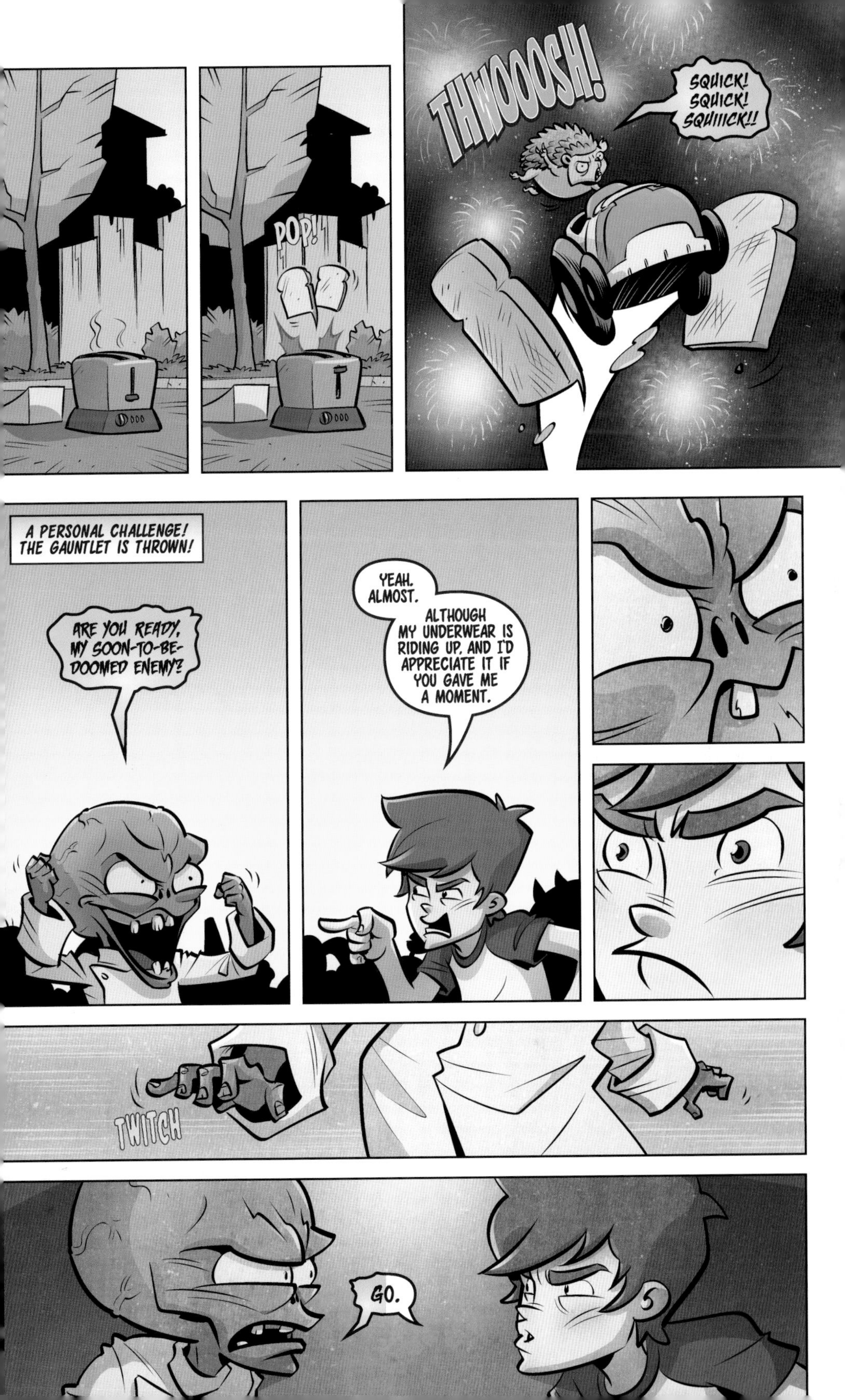
POP!
THWOOOSH!
SQUICK! SQUICK! SQUIIICK!!
A PERSONAL CHALLENGE! THE GAUNTLET IS THROWN!
ARE YOU READY, MY SOON-TO-BE-DOOMED ENEMY?
YEAH. ALMOST.
ALTHOUGH MY UNDERWEAR IS RIDING UP, AND I'D APPRECIATE IT IF YOU GAVE ME A MOMENT.
TWITCH
GO.

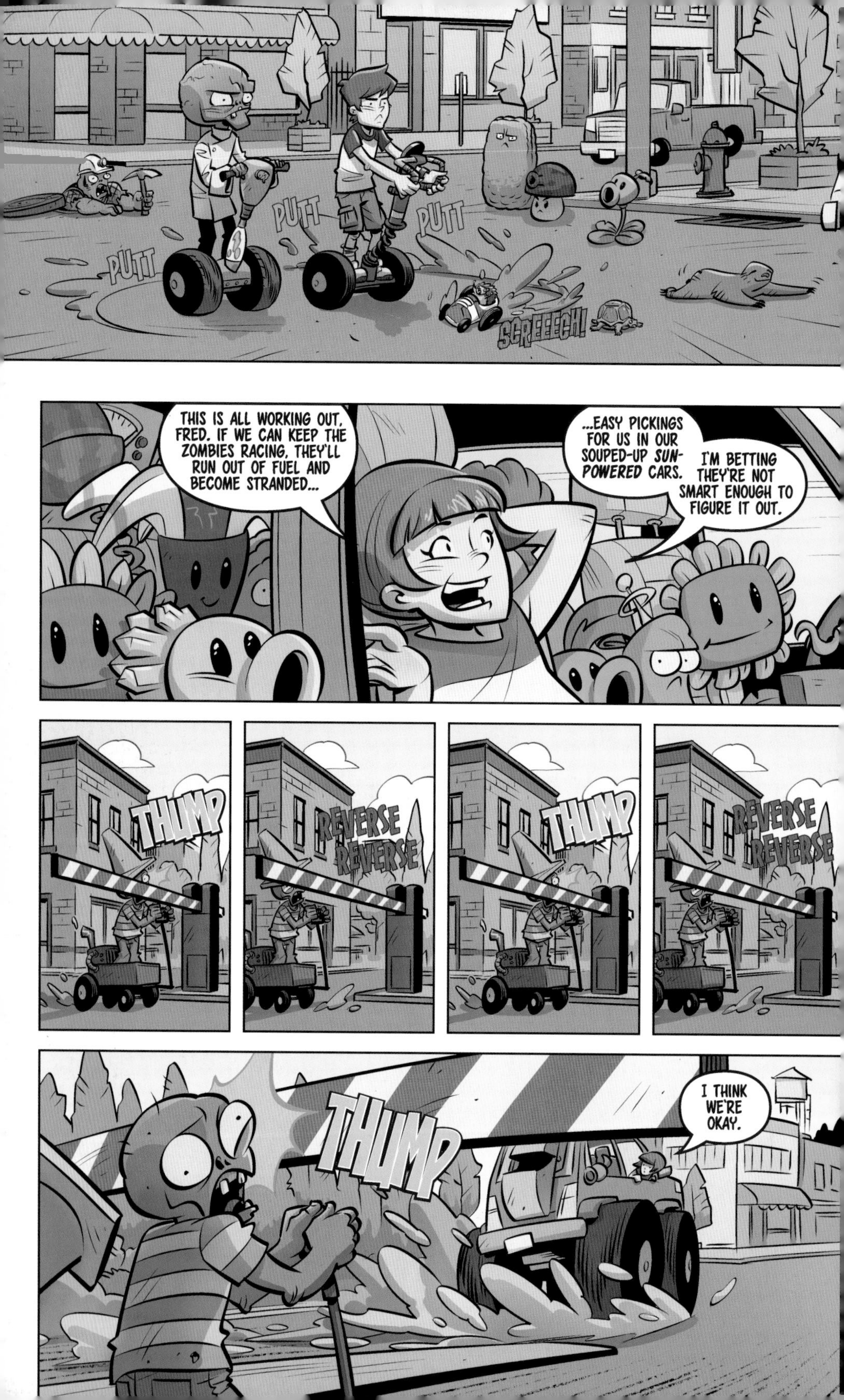
PUTT
PUTT
PUTT
SCREEECH!
THIS IS ALL WORKING OUT, FRED. IF WE CAN KEEP THE ZOMBIES RACING, THEY'LL RUN OUT OF FUEL AND BECOME STRANDED...
...EASY PICKINGS FOR US IN OUR SOUPED-UP SUN-POWERED CARS.
I'M BETTING THEY'RE NOT SMART ENOUGH TO FIGURE IT OUT.
THUMP
REVERSE REVERSE
THUMP
REVERSE REVERSE
THUMP
I THINK WE'RE OKAY.

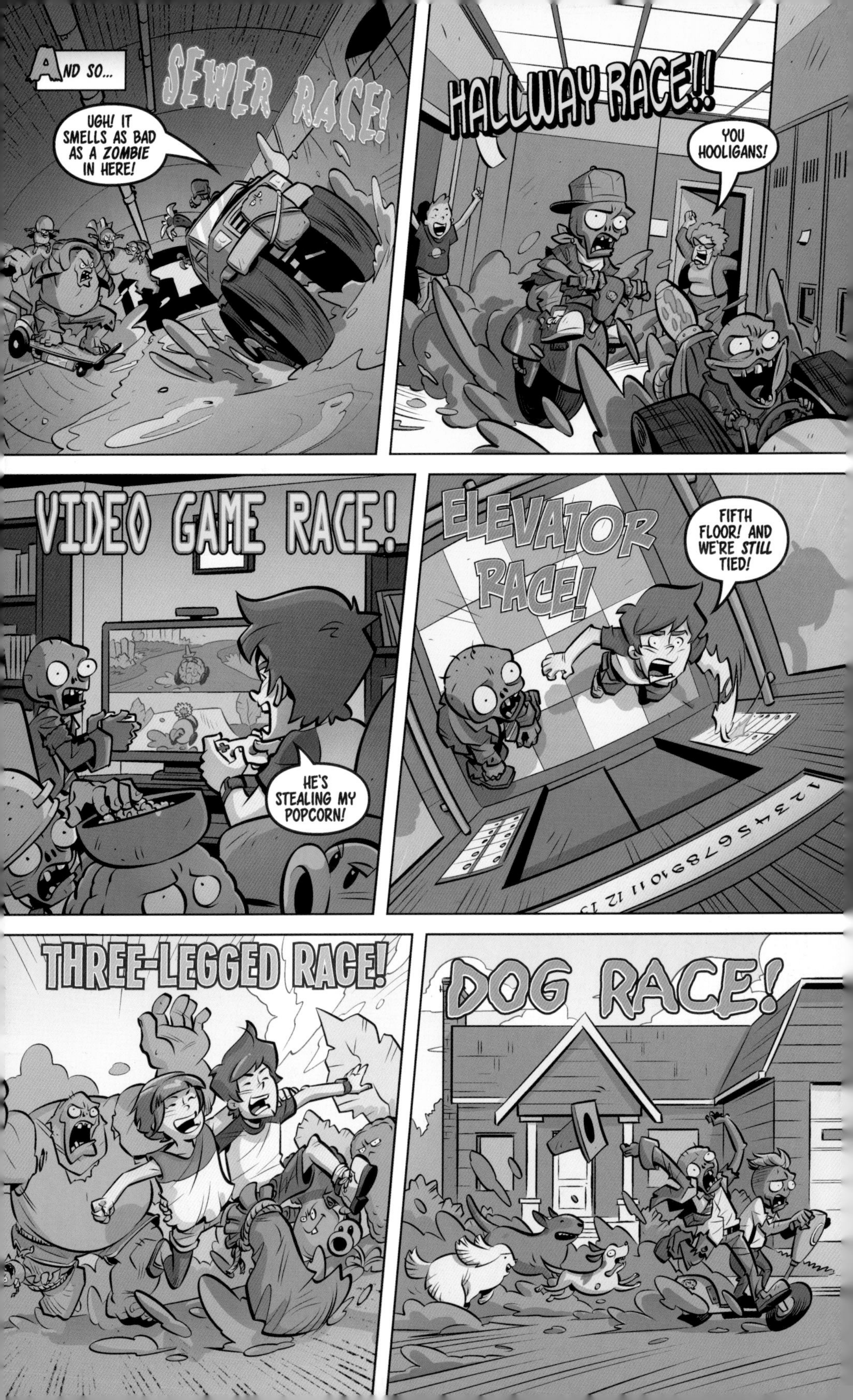
AND SO...
SEWER RACE!
UGH! IT SMELLS AS BAD AS A ZOMBIE IN HERE!
HALLWAY RACE!!
YOU HOOLIGANS!
VIDEO GAME RACE!
HE'S STEALING MY POPCORN!
ELEVATOR RACE!
FIFTH FLOOR! AND WE'RE STILL TIED!
1 2 3 4 5 6 7 8 9 10 11 12 13
THREE-LEGGED RACE!
DOG RACE!

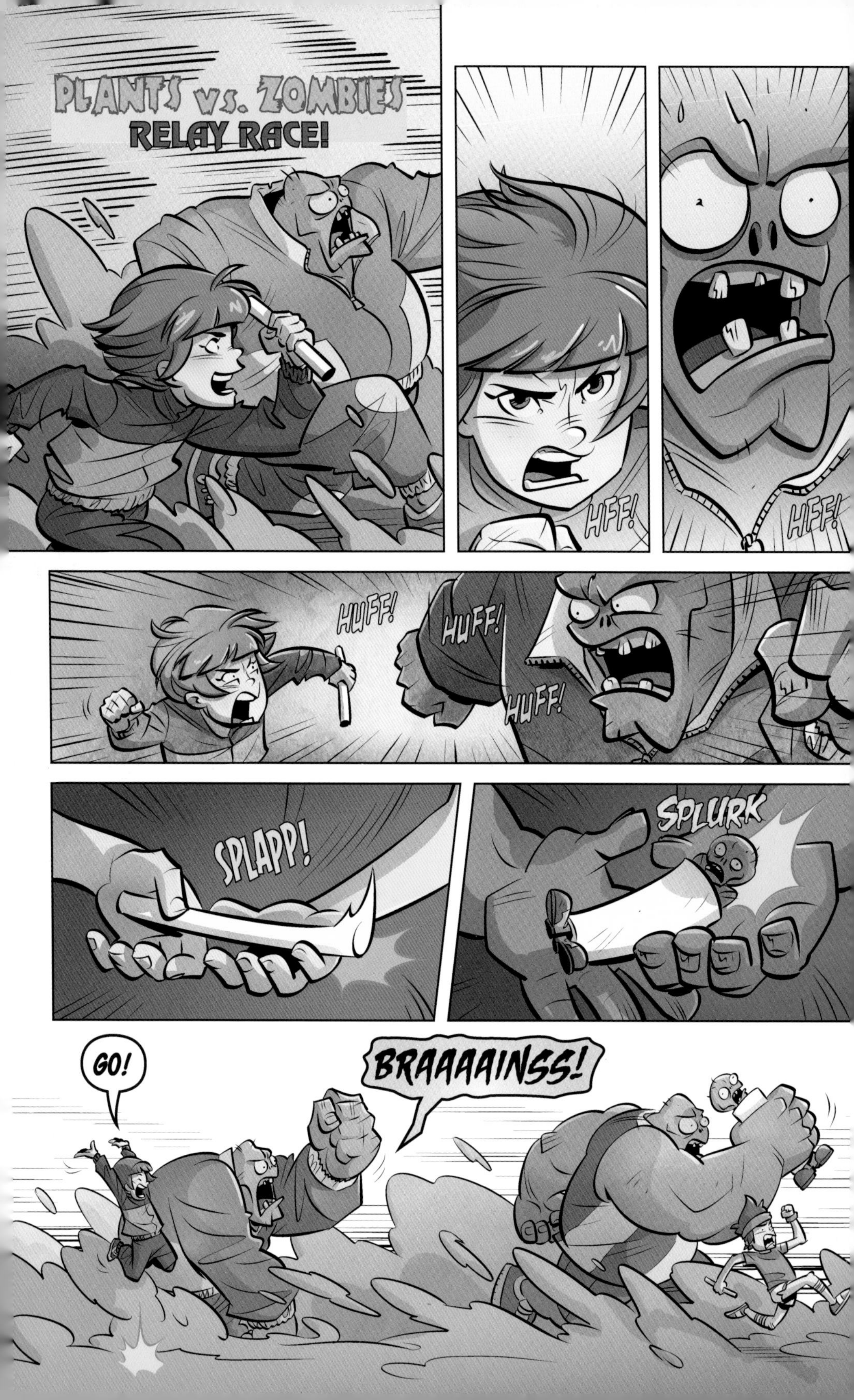
PLANTS vs. ZOMBIES
RELAY RACE!
HFF!
HFF!
HUFF!
HUFF!
HUFF!
SPLAPP!
SPLURK
GO!
BRAAAAINSS!

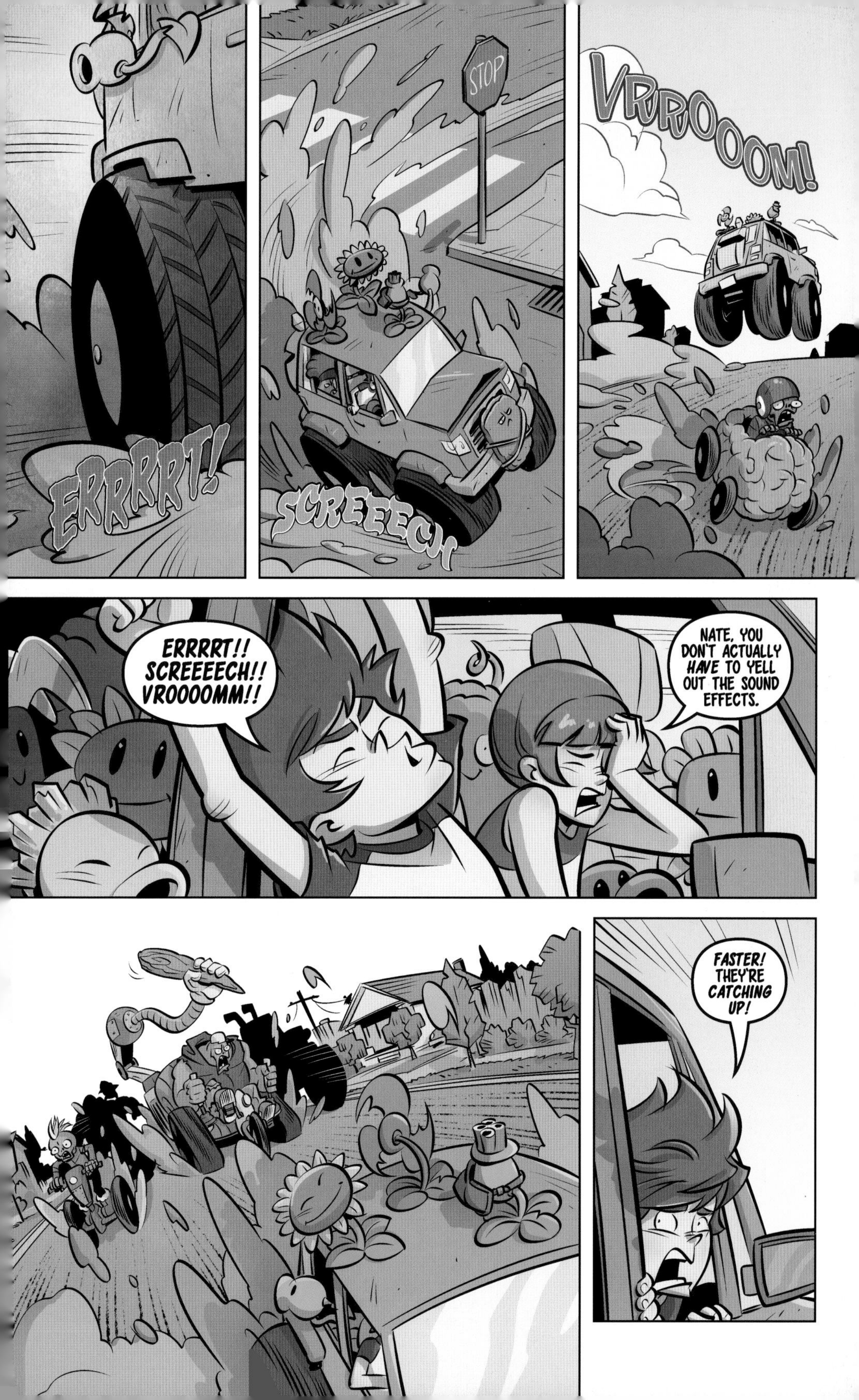
ERRRRT!
STOP
SCREEEECH
VRROOOOM!
ERRRRT!! SCREEEECH!! VROOOOMM!!
NATE, YOU DON'T ACTUALLY HAVE TO YELL OUT THE SOUND EFFECTS.
FASTER! THEY'RE CATCHING UP!

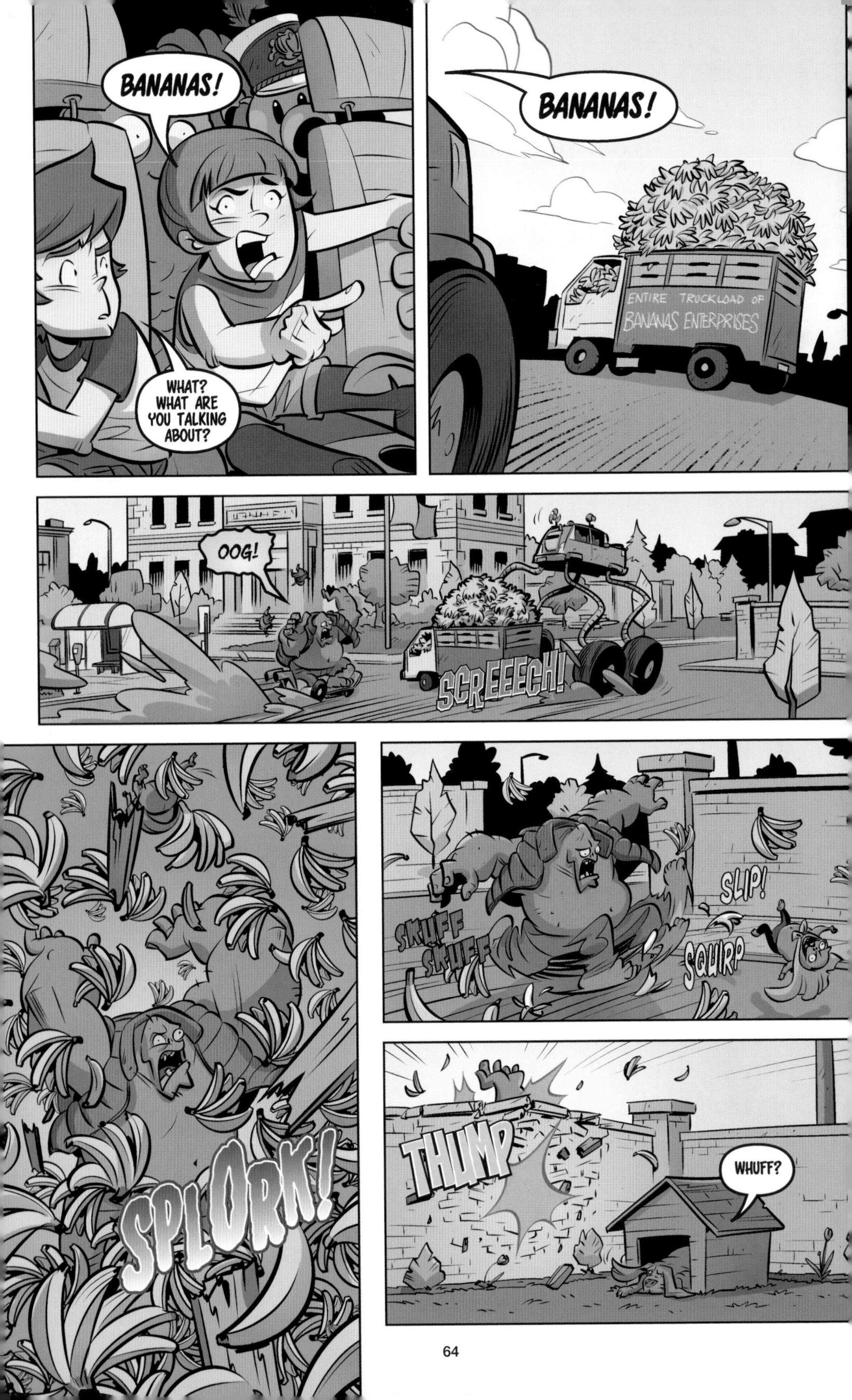
BANANAS!
WHAT? WHAT ARE YOU TALKING ABOUT?
BANANAS!
ENTIRE TRUCKLOAD OF BANANAS ENTERPRISES
OOG!
SCREEECH!
SPLORK!
SNUFF SNUFF
SLIP!
SQUIRP
THUMP
WHUFF?

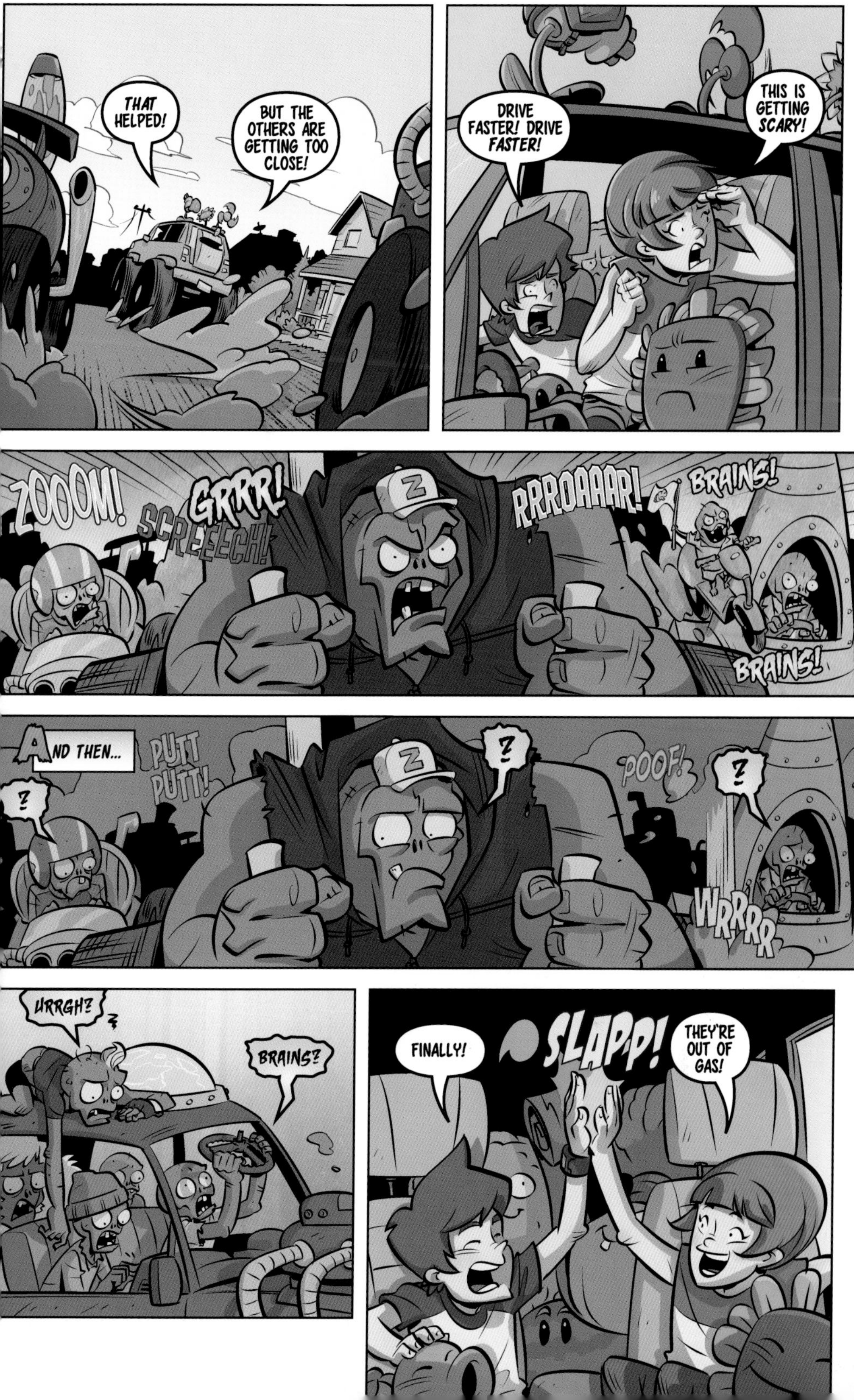
THAT HELPED!
BUT THE OTHERS ARE GETTING TOO CLOSE!
DRIVE FASTER! DRIVE FASTER!
THIS IS GETTING SCARY!
ZOOOM!
GRRR!
SCREEECH!
RRROAAAR!
BRAINS!
BRAINS!
AND THEN...
PUTT PUTT!
?
?
POOF!
?
WRRRR
URRGH?
BRAINS?
FINALLY!
SLAPP!
THEY'RE OUT OF GAS!

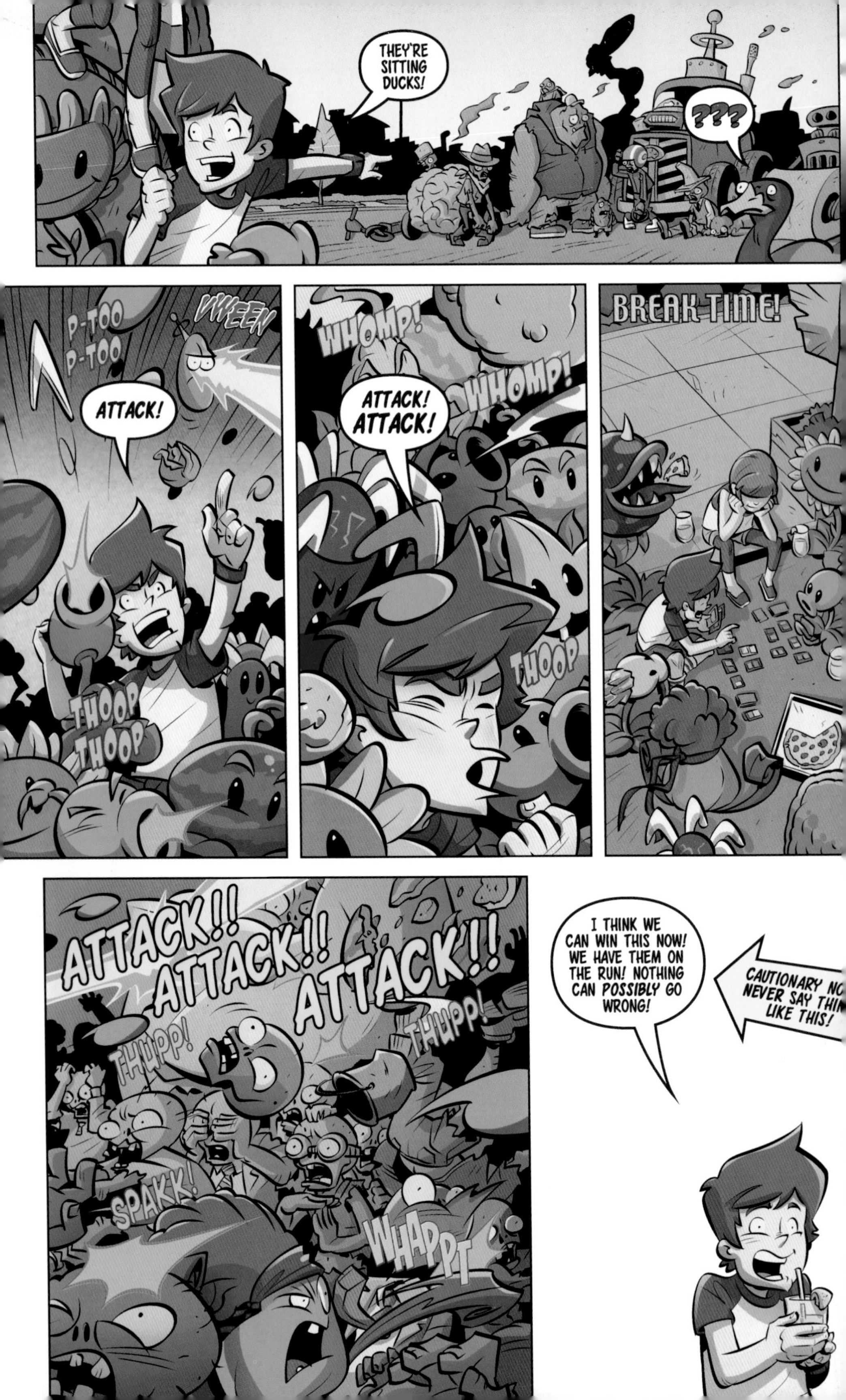
THEY'RE SITTING DUCKS!
???
P-TOO P-TOO
VWEEN
ATTACK!
THOOP THOOP
WHOMP!
ATTACK! ATTACK!
WHOMP!
THOOP
BREAK TIME!
ATTACK!! ATTACK!! ATTACK!!
THUPP!
THUPP!
SPAKK!
WHAPPT
I THINK WE CAN WIN THIS NOW! WE HAVE THEM ON THE RUN! NOTHING CAN POSSIBLY GO WRONG!
CAUTIONARY NO
NEVER SAY THIN
LIKE THIS!

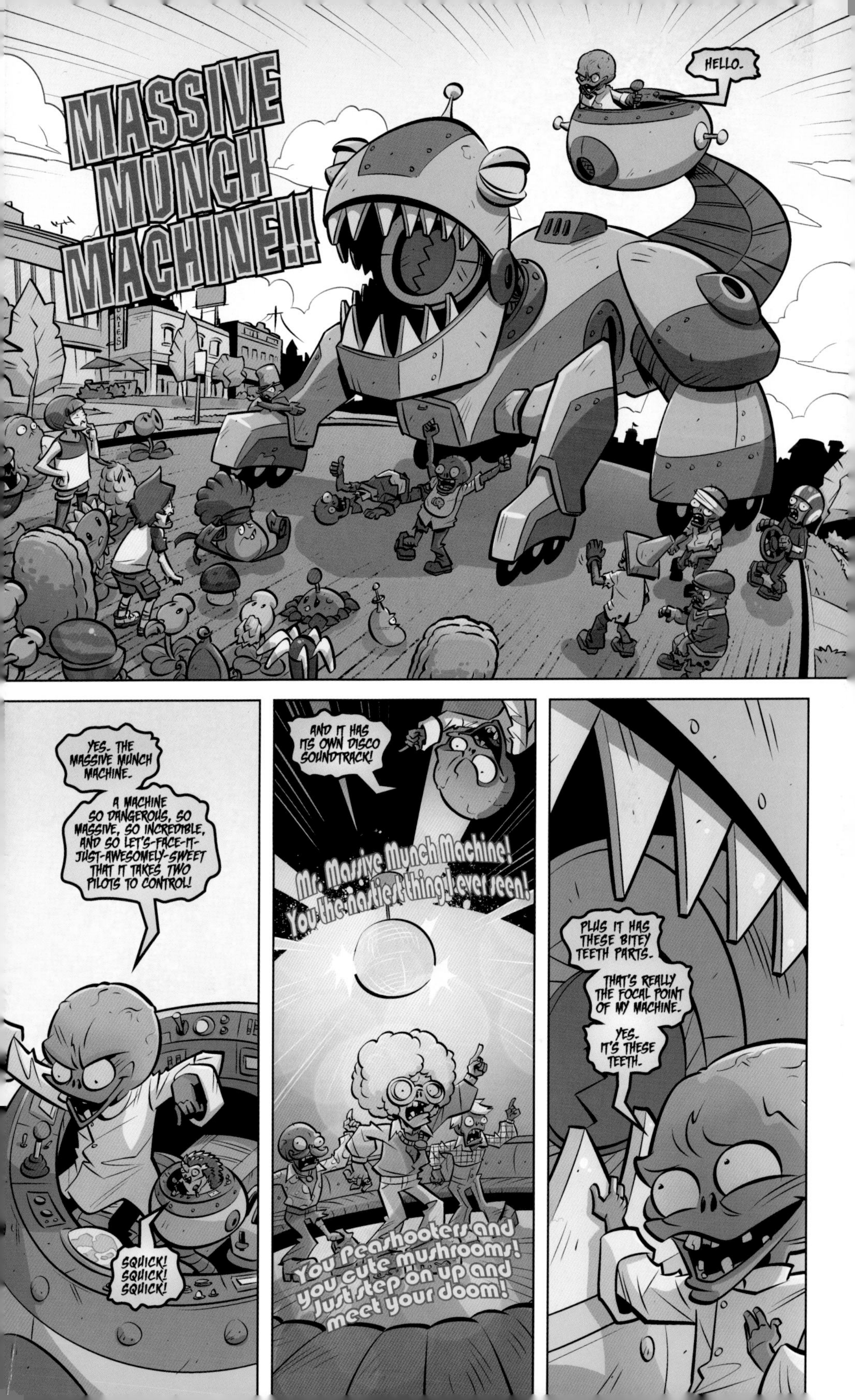
MASSIVE MUNCH MACHINE!!
HELLO.
YES. THE MASSIVE MUNCH MACHINE.
A MACHINE SO DANGEROUS, SO MASSIVE, SO INCREDIBLE, AND SO LET'S-FACE-IT-JUST-AWESOMELY-SWEET THAT IT TAKES TWO PILOTS TO CONTROL!
SQUICK! SQUICK! SQUICK!
AND IT HAS ITS OWN DISCO SOUNDTRACK!
Mr. Massive Munch Machine! You the nastiest thing I ever seen!
You Peashooters and you cute mushrooms! Just step on up and meet your doom!
PLUS IT HAS THESE BITEY TEETH PARTS.
THAT'S REALLY THE FOCAL POINT OF MY MACHINE.
YES. IT'S THESE TEETH.

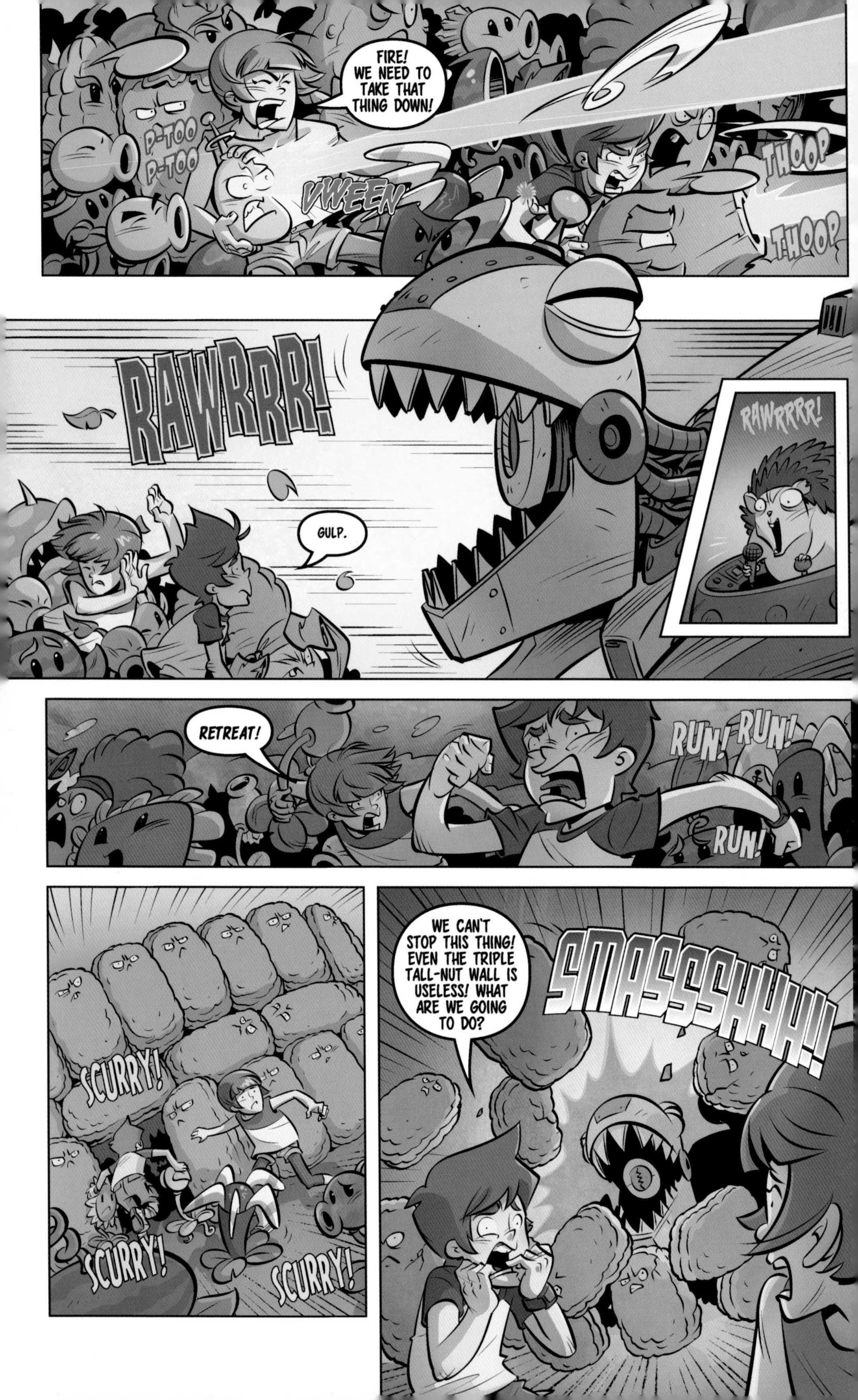
FIRE! WE NEED TO TAKE THAT THING DOWN!
P-TOO P-TOO
VWEEN
THOOP
THOOP
RAWRRR!
RAWRRRR!
GULP.
RETREAT!
RUN! RUN!
RUN!
SCURRY!
SCURRY!
SCURRY!
WE CAN'T STOP THIS THING! EVEN THE TRIPLE TALL-NUT WALL IS USELESS! WHAT ARE WE GOING TO DO?
SMASSSHHH!!

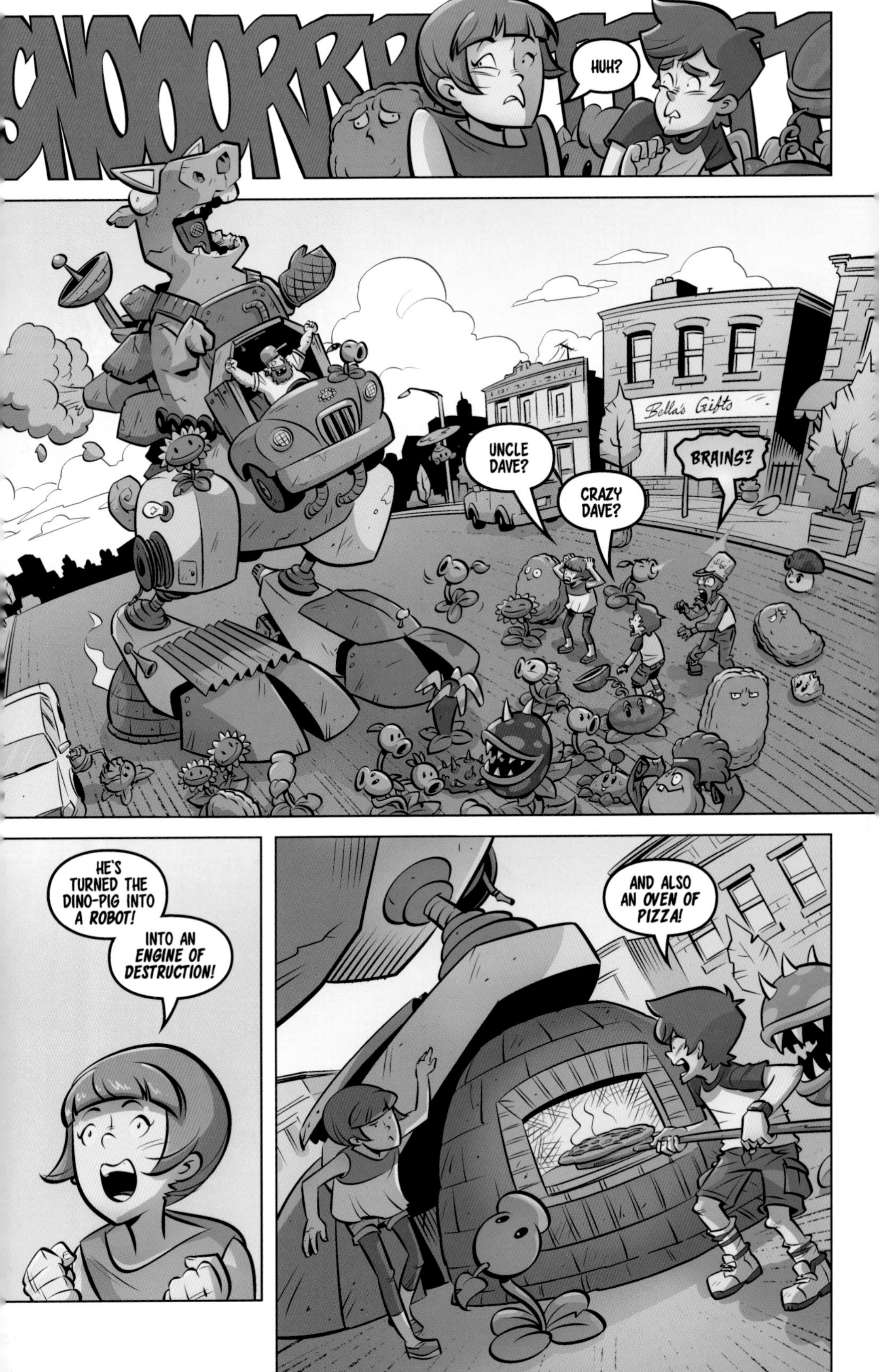
SNOOORRR
HUH?
UNCLE DAVE?
CRAZY DAVE?
BRAINS?
Bella's Gifts
HE'S TURNED THE DINO-PIG INTO A ROBOT!
INTO AN ENGINE OF DESTRUCTION!
AND ALSO AN OVEN OF PIZZA!

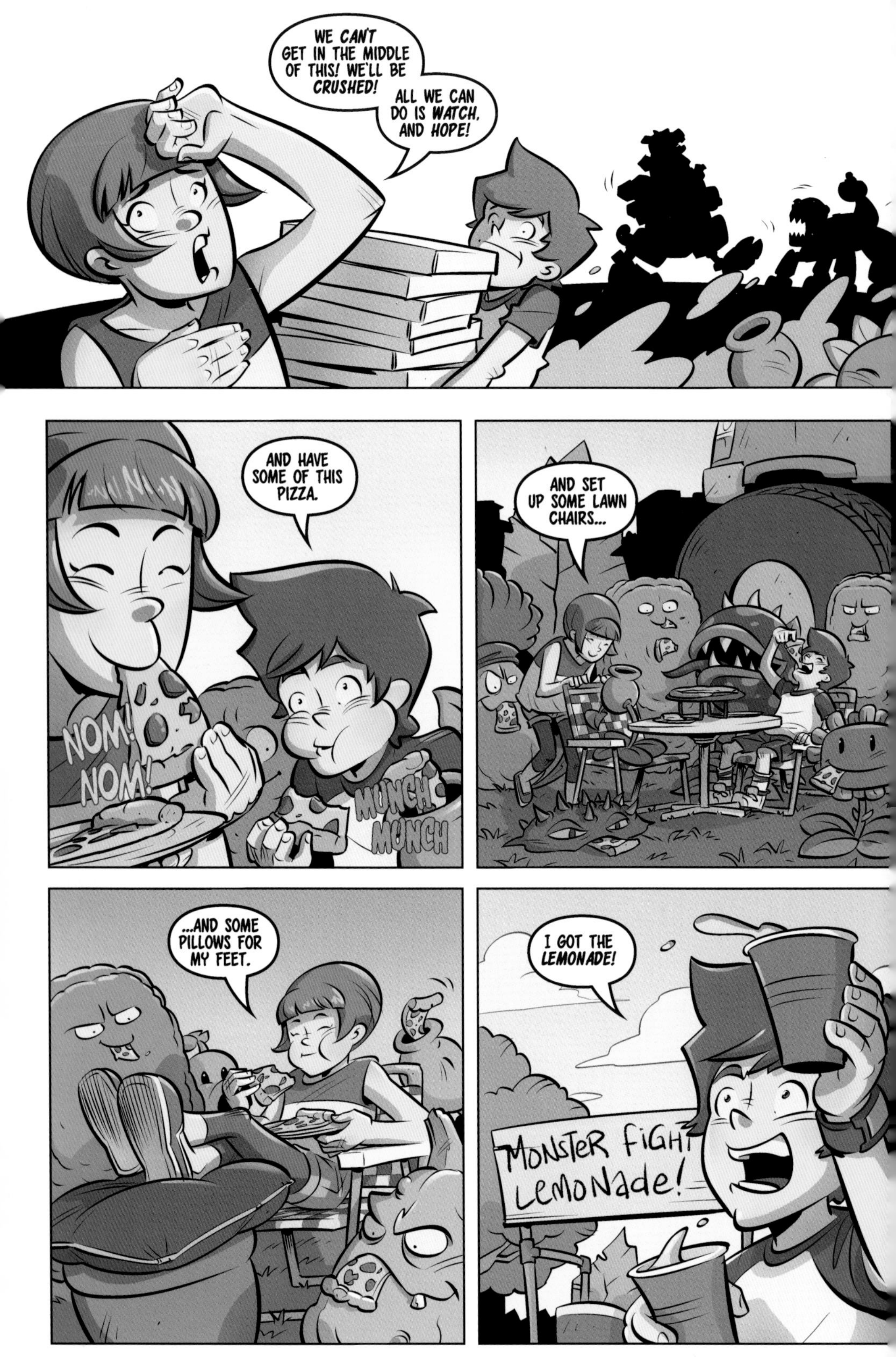

WE CAN'T GET IN THE MIDDLE OF THIS! WE'LL BE CRUSHED!
ALL WE CAN DO IS WATCH, AND HOPE!
AND HAVE SOME OF THIS PIZZA.
NOM! NOM!
MUNCH MUNCH
AND SET UP SOME LAWN CHAIRS...
...AND SOME PILLOWS FOR MY FEET.
I GOT THE LEMONADE!
MONSTER FIGHT LEMONADE!

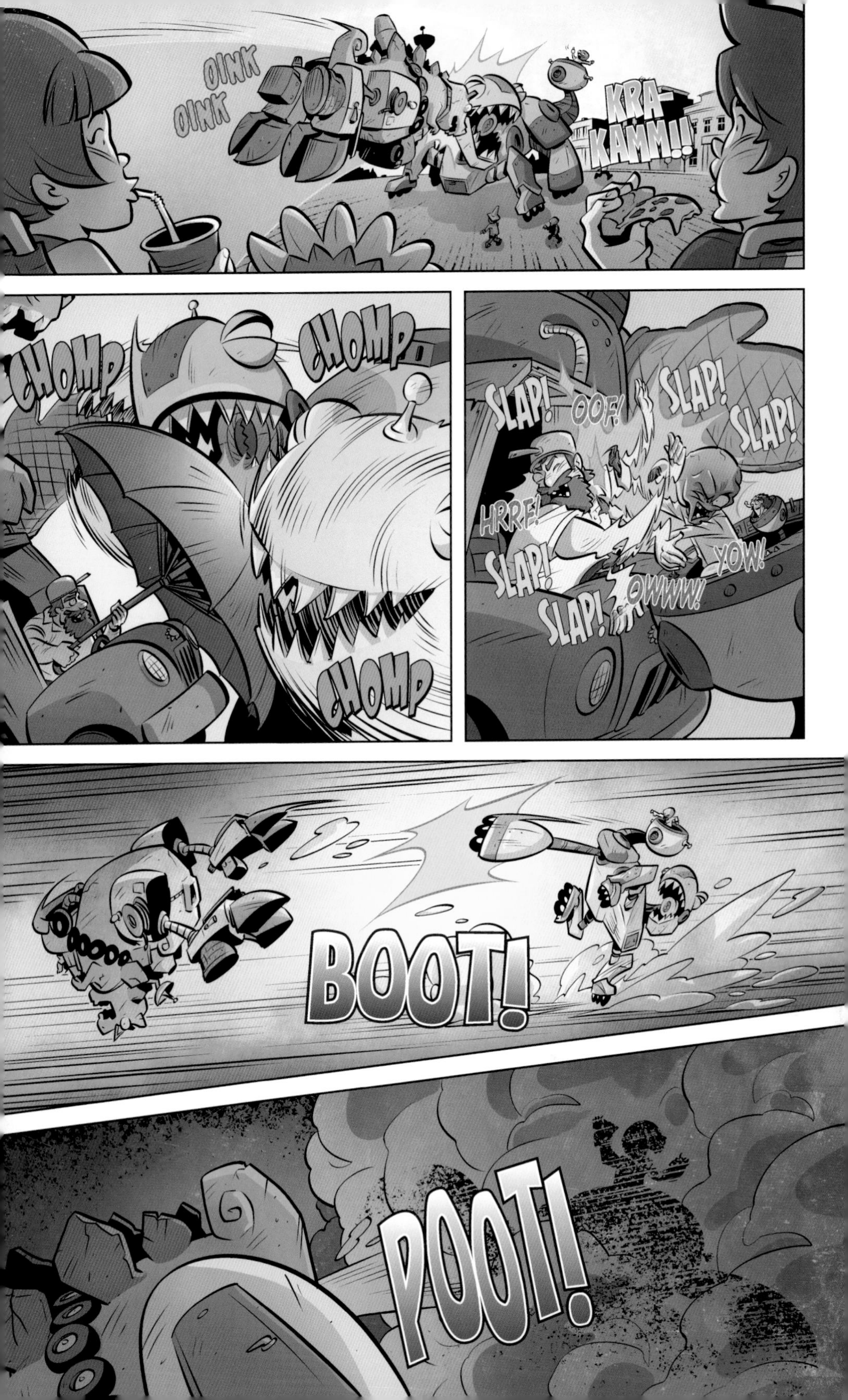
OINK
OINK
KRA-
KAMM!!
CHOMP
CHOMP
CHOMP
SLAP!
OOF!
SLAP!
SLAP!
HRRF!
SLAP!
SLAP!
OWWW!
YOW!
BOOT!
POOT!

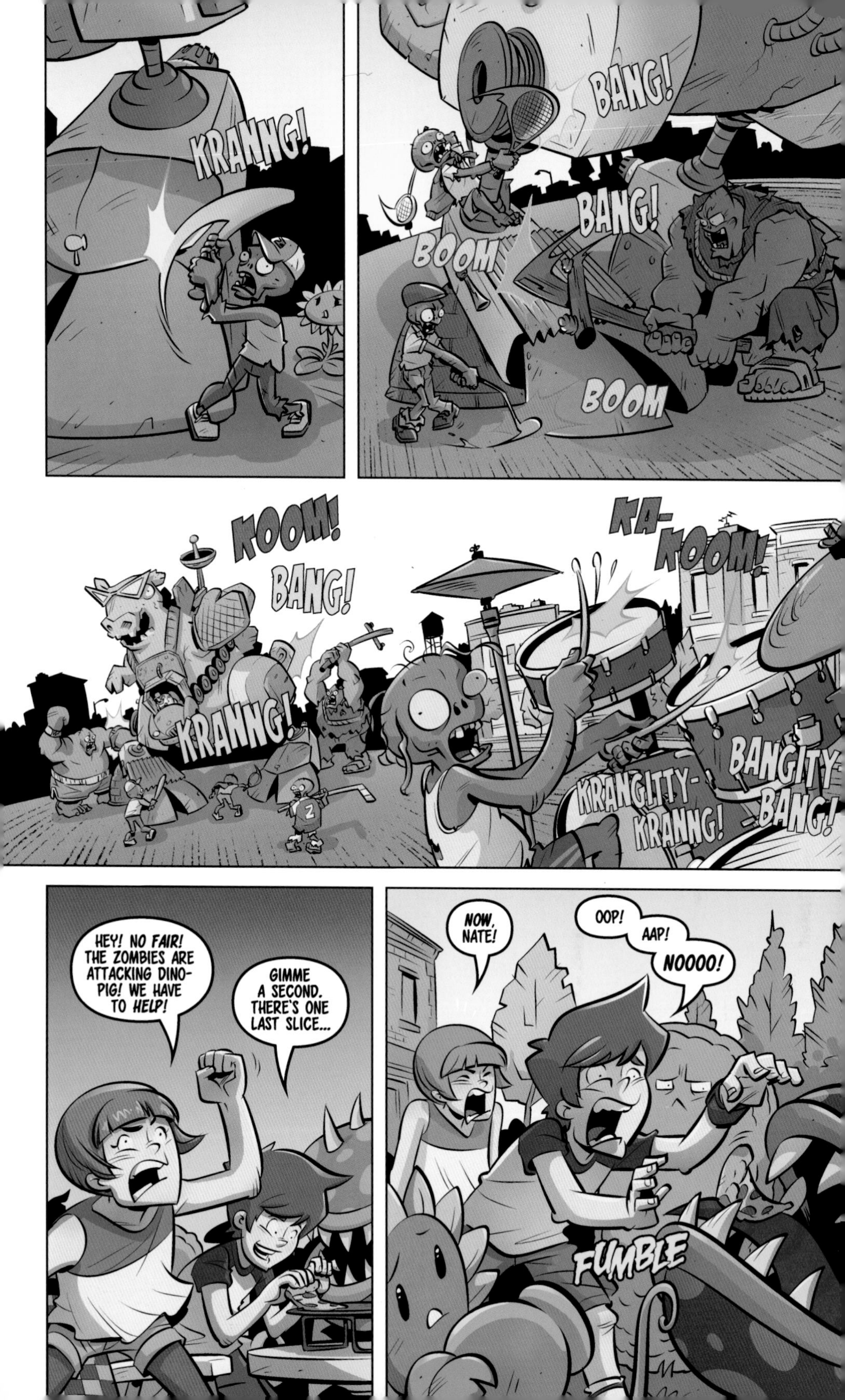
KRANNG!
BANG!
BANG!
BOOM
BOOM
KOOM!
BANG!
KRANNG!
KA-KOOM!
KRANGITTY-KRANNG!
BANGITY-BANG!
HEY! NO FAIR! THE ZOMBIES ARE ATTACKING DINO-PIG! WE HAVE TO HELP!
GIMME A SECOND. THERE'S ONE LAST SLICE...
NOW, NATE!
OOP!
AAP!
NOOOO!
FUMBLE

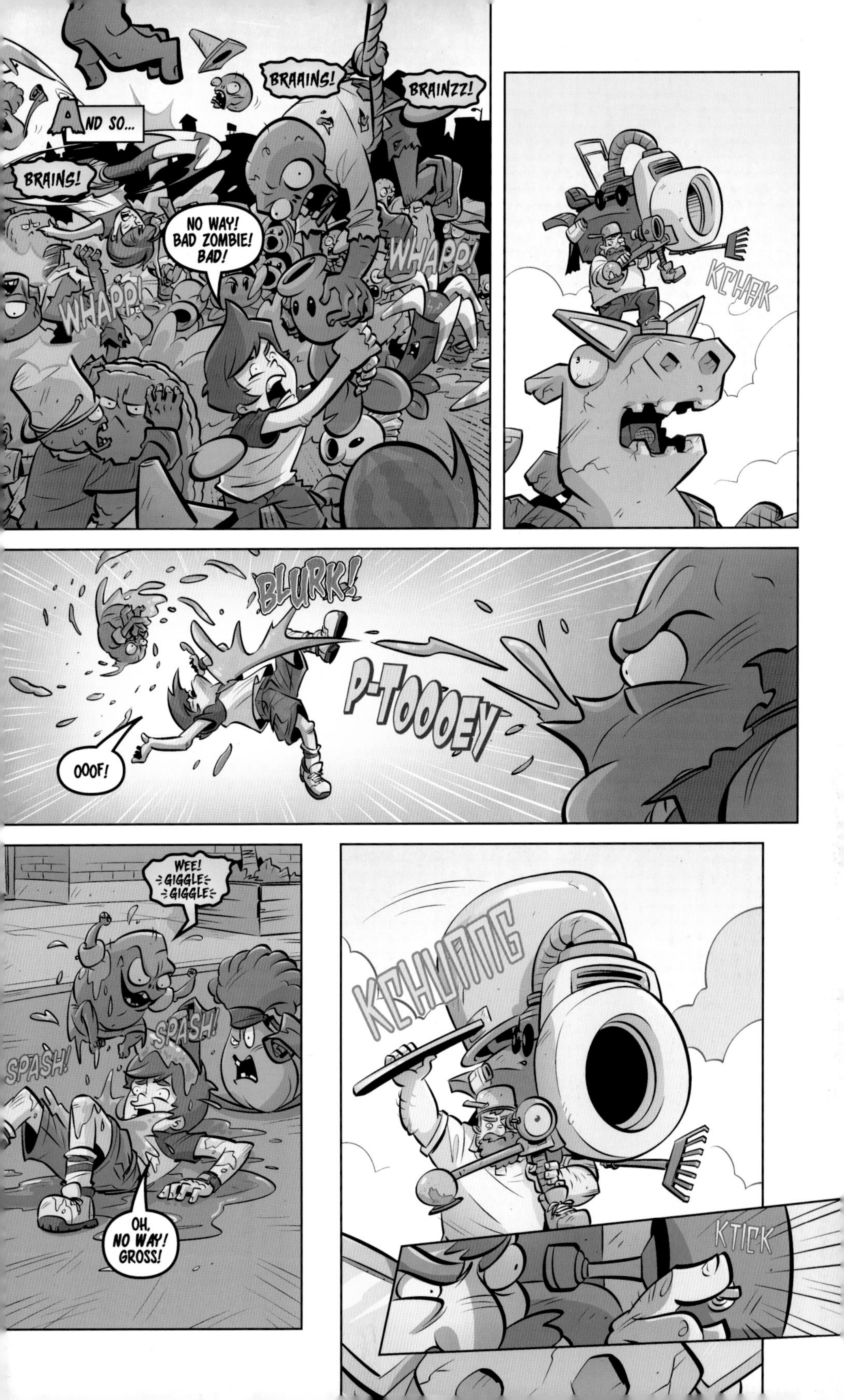
AND SO...
BRAINS!
BRAAINS!
BRAINZZ!
NO WAY! BAD ZOMBIE! BAD!
WHAPP!
WHAPP!
KCHAK
BLURK!
P-TOOOEY
OOOF!
WEE! GIGGLE GIGGLE
SPASH!
SPASH!
OH, NO WAY! GROSS!
KCHUNNG
KTICK

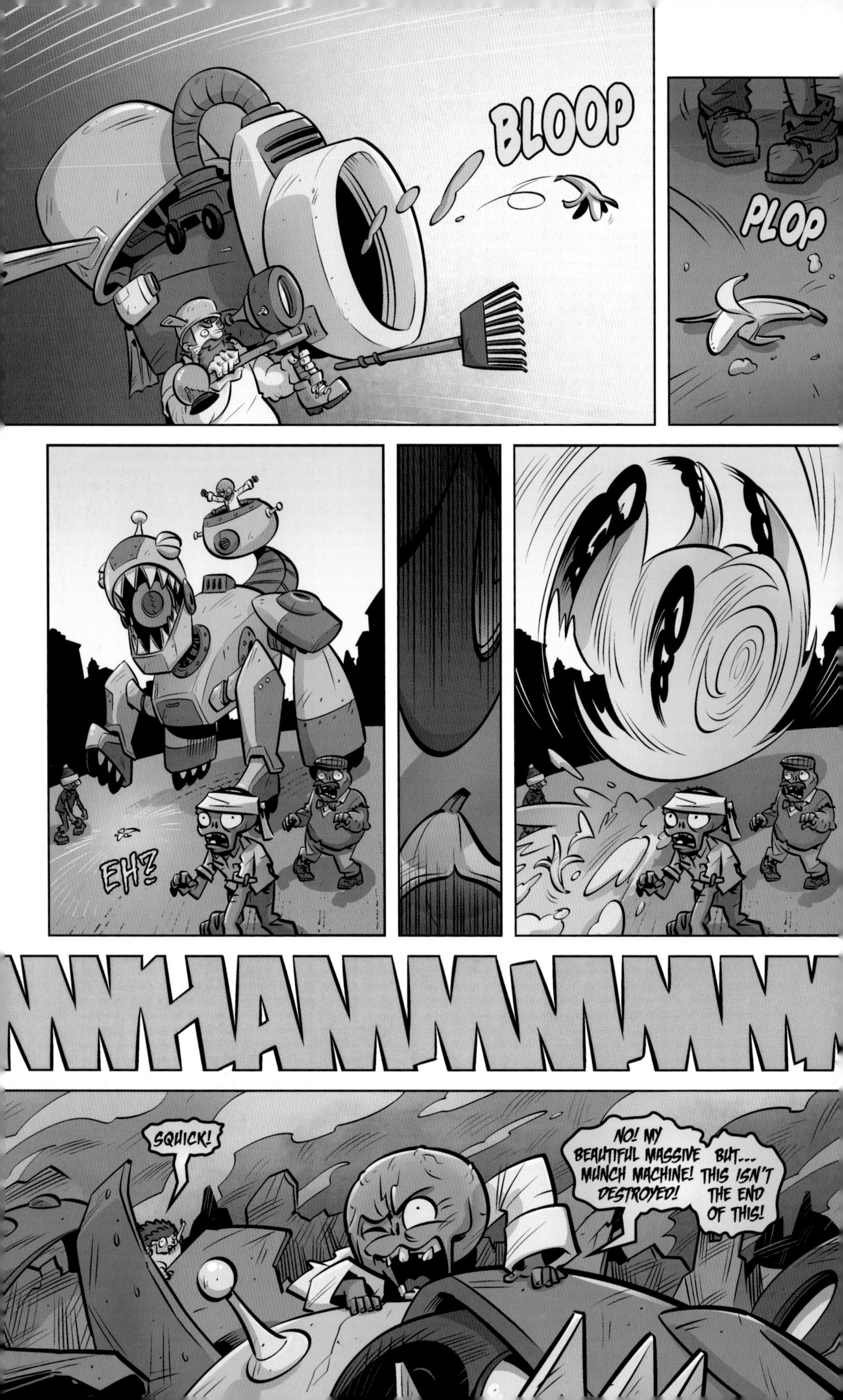

BLOOP
PLOP
EH?
WHAMMMMMM
SQUICK!
NO! MY BEAUTIFUL MASSIVE MUNCH MACHINE! DESTROYED!
BUT... THIS ISN'T THE END OF THIS!

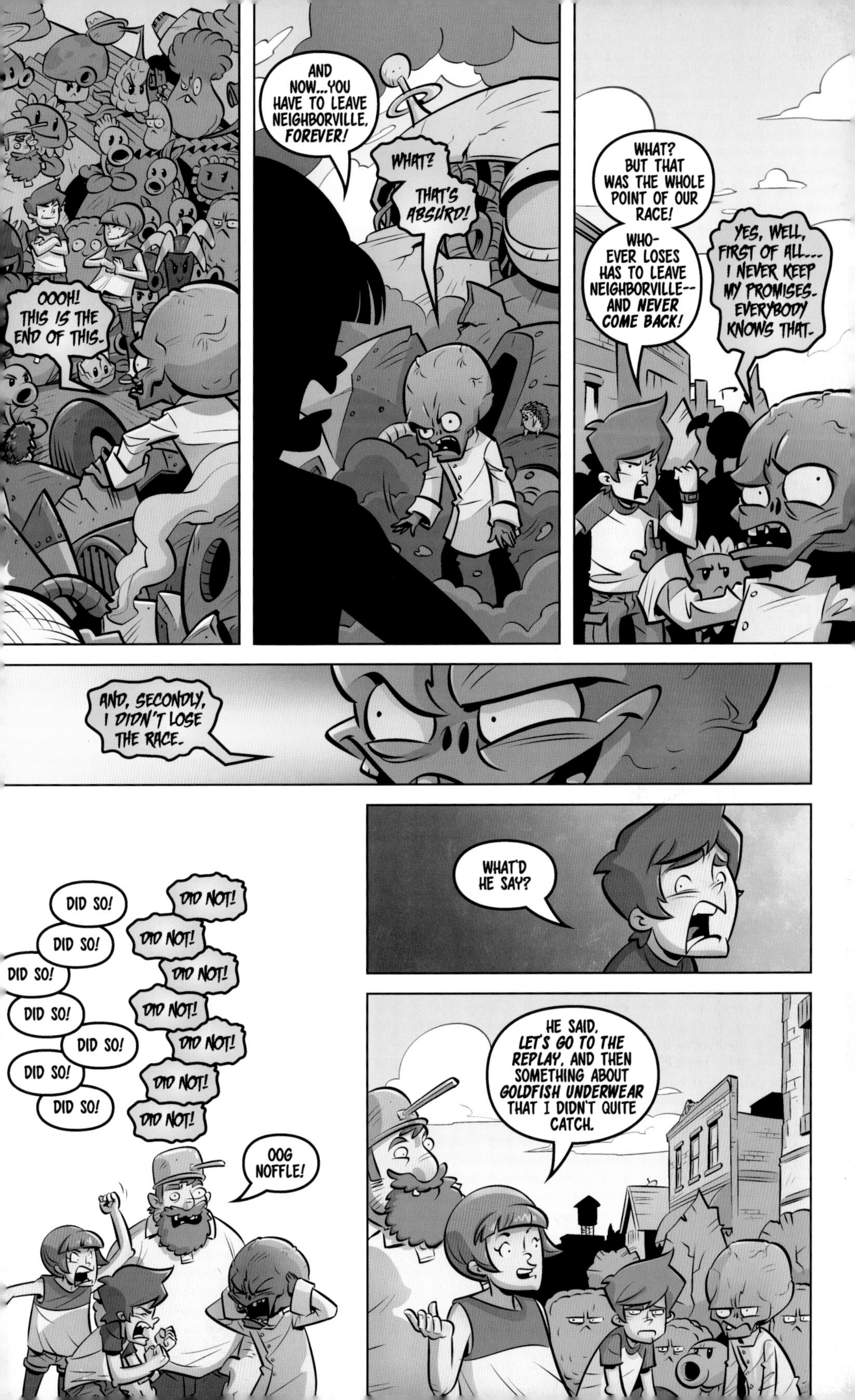
OOOH! THIS IS THE END OF THIS.
AND NOW...YOU HAVE TO LEAVE NEIGHBORVILLE, FOREVER!
WHAT? THAT'S ABSURD!
WHAT? BUT THAT WAS THE WHOLE POINT OF OUR RACE!
WHO-EVER LOSES HAS TO LEAVE NEIGHBORVILLE--AND NEVER COME BACK!
YES, WELL, FIRST OF ALL... I NEVER KEEP MY PROMISES. EVERYBODY KNOWS THAT.
AND, SECONDLY, I DIDN'T LOSE THE RACE.
DID SO!
DID NOT!
DID SO!
DID NOT!
DID SO!
DID NOT!
DID SO!
DID NOT!
DID SO!
DID NOT!
DID SO!
DID NOT!
DID SO!
DID NOT!
OOG NOFFLE!
WHAT'D HE SAY?
HE SAID, LET'S GO TO THE REPLAY, AND THEN SOMETHING ABOUT GOLDFISH UNDERWEAR THAT I DIDN'T QUITE CATCH.

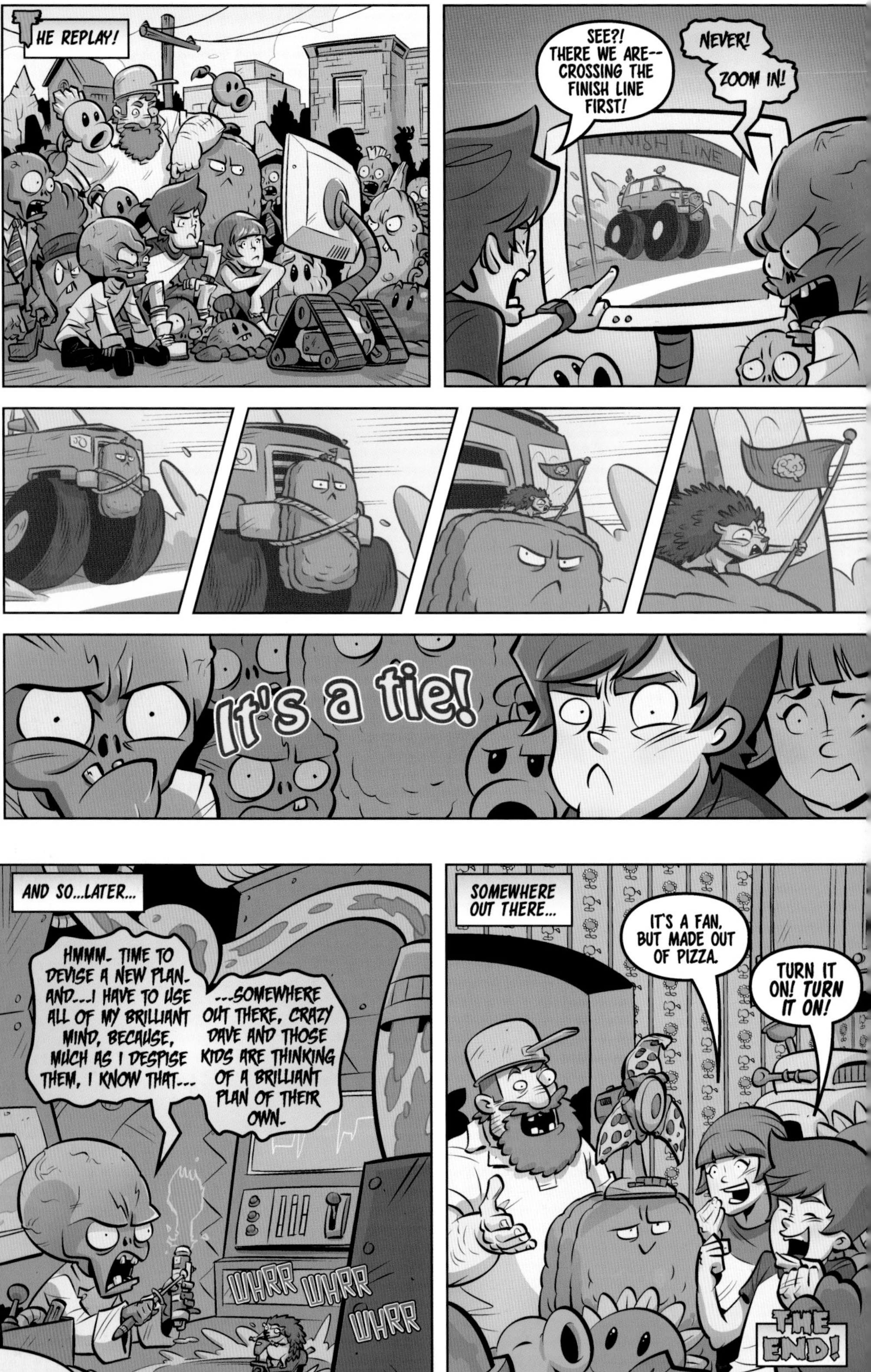
THE REPLAY!
SEE?! THERE WE ARE-- CROSSING THE FINISH LINE FIRST!
NEVER!
ZOOM IN!
FINISH LINE
It's a tie!
AND SO...LATER...
HMMM. TIME TO DEVISE A NEW PLAN. AND...I HAVE TO USE ALL OF MY BRILLIANT MIND, BECAUSE, MUCH AS I DESPISE THEM, I KNOW THAT...
...SOMEWHERE OUT THERE, CRAZY DAVE AND THOSE KIDS ARE THINKING OF A BRILLIANT PLAN OF THEIR OWN.
WHRR WHRR WHRR
SOMEWHERE OUT THERE...
IT'S A FAN, BUT MADE OUT OF PIZZA.
TURN IT ON! TURN IT ON!
THE END!

PLANTS vs. ZOMBIES

THE LADY IN RED

Written by PAUL TOBIN
Art by BRIAN CHURILLA
Letters by STEVE DUTRO

Celebrating 15 Years
FREE COMIC BOOK DAY

The Free Comic Book Day story that
introduced Nate's Shroompoo Shampoo!

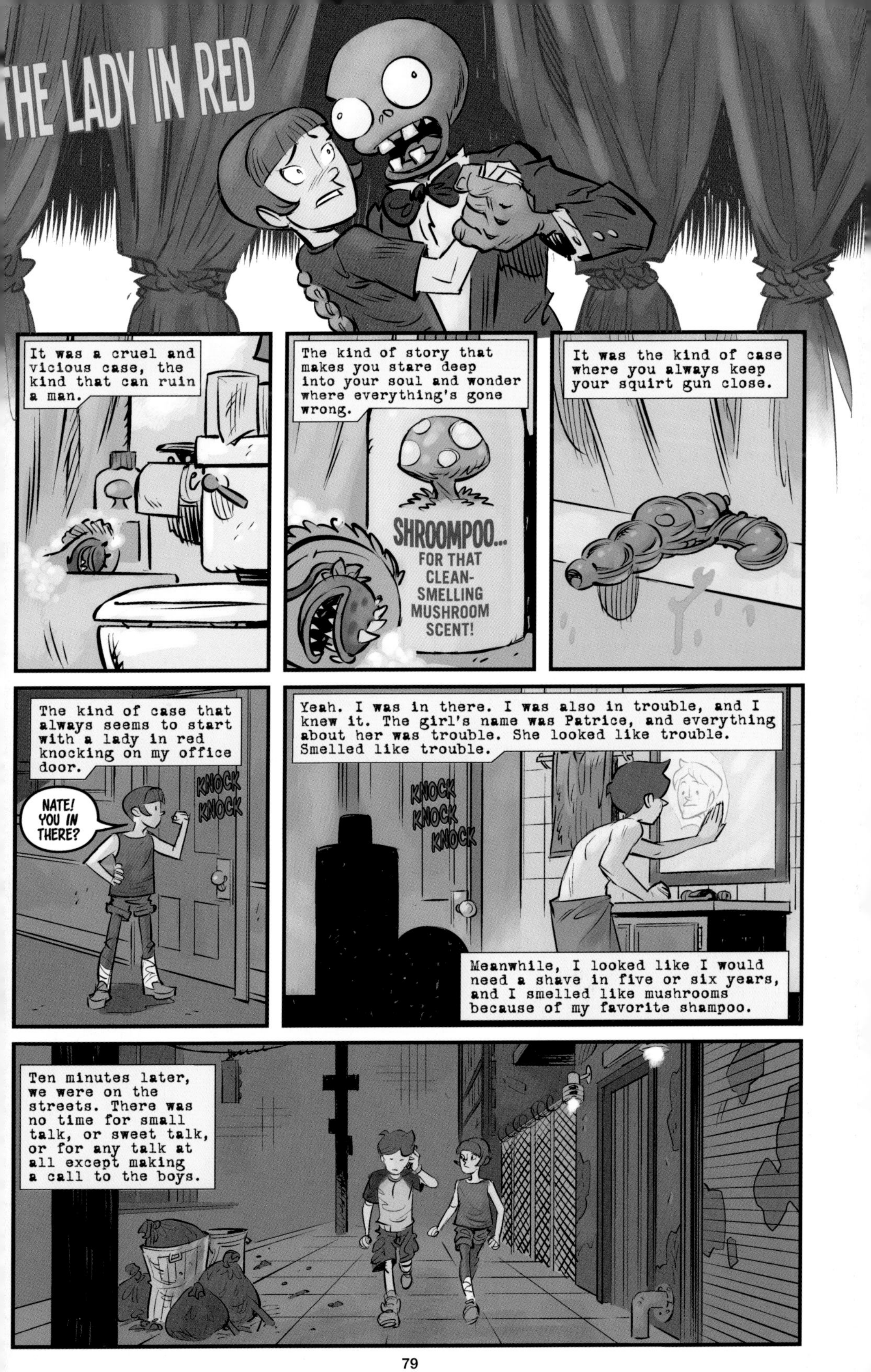
THE LADY IN RED
It was a cruel and vicious case, the kind that can ruin a man.
The kind of story that makes you stare deep into your soul and wonder where everything's gone wrong.
SHROOMPOO... FOR THAT CLEAN-SMELLING MUSHROOM SCENT!
It was the kind of case where you always keep your squirt gun close.
The kind of case that always seems to start with a lady in red knocking on my office door.
KNOCK KNOCK
NATE! YOU IN THERE?
Yeah. I was in there. I was also in trouble, and I knew it. The girl's name was Patrice, and everything about her was trouble. She looked like trouble. Smelled like trouble.
KNOCK KNOCK KNOCK
Meanwhile, I looked like I would need a shave in five or six years, and I smelled like mushrooms because of my favorite shampoo.
Ten minutes later, we were on the streets. There was no time for small talk, or sweet talk, or for any talk at all except making a call to the boys.

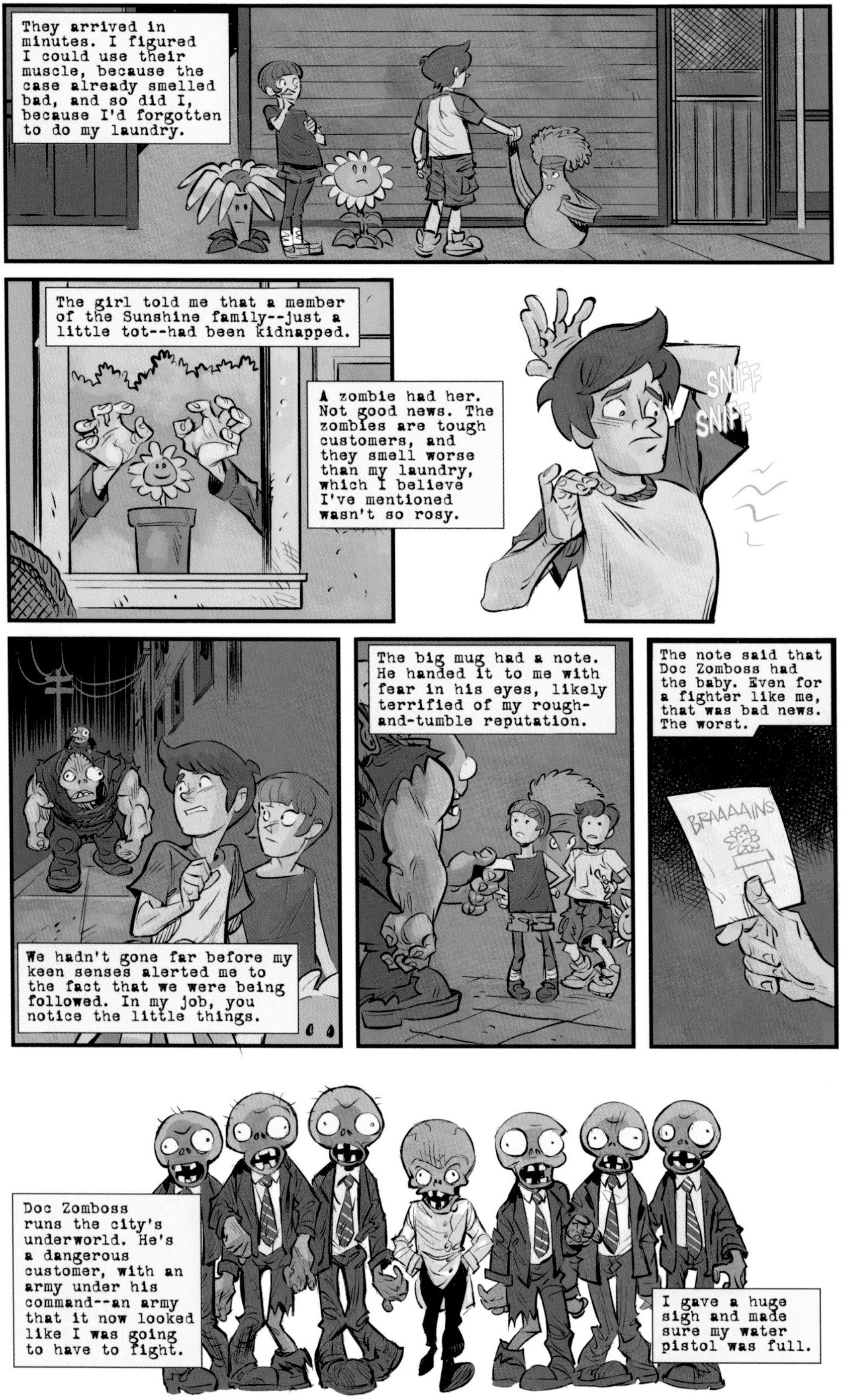
They arrived in minutes. I figured I could use their muscle, because the case already smelled bad, and so did I, because I'd forgotten to do my laundry.
The girl told me that a member of the Sunshine family--just a little tot--had been kidnapped.
A zombie had her. Not good news. The zombies are tough customers, and they smell worse than my laundry, which I believe I've mentioned wasn't so rosy.
SNIFF SNIFF
We hadn't gone far before my keen senses alerted me to the fact that we were being followed. In my job, you notice the little things.
The big mug had a note. He handed it to me with fear in his eyes, likely terrified of my rough-and-tumble reputation.
The note said that Doc Zomboss had the baby. Even for a fighter like me, that was bad news. The worst.
BRAAAAINS
Doc Zomboss runs the city's underworld. He's a dangerous customer, with an army under his command--an army that it now looked like I was going to have to fight.
I gave a huge sigh and made sure my water pistol was full.

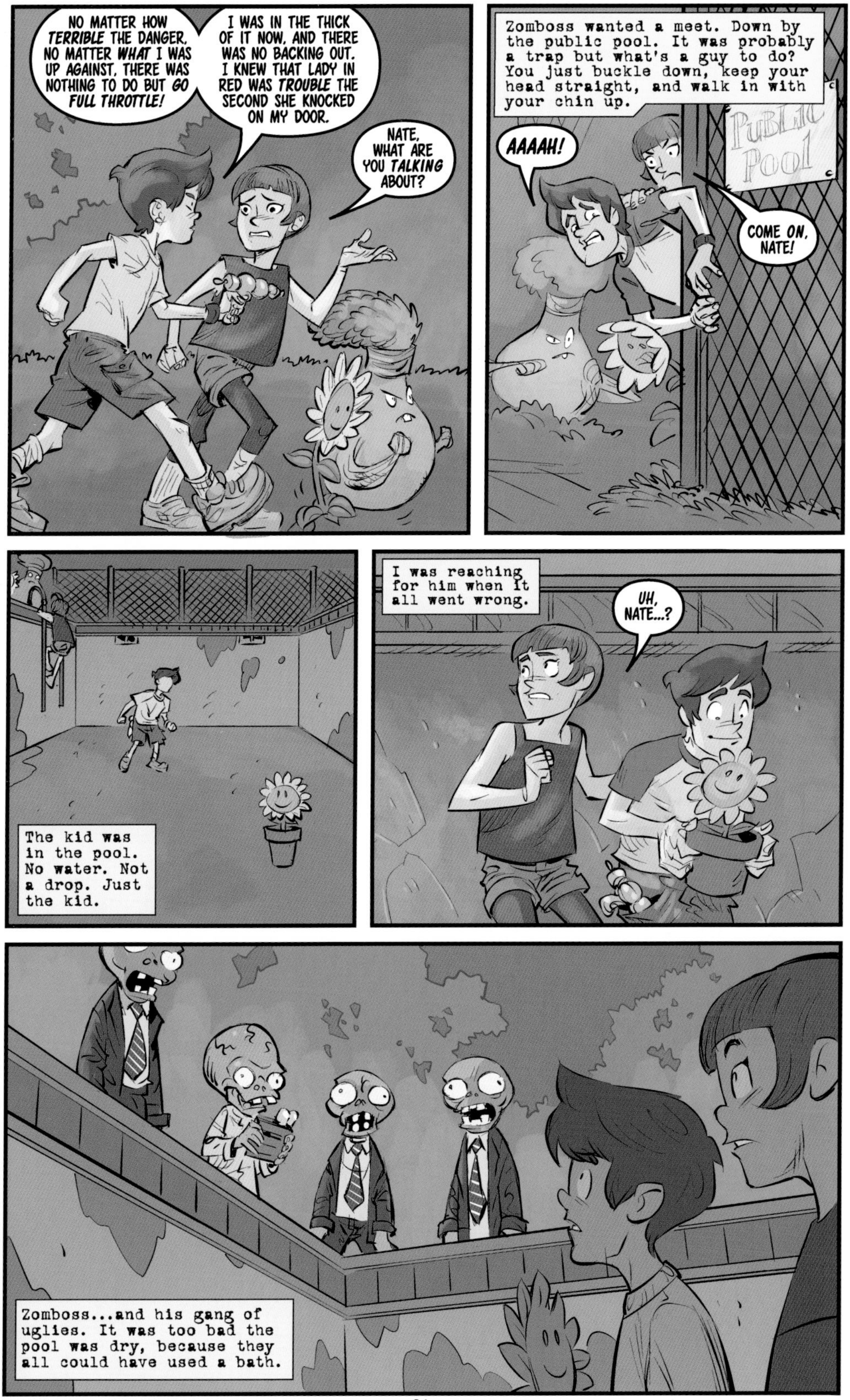
NO MATTER HOW TERRIBLE THE DANGER, NO MATTER WHAT I WAS UP AGAINST, THERE WAS NOTHING TO DO BUT GO FULL THROTTLE!
I WAS IN THE THICK OF IT NOW, AND THERE WAS NO BACKING OUT. I KNEW THAT LADY IN RED WAS TROUBLE THE SECOND SHE KNOCKED ON MY DOOR.
NATE, WHAT ARE YOU TALKING ABOUT?
Zomboss wanted a meet. Down by the public pool. It was probably a trap but what's a guy to do? You just buckle down, keep your head straight, and walk in with your chin up.
AAAAH!
PUBLIC POOL
COME ON, NATE!
The kid was in the pool. No water. Not a drop. Just the kid.
I was reaching for him when it all went wrong.
UH, NATE...?
Zomboss...and his gang of uglies. It was too bad the pool was dry, because they all could have used a bath.

Zomboss started ranting, the way these types do. They all have egos the size of a tree...and mercy the size of a twig.

HA! YOU FELL FOR MY TRAP! AND I'VE SPENT MONTHS ON THIS AMAZING DEVICE, WHICH CAN TRIGGER AN AMAZING VARIETY OF TRULY NEFARIOUS ACTIONS, LIKE...

--SENDING YOU BACK IN TIME, OR MAKING YOU BURP UNCONTROLLABLY, OR TURNING YOUR UNDERWEAR INSIDE OUT, OR SHRINKING YOU TO THE SIZE OF AN ANT, OR MAKING YOU ALLERGIC TO SUNSHINE, OR...

I knew I'd only have one shot at this--

--and I took it.

SPLLURRT!

GLORK!

FIZZT!

FIZZZ!

SPIT!

FIZZLE!

OH, YOU'VE GOT TO BE KIDDING.

I'M GOING HOME.

TOSS!

Ten minutes later, we were at my favorite watering hole, and I was buying a round for the house. Mine was two scoops, the way I like it.

I kept it close, too. I didn't like the way the lady in red was looking at my ice cream.

And I knew that girl was trouble.

THE END.

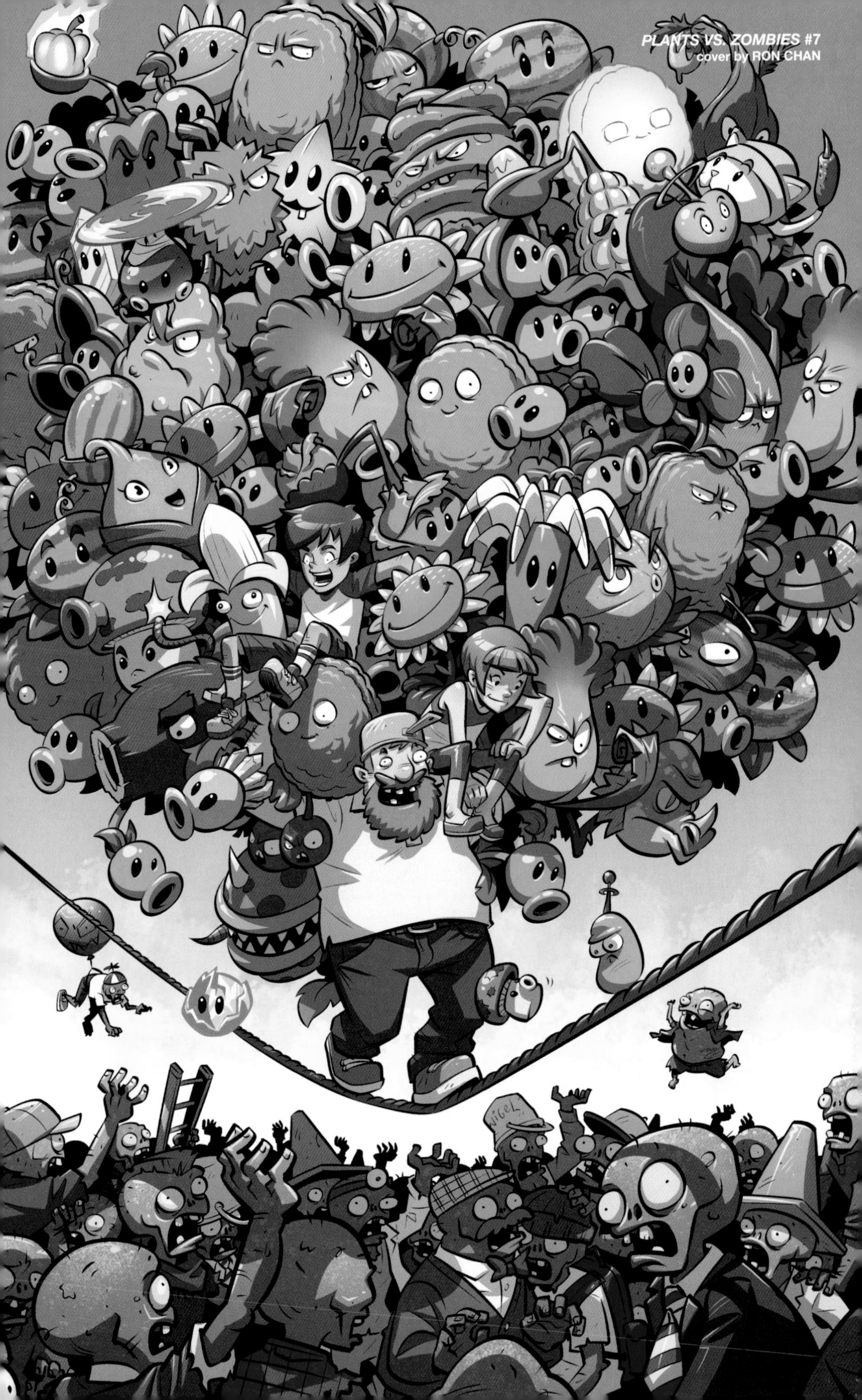

PLANTS VS. ZOMBIES #7
cover by RON CHAN

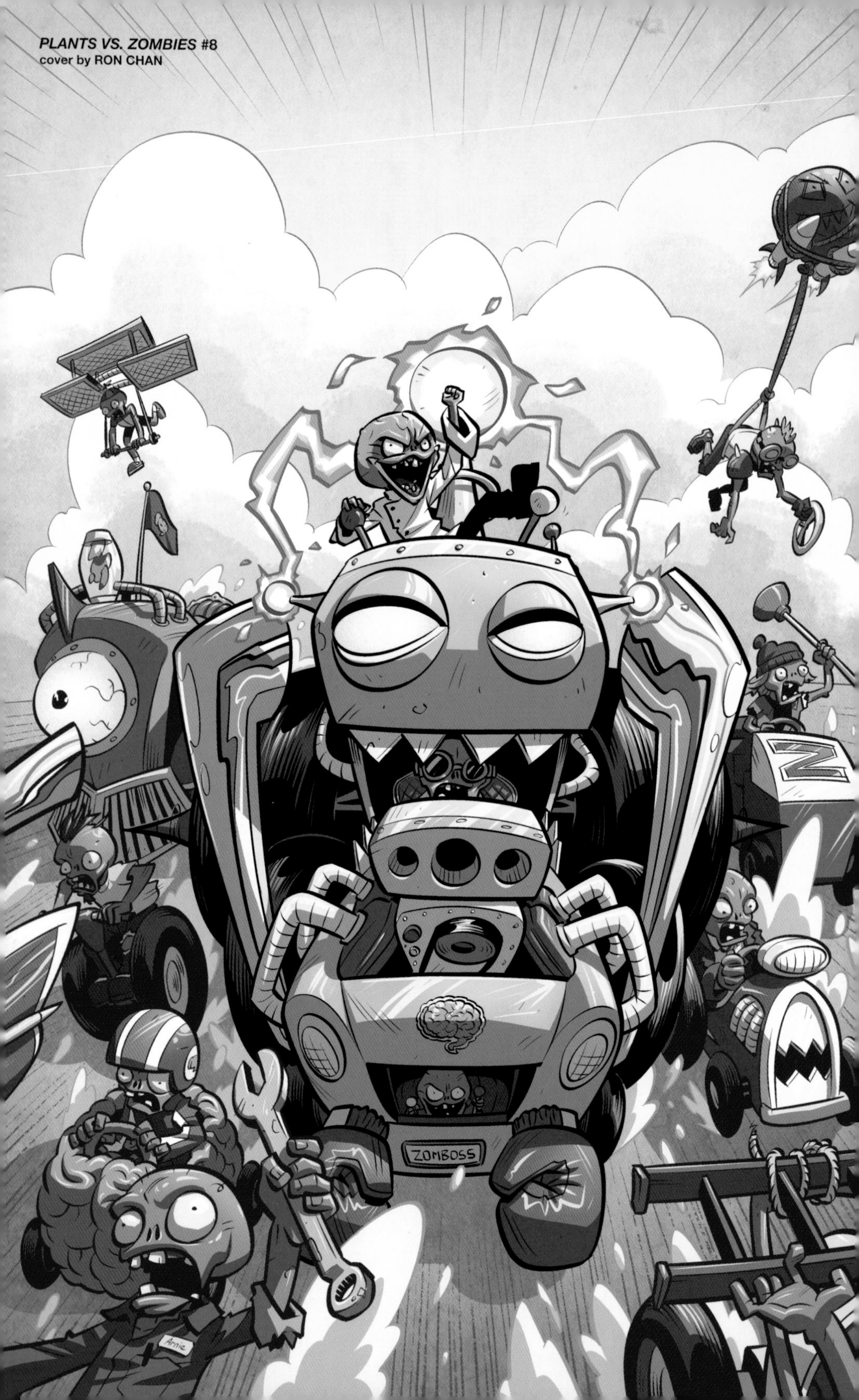
Z
ZOMBOSS
Arnie

PLANTS VS. ZOMBIES #8
cover by RON CHAN

PLANTS VS. ZOMBIES #9
cover by RON CHAN

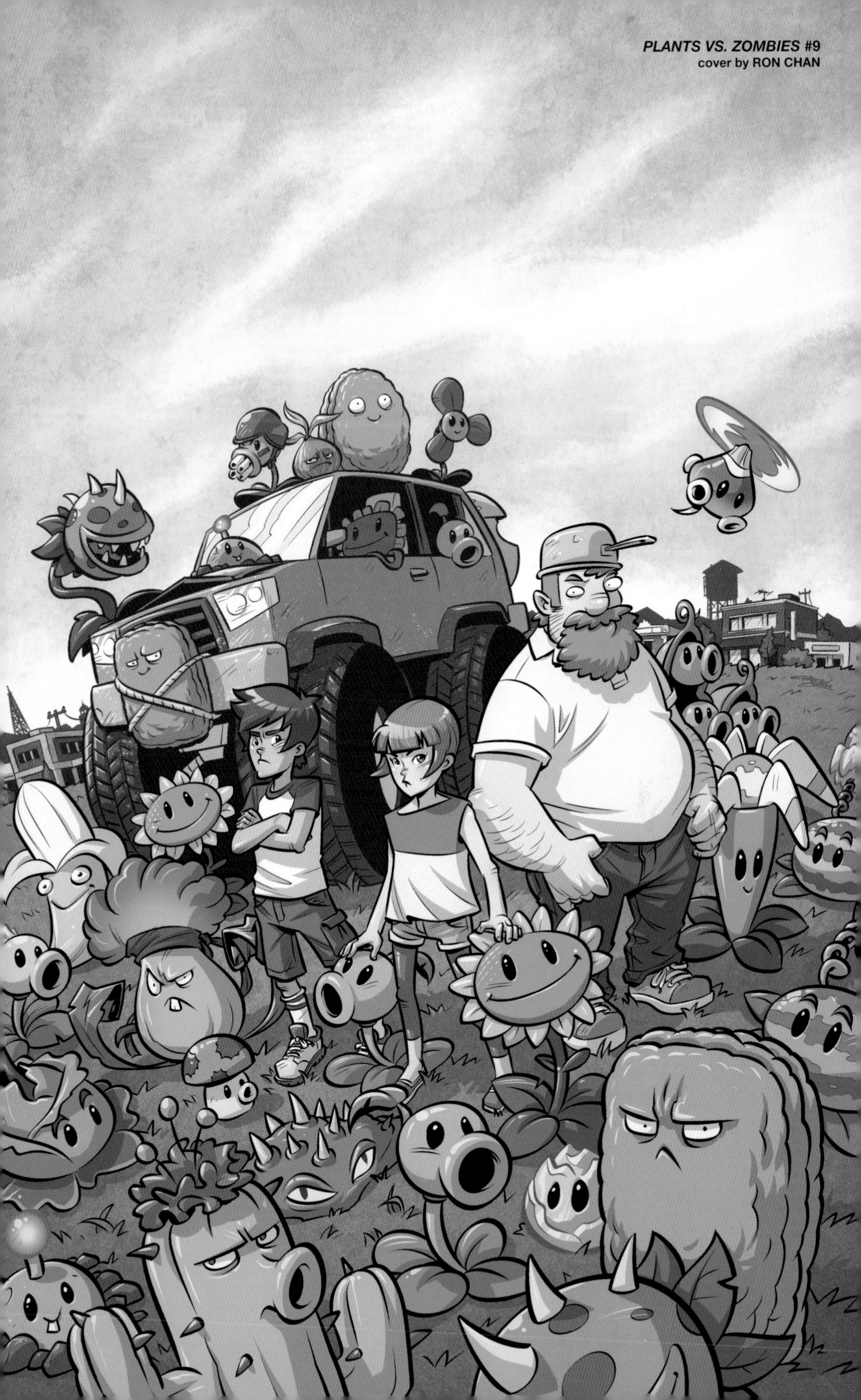

CREATOR BIOS

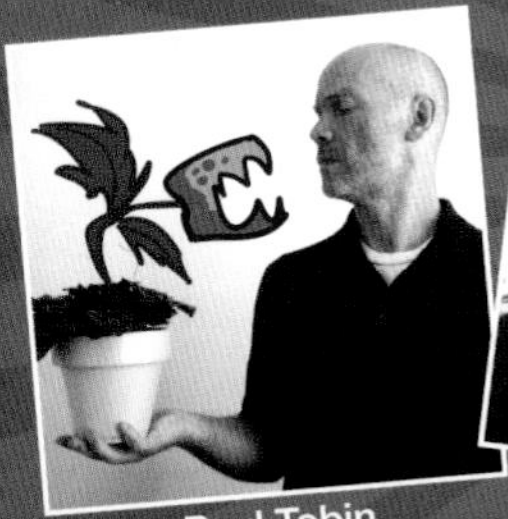
Paul Tobin

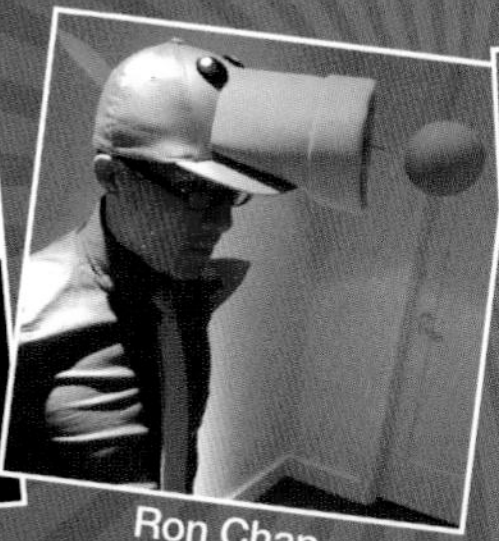
Ron Chan

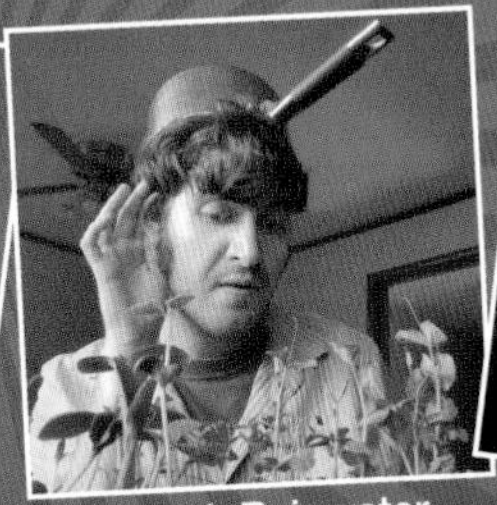
Matt J. Rainwater

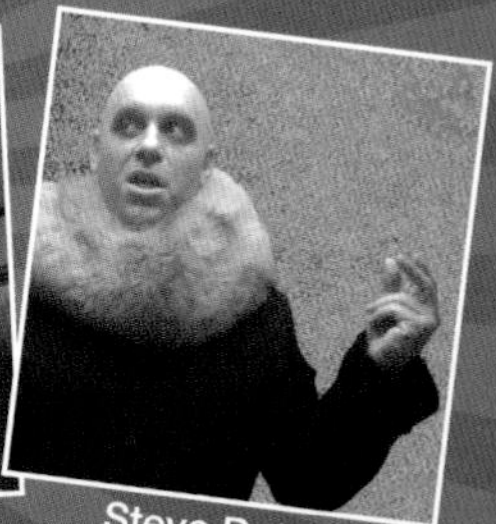
Steve Dutro

PAUL TOBIN is a critically acclaimed freckled person who has a detailed plan for any actual zombie invasion, based on creating a vast perfume and cologne empire—both of which would be vitally important in a zombie-infested world. Paul was once informed he "walks funny, like, seriously," but has recovered from this childhood trauma to write hundreds of comics for Marvel, DC, Dark Horse, and many others, including such creator-owned titles as *Colder* and *Bandette*, as well as *Prepare to Die!*—his debut novel. His *Genius Factor* series of novels about a fifth-grade genius and his war against the Red Death Tea Society began in March 2016 from Bloomsbury Publishing. Despite his many writing accomplishments, Paul's greatest claim to fame is his ability to win water levels in *Plants vs. Zombies* without using any water plants.

RON CHAN is a comic book and storyboard artist, video game fan, and occasional jujitsu practitioner. He was born and raised in Portland, Oregon, where he still lives and works as a member of the local artist collective Periscope Studio. His comics work has been published by Dark Horse, Marvel, and Image Comics, and his storyboarding work includes boards for 3D animation, gaming, user-experience design, and advertising for clients such as Microsoft, Amazon Kindle, Nike, and Sega. He really likes drawing Bonk Choys. (He also enjoys eating actual bok choy in real life.)

Residing in the cool, damp forests of Portland, Oregon, **MATT J. RAINWATER** is a freelance illustrator whose work has been featured in advertising, web design, and independent video games. On top of this, he also self-publishes several comic books, including *Trailer Park Warlock*, *Garage Raja*, and *The Feeling Is Multiplied*—all of which can be found at MattJRainwater.com. His favorite zombie-bashing strategy utilizes a line of Bonk Choys with a Wall-nut front guard and Threepeater covering fire.

STEVE DUTRO is a comic book letterer from northern California who can also drive a tractor. He graduated from the Kubert School and has been in the comics industry for decades, working for Dark Horse (*The Fifth Beatle*, *I Am a Hero*, *The Evil Dead*, *Eden*), Viz, Marvel, and DC. Steve's last encounter with zombies was playing zombie paintball in a walnut orchard on Halloween. He tried to play the *Plants vs. Zombies* video game once but experienced a full-on panic attack and resolved to stick with calmer games . . . like *Gears of War*.

ALSO AVAILABLE FROM DARK HORSE!

THE HIT VIDEO GAME CONTINUES ITS COMIC BOOK INVASION!

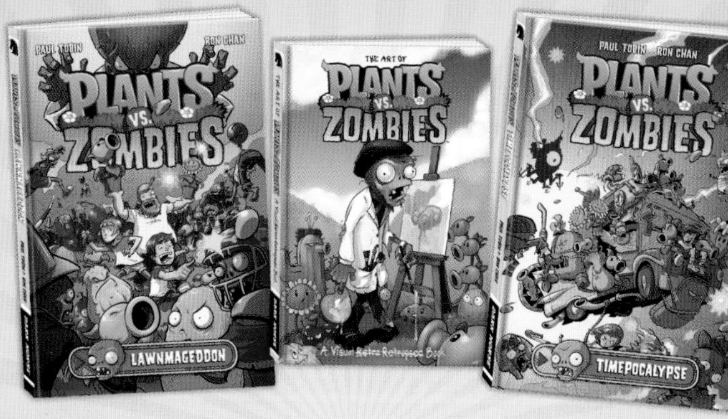

PAUL TOBIN
RON CHAN
PLANTS VS. ZOMBIES
LAWNMAGEDDON
THE ART OF
PLANTS VS. ZOMBIES
PAUL TOBIN
RON CHAN
PLANTS VS. ZOMBIES
TIMEPOCALYPSE

PLANTS VS. ZOMBIES: LAWNMAGEDDON

Crazy Dave—the babbling-yet-brilliant inventor and top-notch neighborhood defender—helps his niece Patrice and young adventurer Nate Timely fend off a zombie invasion that threatens to overrun the peaceful town of Neighborville in *Plants vs. Zombies: Lawnmageddon*! Their only hope is a brave army of chomping, squashing, and pea-shooting plants! A wacky adventure for zombie zappers young and old!

ISBN 978-1-61655-192-6 | $9.99

THE ART OF PLANTS VS. ZOMBIES

Part zombie memoir, part celebration of zombie triumphs, and part anti-plant screed, *The Art of Plants vs. Zombies* is a treasure trove of never-before-seen concept art, character sketches, and surprises from PopCap's popular *Plants vs. Zombies* games!

ISBN 978-1-61655-331-9 | $9.99

PLANTS VS. ZOMBIES: TIMEPOCALYPSE

Crazy Dave helps Patrice and Nate Timely fend off Zomboss's latest attack in *Plants vs. Zombies: Timepocalypse*! This new standalone tale will tickle your funny bones and thrill your brains through any timeline!

ISBN 978-1-61655-621-1 | $9.99

PLANTS VS. ZOMBIES: BULLY FOR YOU

Patrice and Nate have followed Crazy Dave throughout time—but are they ready to investigate a strange college campus to keep the streets safe from zombies?

ISBN 978-1-61655-889-5 | $9.99

PLANTS VS. ZOMBIES: GARDEN WARFARE

Based on the hit video game, this comic tells the story leading up to the events in *Plants vs. Zombies: Garden Warfare 2*!

ISBN 978-1-61655-946-5 | $9.99

PLANTS VS. ZOMBIES: GROWN SWEET HOME

Armed with newfound knowledge of humanity, Dr. Zomboss launches a strike at the heart of Neighborville . . . and also sparks a series of all-star plant-versus-zombie brawls!

ISBN 978-1-61655-971-7 | $9.99

PLANTS VS. ZOMBIES: PETAL TO THE METAL

Crazy Dave takes on the incredibly tough *Don't Blink* video game—and he also challenges Dr. Zomboss to a race to determine the future of Neighborville!

ISBN 978-1-61655-999-1 | $9.99

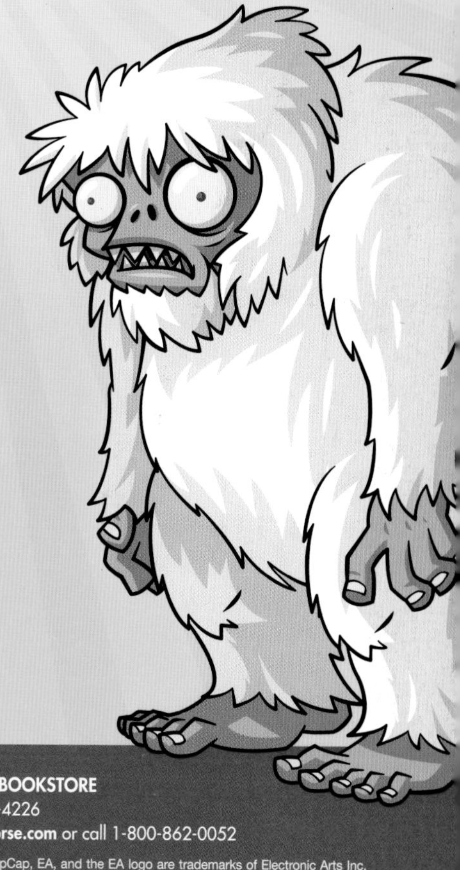

AVAILABLE AT YOUR LOCAL COMICS SHOP OR BOOKSTORE

To find a comics shop in your area, call 1-888-266-4226

For more information or to order direct visit **DarkHorse.com** or call 1-800-862-0052

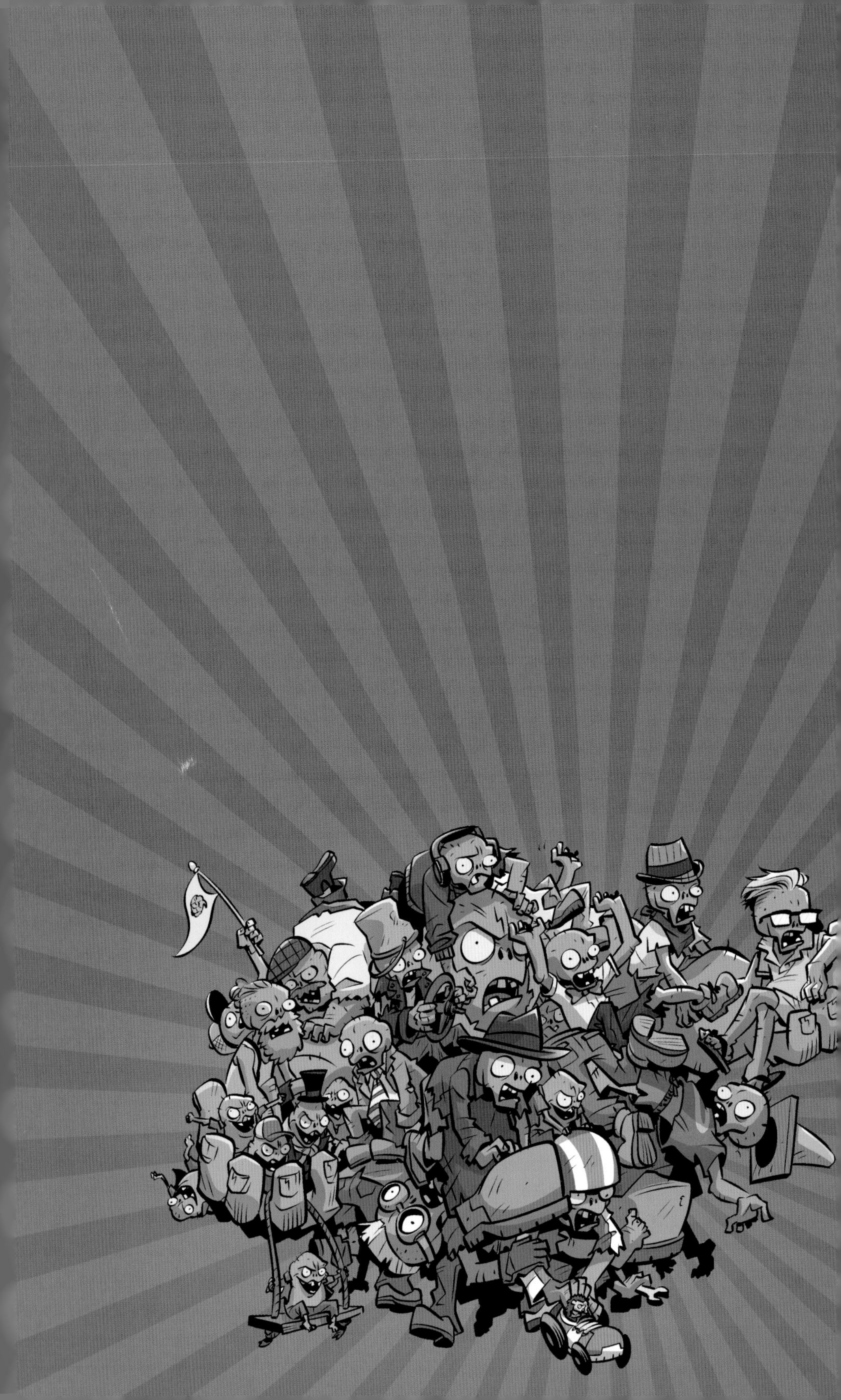

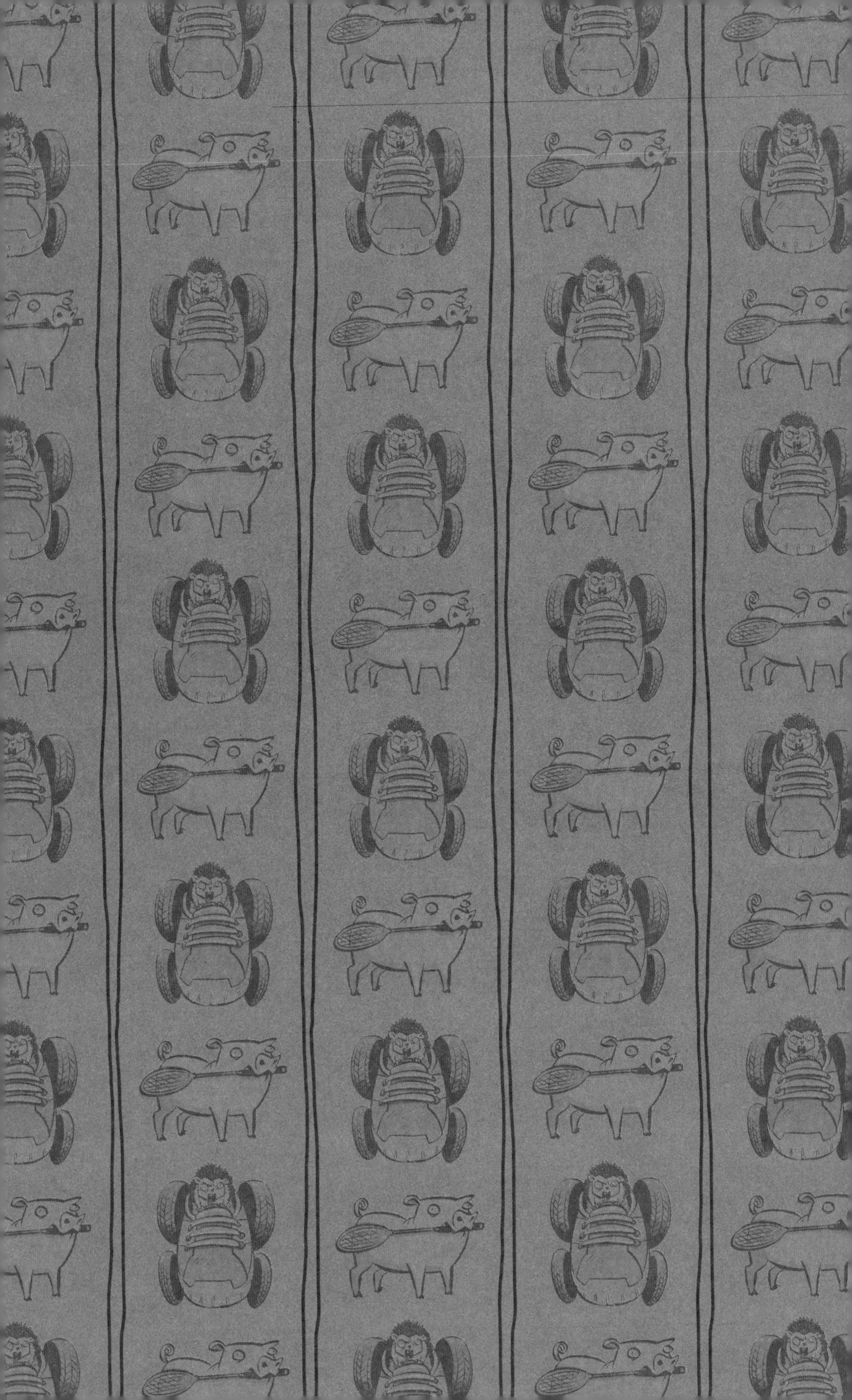